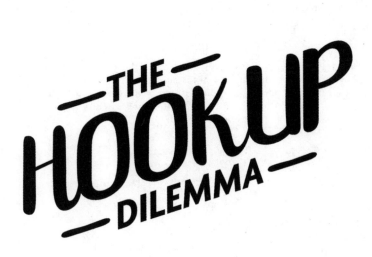

CONSTANCE GILLAM

Entangled Publishing, LLC
10940 S Parker Road
Suite 327
Parker, CO 80134
rights@entangledpublishing.com

Amara is an imprint of Entangled Publishing, LLC.

Visit our website at www.entangledpublishing.com.

Edited by Liz Pelletier and Lydia Sharp
Cover design by Elizabeth Turner Stokes
Cover illustration by Keisha Archer
Cover images ProStock Studio/Shutterstock
Interior design by Toni Kerr

ISBN 978-1-68281-572-4
Ebook ISBN 978-1-68281-594-6

Manufactured in the United States of America

First Edition November 2021

10 9 8 7 6 5 4 3 2 1

ALSO BY CONSTANCE GILLAM

THE LAKOTA SERIES

Lakota Dreaming
Lakota Blood Moon
Under Cover of Night
Lakota Moon Rising

This book is dedicated, as always, to my husband, Jim, for his unwavering support through the headaches, heartaches and triumphs of being an author.

CHAPTER ONE

Elliott Quinn needed a drink—or six. He'd been holed up in his father's office all week. *Again.* He needed—no, *deserved*—a break. After all, today was his birthday.

Dropping his satchel on the polished marble floor of the building's entry, he shrugged out of his suit jacket, ripped his tie from around his throat, and stuffed the offending item into his jacket pocket.

At four p.m., Atlanta bustled with bumper-to-bumper traffic, toxic fumes, and the heavy *thump thump thump* of hip-hop coming from one of the cars. There was a time when he would have been grooving with the best of them, but after a long day at work, jamming was the last thing on his mind. He'd be lucky if he made it from his dinner table to his bed tonight before he passed out. God, he sounded old.

Just as he reached street level, a black SUV pulled up at the curb. The back door opened, and one slender leg appeared, then the rest of the body—a voluptuous form in a pencil skirt and a simple short-sleeve blouse. Masses of dark curls bounced on her head as her long stride brought her closer. Her floral scent wrapped around him, and his pulse spiked.

She sailed past him, keeping her eyes on the building he'd just left. The building that held the offices of Quinn

Enterprises. Interesting. She disappeared inside.

He would have loved for her to have shown up in his office. Would have brightened his day. His life had been a revolving door of sweaty construction workers in jeans and T-shirts for the last three weeks. This was what he'd been missing, though: a beautiful woman.

His lips tugged up into a grin—something that hadn't happened in a while—and he continued his stroll down Peachtree. Up ahead, the flashing display for beer lured him to a dark pub.

Inside, a cacophony of laughter and voices filled the space. A nice change from the stagnant silence he breathed at the office. At the bar, he ordered a Macallan 18 then carried it to the last available booth. He pulled papers out of his satchel then examined the pages that represented his father's current projects. Who was he kidding? He couldn't outrun the chaos of his father's business. All he'd been able to do was change the scenery. He sighed and took a sip of his drink. Fire burned its way down his throat to settle in his stomach.

Like Elliott, his father, Marcus Quinn, was an architect. Though he'd sometimes involved himself in the construction of the buildings he designed, now he was recuperating from a massive heart attack.

The familiar ache of worry ate at Elliott's gut, but it was quickly replaced with agitation. What had the old man been thinking, weighing himself down with so many projects and so much debt? The stress had nearly killed him.

Elliott sifted through a couple of the files. Two high-rises— one three-quarters finished and the other just started. With a sigh, he shuffled through more papers—a sales contract for a property in the Millhouse area. He viewed the picture of the property attached to the contract—a boarded-up two-story building a strong wind could blow away. Was the old man going senile? What would he do with a dilapidated building?

Elliott ran his hand through his hair. This was a nightmare, a nightmare he had to make right. The Quinn men stuck together through thick and thin. It had been that way since Elliott's mother had died.

"Can I offer you anything more?" The impish twist of the waitress's lips and the direct way she regarded him said she was offering him more than a refill.

Although she wasn't his type—he liked a woman with a little more padding—it stroked his ego to know running two companies hadn't sucked all the life out him. "Maybe later."

"Anything you want. Let me know." She pivoted and fought her way through the crowd, her hips swaying to some invisible beat.

Elliott returned his attention to his makeshift office. How was he going to run his own company *and* keep his father's business afloat? Just the thought of the impending workload was enough to give him a migraine. Perhaps he should've taken the waitress up on her offer for a refill. It was going to take at least two more rounds to help him through this mess.

Screw it. Today was his birthday, and he planned to enjoy what was left of it.

He gathered all the sheets representing his father's current work and shoved them into his satchel. He wouldn't worry about it tonight.

While he sipped his drink, he sketched—something he liked to do to wind down. When he finished, the figure he'd drawn on the napkin resembled the woman he'd seen getting out of the Uber.

On Monday, he and his father's lawyer would put their heads together and figure out a way to salvage this wreck that was his dad's business.

Rashida Howard maneuvered to the bar to order a drink. Then, wine in hand, she scanned the crowded room for a seat. It might've been easier finding a spot on a *Titanic* lifeboat.

People were shoulder-to-shoulder and breast-to-chest deep. Every person in downtown Atlanta must've had the same idea—hang out here until the sun went down.

She spied an empty stool and pushed her way toward it. She could almost touch it, but a suit slid onto it ahead of her. In no mood to be nice, she had an urge to grab him by the collar and dump him on the floor.

Breathe, Rashida baby, breathe. Her grandmother's voice rang in her head. That voice of reason was the only thing that stood between her and an assault charge. Rashida's usual calm demeanor had been submerged under the recent changes in her grandmother's life.

Her day had been one disappointment after another, culminating with her last stop at Quinn Enterprises. She'd phoned Marcus Quinn all week. He hadn't the decency to return any of her calls, so she'd decided to forget courtesy and just show up at his office unannounced. No way could he avoid her then.

The plan had been simple. Confront him about his short-sighted plans for the Millhouse area. Get him to admit he was wrong and that he'd withdraw his rezoning application. She'd walk out as he groveled his apology—a smile on her face and his balls in her hands. She'd worn her celebratory heels just for the occasion.

Except when she got there, the office was closed. She'd gone within the hours of operation that were posted on the company's website, but things like "courtesy" and "reliability" didn't apply to Marcus Quinn. Men like that wouldn't recognize business etiquette if it was shoved down their throats.

So she would drown her frustration in a large glass of wine then call another Uber and head home.

This bar reminded her of a New Orleans–styled shotgun property—narrow but deep. The brick-walled booths seated two. And every one of those was occupied.

What did a girl need to do to catch a break? Could she not even get a drink without striking out?

She scanned the booths again, looking for someone who might be settling a tab. No such luck. Of course not, because nothing about today could be easy. But a guy sat drinking alone with his face buried in his phone and his fingers flying across the keypad. He had short, dark brown hair and sported what looked like two days' growth of beard a shade lighter. He looked harmless. Okay, so Ted Bundy had also looked harmless, but at this point she didn't care. She didn't want company or conversation. She just needed to rest her feet.

Because her feet said they'd taken enough abuse from her, she gingerly walked over to the booth then raised her voice to be heard over the din. "Do you mind sharing?"

Without looking up, he nodded toward the empty seat.

A different reaction than she was used to, but after the day she'd had, she was thankful for the nonchalance. She slid in. The cool leather felt heavenly against her bare legs. "Thanks." It was a relief to sit. Now if she could just remove her shoes.

Taking a sip of her wine, she tried to look anywhere but at the man across the table. He must be saving the world with that text message. Even the ice in his drink had melted from his neglect.

Since he wasn't paying attention to anything but his phone, she slipped both feet out of her heels. Every tightened muscle in her body relaxed, and she sighed as the cool air drifted across her very tired and aching toes.

She surveyed the other customers. Like Atlanta, the patrons were all ages and races. The rumble of conversations and the music took her mind off Quinn Enterprises and their proposed changes to her grandmother's community.

Being as subtle as she could, she tried to stretch out her legs. But she bumped Mr. Text Guy's leg—the fabric of his pants was a whisper of softness against her skin—then jerked away. It was quick, but the intimacy of the gesture sent chills over her bare arms. "Sorry."

He didn't look up, just continued tapping on his phone.

She eyed him from beneath her lashes. Even though she didn't want conversation, she wasn't used to being ignored. Men found her attractive and sometimes fell all over themselves to get her attention. Even Alex had been attentive in the beginning—

Her eye twitched as Alex's face flashed before her. She shoved the thought of her ex-boyfriend to the back of her mind. She didn't want to give thoughts of him any energy from even one of her brain cells.

This guy across from her appeared to be in his early to mid-thirties, with clean, short nails, square palms, long fingers, and no tan line around the ring finger of his left hand.

She had a thing for hands and butts. Too bad he was sitting.

Taking another sip of her wine, she debated asking him if it would be okay if she rested her feet on the seat next to him. If he said yes, she'd be in heaven.

The least he could do was offer up a little conversation. Hadn't his mama taught him better?

"I'm Rashida."

He dragged his attention from his phone, looking over at her. His eyes widened, and something shifted in the mossy-green depths. She'd never been an outdoorsy type—the humidity did crazy things to her hair—but she suddenly had the urge to go hiking in the forest.

"Elliott," he said, wrapping his large palm around hers for a handshake.

Calloused fingers brushed against her hand, making the hairs on her arms tingle. His skin was slightly cool against hers, his grasp firm. She wondered how those same fingers would feel running over her body. She didn't dare look at him now, because that thought and the subsequent heat would show in her eyes.

She played a mental game of guessing his profession. Those rough fingers made her think of manual labor, like construction. No. He wore a dress shirt, and she'd spied a suit jacket hanging on a peg just outside the booth. Office worker? Maybe. CEO? She liked the sound of that better.

"Is this place always so crowded?" she asked.

"It's hot outside." Elliott picked up his drink. Holding her gaze, he swallowed the last of the amber liquid in his glass. Had they turned off the air conditioning in the bar? Her body suddenly felt overheated. Her cheeks flushed.

She seemed to have his full attention. What would he do if she brushed her leg against his again? *He could be a serial killer, Rashida. Don't do it. Leave this man alone.*

Did she listen to herself? Nope. "Do you work around here?"

"I do," he said—and nothing else.

Okay. She was trying too hard at this one-sided conversation. She needed to finish her wine then leave.

Using her toes, she hunted around for her shoes on the floor. She found one of the heels then tried to wriggle and waggle her foot back into the shoe. It wouldn't fit; her feet had swollen from wearing these damn heels all day. *Holy moly.* What was she going to do now? No way could she hobble out of here shoeless. She'd suffer third-degree burns from the sidewalk, because Elliott was right. It was hot as hell out there.

He lifted his head, finally giving her his full attention. "What's wrong?"

My God. Did I groan out loud?

"I, uh...I can't get my foot back into my shoe."

He peered under the table. "Why not?"

"It's swollen."

One eyebrow shot up, and he threw her a questioning look—a look that made her blood boil. "I don't have a parasitic infection." She huffed out a breath. "My feet are swollen because I've been standing in heels all day."

"You just need to elevate your feet." He patted the seat next to him then added, "Wait—do they stink?"

Damn was he rude. "My feet do not stink."

"I was kidding." A smile tugged at the corners of his mouth.

Her shoulders relaxed. Who knew Mr. Text had a sense of humor?

Defiantly, she put one leg then the other on his side of the booth.

He studied her feet then gave the air above them a sniff.

She gave him a haughty glare. "My feet do *not* stink."

"If you say so." He laughed. The sound left a trail of liquid fire over her body. "I'm going for a refill. You want another?"

She might as well. She was stuck here until her feet could no longer be mistaken for Daffy Duck's. "Please." She dug into her purse for her card.

"On me," he said. "What are you drinking?"

Typically, she preferred to purchase her own drinks. She did okay for herself and didn't need a man to take care of her. However, that glint in Elliott's eyes made her swallow her pride and accept his offer. She'd had a hard day and deserved a little kindness. "Chardonnay."

He nodded then disappeared into the crowd.

His ass did not disappoint.

D rinks held high to prevent a spill, Elliott weaved his way back to his booth. He'd been given a gift—the woman from the Uber. It was as though he'd sketched her appearance into this very bar as a birthday present to himself. But his drawing couldn't capture the real woman—the dimple at the side of her generous mouth or the smooth skin at the base of her throat that made his heart hammer like a teenager at the thought of kissing that spot.

Customers were wedged in tighter than a tongue and groove joint. The place probably violated fire code—

His eyes rolled back into his head before he could even finish the thought. He might have left work early, but he'd brought the job with him.

He placed the drinks on the table and slid in. Rashida's feet still rested on his side of the booth. Long, beautiful legs led to trim ankles to high-arched feet capped off with blue toe polish, which glittered and contrasted against her honey-brown skin.

"Thank you." Slender fingers reached for her glass.

"Do you work around here?"

"I work from home."

Earlier, her chatter had intruded on his texts with one of his father's competitors, but now she appeared reluctant to speak. Hopefully, he hadn't put her off with his comments about her feet.

"Doing what?" he said, keeping his tone light.

She ran a finger around the rim of the glass. "I'm a food critic."

That was not what he'd expected. From the way she carried herself outside his father's office building, shoulders back with a confident stride, he'd thought lawyer or the head of some corporation.

He took a sip of his whiskey. "So, do you just appear at these restaurants unannounced?"

"If you mean do I let them know I'm coming to critique their restaurant, then no. I make a reservation and have a meal just like any other customer."

He chuckled, imagining a restaurant owner's surprise when a not-so-good review showed up. "Until your review appears...? Where?"

"*Atlanta Magazine.*"

Elliott studied her with unapologetic interest. This woman, all long legs and good posture, was like a cat—no, more like a lioness. She must have gotten hot since he saw her earlier, because now her thick dark hair was gathered on top of her head with stray strands brushing the back of her neck. Around her throat looped several fine gold chains—one trailed and disappeared in her cleavage. *Wonder how far that chain travels down her body.* He imagined following the path with his tongue.

He forced himself to stop ogling. Her big, chocolate-colored eyes observed him with amusement hidden in their depths. A message was sent by her and received. She could have him with a crook of her finger.

She was absolutely right.

When he'd left work, he had no idea he'd be sitting across the table from this beautiful woman, thoughts of taking her to bed running through his brain.

"What about you?" Rashida asked. "What do you do?"

"I'm an architect."

"Oh, what do you build? High-rises?"

His cell pinged. A reply to his irate text had come. He flipped the phone over. He'd deal with it later. "I design new homes."

His phone vibrated. He picked it up to make sure it wasn't his father's nurse calling. It wasn't, so he let it go to voicemail, but then a pang of guilt shot through him. He hated to ignore his father's colleagues, no matter how much they made him want to change his name and skip town, but he deserved some time to himself. Time to enjoy this beautiful, witty woman the Fates had dropped into his workaholic life.

"I guess I should be going," Rashida said, eyeing his phone.

Something heavy settled on his chest. He wasn't ready to say goodbye. They'd exchanged enough information to not be complete strangers but not enough to have a reason to contact each other again. He needed more time with her.

She made no move to put on her shoes, though. Maybe she felt the same. Maybe she wanted more time with him, too.

"How are they doing?" He glanced over at her feet. He never thought of himself as a foot man, but he had the insane desire to reach out and touch her bare toes and to let his hand travel up her leg. Boy, he'd bet that would put a quick end to the evening. *Cool it, Elliott, before she runs out of here screaming.*

She wriggled her toes. "Guess I won't know until I try." With some effort, she managed to get her feet into her shoes, then she reached for her bag.

His stomach sank. *Quick, think.* He couldn't let her slip away. "How about dinner?"

Arching an eyebrow, she asked, "What?"

"Dinner. You know, food. Sustenance. I thought you might be familiar with it considering your job and all."

She hesitated, not cracking a smile at his poor attempt at a joke.

He held his breath.

"Where?"

He expelled the air from his lungs. "Across the street."

She leaned out of the booth and peered out the window. The happy hour crowd had thinned, and it was now possible to glimpse the street.

"The Ritz Carlton?" she said, turning back to face him.

He shrugged. "They have a nice restaurant." *Say yes.*

She leaned back in her seat and studied him for what seemed like a lifetime. Then...

"Yes."

CHAPTER TWO

Her whole outfit was a study in contradictions. Demure white blouse, pencil skirt, but fuck-me heels and delicate chains that snaked between breasts that would fit perfectly in the palms of his hands.

Her flowery scent and the hypnotic sway of her hips lured him out of the restaurant like a pied piper.

The sun, leaving purple and orange streaks across the sky, had taken little of the humidity with it as it dropped below the horizon. At the street corner, he grasped her elbow, using the fast-moving traffic as an excuse to touch her. He didn't remove his hand from her arm when they entered the restaurant.

The maître d' watched their approach.

"Two for dinner." Elliott was prepared to slip the man a huge tip for a good table. He wanted this dinner to be a prelude of things to come. And if they didn't end up in bed tonight, then he wanted to see her tomorrow and the next day after.

The man's smile faded from politeness and morphed into what Elliott could only call concern. "Excuse me a moment." He stepped away.

"That was weird."

"Sorry." Rashida gave a tiny shrug.

Why was she apologizing? Elliott moved away from the

station then searched for the maître d' among the tables. He found him conferring with another man.

Back at Rashida's side, Elliott said, "I assume you've critiqued this restaurant before?"

"It was a good review. But the sea bass was a little off."

He could almost see the havoc that critique had produced. "So are they going to spit in our soup?"

Before she could answer, the maître d' reappeared with the second guy in tow. The two men acted more nervous than a novice construction worker on a hot tin roof.

The second man with his overly bright and solicitous smile said, "Wonderful to have you with us again, Ms. Howard."

"Pleased to be here, Mr. Applewhite." Her smile was gracious and genuine. Not at all like a woman who held all the power.

"If you will follow me, I'll be happy to seat you."

Applewhite led them deep into the restaurant to a secluded table. He held out a chair for Rashida.

After she was seated, he said, "Enjoy your dinner. Your waiter will be right with you."

"Thank you."

She studied the menu, and Elliott studied her. As she gnawed on her lower lip, he imagined tasting that plump bit of flesh. He could almost—

He jerked. A light touch had settled on his leg, sending a jolt of electricity to his cock. Rashida nonchalantly considered the menu as her foot stroked him. Up and down...up and down...

He took a deep breath then picked up his own menu, hoping thoughts of food would take his mind off the lazy sweep of her leg against his. It didn't. It brought up images of them sliding across silken sheets, her under him and him plunging into her hot, wet—

"Are we ready to order?"

Elliott flinched. He'd been lost in his lust and hadn't noticed the waiter's approach.

He put down his menu. He didn't want food. He wanted to take her upstairs to one of the rooms, lay her on a bed, and consume her like a five-course meal. But he'd invited her to dinner...

"Are you hungry?" he asked.

She looked up, and with a twinkle in her eyes, said, "Ravenous."

His pulse and his cock leaped. "Me, too."

"Then might I suggest the..."

The waiter's voice was like a drone in Elliott's ear. His eyes charted a course over her broad forehead to her angular jawline up to her full, sensual lips. Individually, her features were ordinary, but taken as a whole, she was gorgeous.

"...the dry-aged ribeye..."

"Sounds delicious," Elliott said, his gaze traveling the path of her necklace again down to her breasts. He wanted to feel their weight in his hands.

"And for you, ma'am?"

"The halibut."

"Good choice. If I may have your menus." After handing them over, the waiter turned and left.

"Those are not on the menu," Rashida said.

Her voice broke into his thoughts, and she watched Elliott with a half smile and a raised eyebrow.

"What?"

"My breasts are not on the menu," she repeated.

Heat rose in his face like the blast from a welding gun. "Sorry." He shook his head. "Actually no, I'm not."

"I've been told they're my best feature." There was a hint of laughter in her voice.

"They're not." *Damn.* "I mean, they are one—two—of many."

"Nice save." She fingered the flatware. "You seemed pretty intensely involved with your phone back at the bar. Everything okay?"

He shrugged off her concern. He would not let the sorry state of his father's business intrude on this evening. "Work related." He needed to bring this conversation back to the two of them.

"So, where are you from?" he asked. "I detect something in your voice."

"Good ear. Born in Miami, but my family is from Tobago." She leaned forward. "Ever been?"

"No. Never. Do you get there often?"

Her smile was whimsical. "Never been. But I'd like to visit someday. And you? Where are you from—here?"

"Born and bred. My family has been in Atlanta for over a century. In fact, I was born right down the road at Piedmont Hospital." He wanted to thump himself in the head. He sounded like a paid announcement for the Chamber of Commerce.

The waiter arrived with their salads then soon departed again.

Elliott shrugged. "Sorry. I love the city."

"Don't apologize. It's great you care so much about Atlanta." She drizzled salad dressing over her greens. He'd been so wrapped up in admiring her attributes he'd missed that she'd ordered her oil and vinegar on the side. His salad was drowning in dressing just the way he liked it.

"Are both your parents from Tobago?" He speared lettuce on his fork and glanced up for her answer.

"Yes."

He didn't miss the slight hesitation nor the shadow that passed over her face and flickered away just as quickly.

The waiter reappeared. Again interrupting them. "Have you selected a wine to go with your meal?"

After they made their selection and the waiter left, Elliott decided not to ask more about her family. He sensed pain underneath her jocular exterior.

"What—"

"My fa—"

They'd both spoken at the same time, but their laughter seemed to ease the awkwardness between them.

She shrugged. "The topic of my family is always a speed bump in conversation." Her mouth lifted at the corner. "My parents divorced when I was a baby." She moved her knife closer to her fork on the table. "I haven't seen my father since I was maybe three. I have very few memories of him."

He hung on her words, wanting to know more about her and her family. Not because he wanted to get her into bed—yes, he wanted that more than anything—but because her face was so expressive when she spoke, and that low, gravelly voice got him in his gut.

He'd known her for a couple of hours, but he liked her more than some of his acquaintances he'd known all his life.

"Nice hotel," she said, looking around. "I've only been in the restaurant."

He recognized the words for what they were. A change in

topic. "Yes, I've heard the rooms are luxurious."

"You've never stayed here?"

He shook his head. "Not this Ritz, but in other cities."

"I'll have to check out the rooms sometime."

Elliott's pulse did a booster into the stratosphere. He put down his fork. "I'd be happy to take you on a personal tour."

She toyed with the leaves of romaine on her plate. Her gaze speared his. "I'd like that."

Her words were low and suggestive. He took them as an invitation. "Would you like the tour after dinner tonight?"

"I'd love it."

B eyond the hotel's floor-to-ceiling windows, the Atlanta skyline blazed against the night.

"Beautiful," Rashida said then turned away to take in more of the hotel suite.

Elliott leaned casually against the closed door, legs crossed at the ankles. "Yes, you are."

Her pulse fluttered in her throat, making it hard to breathe. Why did he affect her this way? He was no more handsome than any of the other guys she'd seen recently. She did love the glints of auburn in his dark hair, the broadness of his shoulders, the solidness of his body. Okay, so maybe he was a little bit more handsome.

Some gossamer of connection drew her to him. Something she couldn't define. Something that caused heat to spread through her system like wildfire, burning a path to the throbbing area between her legs. This was impulsive, her being here. She'd just met the guy.

He pushed away from the door and moved toward her, his suit pants stretched taut across his…his… *Damn.*

He could have stepped straight out of the pages of *GQ* with his broad shoulders and well-tailored suit. She wanted to run her hands over his skin, over those well-defined muscles hinted at beneath his white shirt, over the pulse that beat wildly in his throat.

Her stomach pitched like a boat on choppy water. He was nervous. The realization relaxed her and at the same time gave her a sense of power.

She slipped out of her shoes and padded toward him. His eyes, a window into his thoughts, his feelings, changed from emerald to almost onyx as she walked into his arms.

She loved the solid feel of his chest against her body, his thighs against hers, and the bulge of his sex against her stomach.

Rising on her tiptoes, she whispered in his ear, "I want to see you naked."

He leaned back so he could look at her. "In a minute." His gaze traveled over her features before settling on her mouth. "I've been waiting all evening to do this."

The scent of whiskey fanned across her face as his tongue touched first one corner of her mouth then the other. She leaned into him, anticipation making her body limp and her legs weightless.

His tongue skimmed along the crease of her lips. She parted to let him in, and his tongue danced with hers, sucking, biting, then soothing.

Goose bumps skittered over her skin. Her breath labored in her chest. *Jesus…*

She tightened her arms around his neck, kissing him with

all the sexual need that had been building all evening.

The scent of him, the rightness.

She tore her mouth from his to draw in much-needed air.

While she panted, he shrugged out of his suit jacket. He dropped it on the entry table. His hands went to the buttons on his shirt, but he moved too slowly. She pushed his fingers out of the way. "Let me."

His hands dropped away. "Be my guest."

It seemed to take forever before his bare chest was underneath her hands. The warmth of his skin, the woodsy scent mixed with his natural musk, made her want to sink into his body. She buried her nose in his throat and inhaled instead.

As she'd predicted, his abdomen was a series of dips and ridges. A fine dusting of dark hair covered his chest and trailed down his body before disappearing into his pants.

His finger lifted her chin. "My turn."

The hunger in his eyes made it difficult to breathe. Each shallow inhale pushed her nipples against her bra in exquisite torture. Dreamlike, she wondered if she was in over her head.

He made fast work of the buttons on her blouse. He pushed the material off her shoulders, and it fluttered to the floor. His finger traced the scalloped edge of her bra then trailed down to circle an engorged nipple.

She moaned on an exhale of breath.

His lips replaced his finger, sucking on the bud through the fabric of her bra. Her sex clenched and unclenched as tension started to build between her legs.

"Turn around." His voice was low, rough.

She complied, anticipation making her light-headed.

Kneeling behind her, he unzipped her skirt slowly until it joined the blouse. She stepped out of the puddle of clothes.

Goose bumps rose on her skin.

Hooking his fingers in her thong, he lowered it slowly. Cool air hit her ass. Then the hot, rough press of his tongue between her legs.

Oh. My. God. She sagged against the door. The cool metal felt good against her heated forehead, while her nerve endings shot off mini volts of electricity through her. She centered her focus on his warm tongue, a tongue which stroked her from her slit to her clit and back.

"Please." She didn't know what she begged for. Stop? Don't stop? Her heart hammered in her chest like a battering ram.

As his mouth worked on her tight bundle of nerves, his fingers plunged repeatedly into her. He groaned, the sound almost a hum emanating from his chest.

Tightness built in her core like a ball of molten lava, growing larger with each plunge of his fingers and pull of his lips. She closed her eyes and held on, concentrating on breathing. For once in her life, she wasn't in control of the situation. It scared her, this lack of control, but in a strange way it was exhilarating.

"Elliiiott." It was a warning before the tension in her belly broke, sending a tsunami of heat flashing through her body and a gush of wetness flooding her pussy.

He didn't give her a moment to recover, just turned her around, lifted her so her legs wrapped around his waist, which was a good thing since her legs were too weak to support her, then strode easily toward the bedroom.

A fine sheen of sweat beaded his face, and his skin was hot beneath her fingers.

He lowered her onto the bed then began to shuck out of his pants and shirt, almost falling in his haste. His cock sprang out of his boxers. Long and thick, it stood at attention, the head bulbous and broad.

Reaching down, he removed a condom from his wallet. Using his teeth, he ripped the package open. His hands shook as he attempted to roll it over his erection. Her stomach gave a queer twist.

Sitting on the bed beside her, he asked, "Are you okay?" The once emerald eyes had turned dark as a sky before a storm. Sweat beaded his face.

She could only nod, the rapid *whoosh* of her pulse in her ears making her mute.

"Lay back," he whispered.

She stretched out on the sheets. He took in her features one by one, then her breasts, her stomach, and finally the strip of hair that covered her sex.

His gaze lingered.

Did he like what he saw? No amount of crunches had made her stomach as flat and firm as she wanted. But the rapt way he inspected her body banished her insecurities. Made her feel beautiful.

She opened her legs.

He breathed slowly, in and out, his broad shoulders rising and falling with each breath. Supporting his weight with one hand, he hunkered over her, using the other hand to guide his cock to her opening. Slowly, he eased into her, pausing with each inch, giving her time to grow accustomed to his girth.

Once fully seated, he paused, searching her face.

She was about to come out of her skin. "Fuck me."

He closed his eyes briefly, seeming to gather himself, then began to move, stroking her inner walls with his thickness. Her muscles clenched around his cock, threatening to hold it hostage. She wrapped her legs around his waist as the tightness began to build again in her core.

It was like a meal she'd waited days to taste. She couldn't get enough. She clutched at his shoulders, digging her fingers into the muscles.

They screwed like it was a battle neither of them wanted to lose.

"God." His voice strained above her. The cords of his neck stood out in relief against his flushed skin. Sweat coated his face and dripped onto her breasts. He quickened his pace, and she met him thrust for thrust.

"Deeper. De—" Her throat closed over the chant as another orgasm tore through her like a category five hurricane, leaving her drenched and unanchored from her moorings. He pumped with two or three more deep thrusts, then his body locked in a spasm.

Moments…minutes…later, the bed shifted as he dropped onto the mattress beside her.

She closed her eyes, holding on for a minute to the weightlessness of her limbs and the silence in her brain.

"You okay?" he asked.

"Hmmm."

His finger feathered across her lips. Leaving a light kiss, he said against her mouth, "Give me a minute."

The bed shifted as he rolled off and padded away.

She watched him walk toward the bathroom. *What happens now?* This had been the best sex of her life, but this wasn't real. Did they part in the morning promising to call each other but never did? Would she be okay with that?

The toilet flushed, water ran in the sink, and a minute later, he wrapped his arms around her, pulling her into his body.

His nose nuzzled her ear. "You smell wonderful."

She pushed her unease away and sank into the comfort of his body. "So glad I don't stink."

His chuckle filled her head. "You smell like the best Scottish whiskey and taste like honey."

She turned so she could see his face better on the pillow beside her. "I'm not sure that's a compliment—the Scottish whiskey part."

"It is. The Scots make some of the best whiskey in the world and have for several centuries."

"Expensive, I bet."

"Very."

The whispered word made tiny eruptions break over her skin and her nipples pebble. What was it with this man? She loved the chase but didn't fall into bed with every handsome guy who crossed her path. In fact, screwing someone the day she met them wasn't her modus operandi.

He closed the distance between them then touched her lips softly with his. Just the slightest of touches like the wings of a butterfly. He broke the contact until his lips hovered over hers. She couldn't stand not touching. Reaching up, she pulled his face closer then closed her eyes and sank into a kiss that was all tongue and teeth and heavy breathing.

Soft but firm, his mouth moved over hers. His large hands traveled up her back, leaving a trail of heat and creating a throbbing that was almost an ache. He mapped her mouth like his hands traveled the territory of her body.

Cradling her face in his large hands, he deepened the kiss. Someone moaned. She wasn't sure if he'd made the sound or she had. Lost in the kiss, she was aware of the heat of his body, the scratch of his stubble, his chest hairs rubbing her sensitive nipples.

Sometime later, he turned off the bedside lamp then pulled her close, his front to her back. She closed her eyes and sank into his warmth. His breath stirred the hair at her temples. She must have looked a hot mess.

"It's been a great birthday," he said.

She shifted in the bed to face him. "It's your birthday?"

He reached over and picked up his watch. The numbers were illuminated in the dark. "*Was* my birthday."

She sighed. "Happy birthday."

"Thank you. You made it a very special one." He bent his head and captured one of her nipples between his warm lips and sucked. A corresponding tug sparked and caught fire in her core, molten heat spreading through her body. She threw her leg over his hip and gave in to the sensations created by his lips.

He kissed his way up her neck to capture her mouth with his. This time when his cock entered her, it was with slowness. As though he wanted to make this one moment in time last forever.

But she knew nothing lasted forever.

CHAPTER THREE

Seated in a secluded area of The Grill, a restaurant she'd critiqued last year, Rashida waited impatiently for her sister to arrive. Karla, a real estate agent, was crucial in Rashida's plan to stop Quinn Enterprises. Without her help, Rashida would be floundering at sea like a boat without oars.

It had been her sister who'd alerted Rashida to what was potentially happening in her grandmother's neighborhood. Karla who'd told her Quinn Enterprises had filed a change in zoning application. Now that she'd lit a fire under Rashida, her sister didn't seem to care what could happen to Grammy's little bit of paradise.

Rain slid down the restaurant's windows, blurring the traffic that inched by. She'd been surprised by the rain when she'd stepped out of the Ritz this morning.

She cringed thinking about her behavior the previous evening. This fight with Quinn Enterprises had turned her into another person. Everything about her was ramped up. She was quick to anger, quick to defend, and based on the previous night with Elliott—quick to have carnal knowledge of an unknown man's body.

Elliott was charming, funny, and sexy. And he'd touched her like no man ever had. And that scared her. Scared the shit out of her. So, while he'd slept, she'd dressed and crept out of the suite like a thief in the night, leaving nothing behind, especially not her cell number.

"Sorry I'm late." Karla slid into the opposite seat. She glanced around the restaurant. "Where's the waitress? I've a client coming in an hour."

Karla Howard-Buckley was co-owner of a real estate brokerage firm with her husband, Kenneth.

"Relax," Rashida said. "I ordered you a salad with lemon slices."

Her sister ate like a mouse, nibbling at the corners of her meal to maintain her size zero figure. *Probably for that scumbag she calls a husband.* Life was too short for all that deprivation and especially for a man who didn't appreciate it.

Rashida wished she could help her sister, but what advice could she offer? She wasn't any more successful in her own love life.

"So, what's been happening?" Karla asked.

No way was Rashida going to tell her sister about hooking up with a man she'd just met. There were not enough hours in the day for the lecture that would result from that reveal.

Karla forked the lemon from her water glass and placed it on a bread plate, then she dissected the fruit with a knife and fork like it was prime rib and speared a tiny wedge into her mouth, chewing slowly.

"You're weird."

Karla smiled with lips closed as she continued to chew. After swallowing, she said, "You should try it. It cleanses the palate, *Ms. Food Critic.* And don't talk about weird, with your one food item per plate."

"Yeah, whatever." Rashida lined up her fork and knife. "I

went by Quinn Enterprises yesterday."

This got her sister's attention. "Why?"

Why do you think? But Rashida bit back the response. She couldn't afford to get on the wrong side of her sister, because she needed Karla's help, even though at times, she irked Rashida to no end. "I want them to withdraw their re-zoning application."

"And they said they'd jump right on it?" Karla asked with a smirk.

"Quinn wasn't there. I'm going back on Monday. I'll fight this until my last dying breath if I have to."

Karla rolled her eyes. "Stop being so melodramatic." She leaned forward. "The neighborhood is close to downtown. Any good developer would jump at the opportunity to lure young professionals into the area. I only wish Kenneth and I had thought of it. Plus, Grammy's house requires too many renovations for her to do on a fixed income."

"A little callous, isn't it?" How could her sister not be upset by what was happening in Grammy's little neck of the woods? Where was the caring sister she once knew? The one who fought for the underdog.

Rashida knew the answer, though. Kenneth Buckley happened to her.

"Where is the waitress?" Karla glanced around. Not spotting the server, she turned back to Rashida. "I'm not callous, just realistic. The Millhouse area is going through a transition. When it's finished, those homes will be worth a lot of money."

Rashida tilted her head. "Transition?" The word came out louder than she intended if the looks she was getting from other diners were any indication. "This is our grandmother's neighborhood. Her property will be affected."

Karla waved Rashida's protest away. "If she sells, she'll make a nice profit."

"*Profit?*" Rashida was practically vibrating in her seat. "Who cares about profit? Okay, maybe you and Kenneth do."

As soon as the words were out of her mouth, she wished she could call them back. Her sister's face went tight.

Shit. Honey. Honey. Not vinegar. She'd forgotten her grandmother's words. Deep breath.

"What do you think will happen if Grammy has to sell her house and live with Mom?" Rashida asked.

The waitress reappeared with their lunch. She set Karla's salad plus a saucer of a half dozen lemon wedges in front of her. The waitress carefully placed Rashida's plate with only the bourbon-glazed salmon on the table. Next to the fish, she added two bread plates—one with string beans and the other with new potatoes.

"Anything else, ladies?" the waitress asked.

"No. Thank you," Karla added with a smile.

Rashida arranged the plate with the string beans at eleven o'clock and the potatoes at one o'clock to the main entree.

Karla eyed Rashida's meal.

"What? You know I don't like anything to touch," Rashida said defensively.

With a weary sigh, her sister shook her head. She squeezed lemon juice over her salad. "Where were we? Oh, yes. There'll be a period of adjustment for both, but they'll be fine living together."

Karla sighed then leaned forward. Her features were arranged in a conciliatory but weary expression. "Look this was bound to happen. The area has access to MARTA, and it's minutes from downtown. I'm just surprised it didn't happen sooner."

Rashida eyed her salmon. It stared back at her like a slab of pink Play-Doh. She pushed her plate away then took a big gulp of water. Why was she having this conversation with Karla? Her sister saw everything in dollars and cents. Why had she deluded herself believing that Karla would help with the fight against Quinn Enterprises?

"Trust me. Grammy will be okay and a whole lot wealthier. If she wants to sell, I'll handle it personally."

When Rashida opened her mouth to protest, Karla held up a hand. "I'll do it without charging her a cent."

Rashida moved her knife and spoon until the end of each utensil lined up. She put her hands in her lap. When she was upset, she took to arranging and rearranging anything within arm's reach. "I want you to go with me on Monday to talk to Marcus Quinn." *Pretty please.* She held her breath.

Karla shook her head. "Can't. My day is chock-full of showings."

Rashida gripped her hands tighter. "Can you at least attend the zoning meeting on Tuesday?"

Karla speared a couple of leaves of lettuce with her fork. "Kenneth and I are meeting with some of the committee members Tuesday evening to finalize plans for the Atlanta Symphony benefit."

Rashida's heart sank. The written word was her forte, not public speaking.

But it looked like saving the Millhouse area was going to fall on her shoulders alone.

• • •

Windshield wipers swished hypnotically as Elliot drove through stop-and-start traffic on his way to his father's home. When it rained in Atlanta, motorists forgot how to drive.

Garth Brooks's distinctive voice floated out of the speakers. Elliott's mouth tightened, and he lowered the volume on the satellite radio station. He loved Brooks's style and delivery, but tonight he wasn't in the mood for a mushy love song.

He was irritated at himself for being irritated. Rashida had left sometime in the early morning without saying goodbye or leaving her number. He preferred this type of arrangement with the women he wined and dined. So why was he in such a funky mood?

When he arrived at his dad's house, Elliott jumped out of the car, and before he could insert his keys in the lock, Rebecca Scott, his father's nurse, opened the door.

"Good evening." Young, courteous, and unassuming, she was the complete opposite of his dad's secretary.

"How are you?" He dropped his keys on the small Queen Anne entry table.

"I'm fine."

The dark circles under her blue eyes called her a liar.

"Are you sure? I know he can be demanding."

She shrugged. "I've had worse."

She was his father's third nurse in six weeks. Elliott didn't want her to quit. "I thought the staffing agency rotated you with two other nurses so you'd have days off. I've seen you every day this past week."

She flushed pink then bowed her head to inspect her Crocs.

"What? What is it?"

Her high ponytail bounced when she glanced up. "None of the other nurses will work with your father," she whispered.

"Word has gotten out that—"

"He's difficult?"

She didn't respond, which gave him the answer.

He rubbed the back of his neck. Irritation ran like a live-wire through his body. Everything chafed under his skin today. "I'll talk to him. Is he awake?"

"Yes. I was just on the way to the kitchen to make him some chamomile tea."

"Take your time. I'll stay with him for a while."

Her lips lifted, but the corners of her mouth quivered, and the smile was lost. "Thanks." She moved off in the direction of the kitchen.

Jeez, Dad. Elliott climbed the stairs to his father's bedroom. He eased open the door and peered in.

"I'm awake," his father announced.

"How's it going, old man?"

"Nice of you to visit." The twist of his father's lips and the bite to his words spoke of his frustration. He was a man who played golf, smoked expensive cigars, and headed a multi-million-dollar empire, but now he was sidelined by a massive heart attack.

His father's fingers fumbled until he found the button that lowered his hospital bed. "Help me out of this contraption, would you?" He swung his thin legs over the side.

Elliott placed an arm around his father's waist. Gone was the robust man with the thick hair and booming voice. Left in his place was a bag of bones with wisps of thinning white hair sticking out from his head.

According to the doctor, his father should be moving around more, building his strength. Although he professed that he wanted to return to work, he'd refused to go to cardio rehab and spent more time in bed than he should.

Elliott led his father to a chair a short distance from the bed. The old man fell into the seat as if the muscles in his legs had been cut.

He batted Elliott's hands away. "Robert says a zoning meeting is coming up. Are you ready?"

Elliott backed up and sat on the edge of the bed. "Of course."

He made a mental note to ask his dad's attorney to filter the information he gave the old man. The last thing his father needed was a day-by-day account of how strapped his business was for capital.

"Are you going easy on the nursing staff?"

His father angled a look at Elliott with eyes still sharp with intelligence. "That girl should be in preschool. If I say boo to her, she cries."

Elliott rubbed the area between his eyebrows, hoping to stave off a headache. "Dad, she's a good nurse. Please, go easy on her."

His father eyed him. "Are you interested in her? I thought you liked them with a little more spunk."

Elliott thought about Rashida getting out of that Uber—bold, confident, and ready to take on the world. "She's not my type. Just go easy on her. Okay?"

"You know I was married and had you by the time I was thirty-four." His father studied him with shrewd eyes. "At least tell me you're getting laid regularly."

Elliott suppressed the images of Rashida's naked body above him, under him, open to him. "Hey, old man. Focus your attention on getting better and not giving your nurse a hard time. And in answer to your other question, I don't have time to do anything but work."

His father's large, bony hands opened and closed on the arms of the chair. "I'll be back to work soon. A week or two. I might be up to going to the zoning meeting with you."

Elliott hoped his expression didn't show his doubt. "Trust me. Erickson has tutored me well. I'm ready for the meeting on Tuesday. You concentrate on getting well. I've got everything under control."

He wondered, not for the first time, why his father had started a new project when his business didn't have the capital to complete the projects already underway. But he kept the thought to himself. If his dad thought Elliott wasn't running the business the way he wanted it to be, he'd be out of this bed and back to work before Elliott could blink. As much as he and his dad were at odds, he didn't want his father to suffer another heart attack.

The next one might be fatal.

Sunday afternoon, Rashida inched her Toyota a couple more feet along the road. This traffic delay was eating into her day. She had a blog post to put up.

She craned her neck to see beyond the car in front of her. What was the hold up? This wasn't rush hour on I-85 or I-20. This was a small side street in a quiet residential neighborhood. Rashida spotted the flashing lights of an ambulance. Must be serious.

Finally, after fifteen minutes of moving forward at a snail's pace, she spotted the problem—a fender bender. Like everyone else, she rubber-necked to see the accident.

One car was a Porsche Carrera. She recognized the luxury vehicle immediately because it was her dream car. The other vehicle looked suspiciously like her grammy's 1976 Detroit gas guzzler—

Rashida's stomach flipped like a pancake on a hot grill. It *was* her grammy's 1976 Detroit gas guzzler.

She scanned the small knot of people on the side of the road. *Please don't let her be in that ambulance.* She almost collapsed against the Toyota's steering wheel when she saw her grandmother going toe-to-toe with a police officer on the sidewalk. Rashida groaned. She could almost read the exasperation on the officer's face.

She maneuvered her car around the broken glass and the sports car's molded plastic bumper, which now lay in all its wrecked glory on the asphalt. After finding a parking space a little way up from the accident, Rashida grabbed her purse and jumped out of the car.

"I tell you, Officer, it was not my fault." Eula Mae Robinson's singsong island lilt drifted to Rashida. She speed-walked toward her grandmother, ignoring the stitch in her side. She really had to get back to the gym.

"I need your license and proof of insurance," the officer said.

"Ah, there's my granddaughter."

The officer turned and watched Rashida approach. His eyes lingered on her for a second before turning his attention back to her grandmother.

"Grammy, are you okay?"

Her grandmother drew herself up to her full five foot nothing height. "Of course, I'm okay." She resettled her purse between her arm and her body. "I was driving to the grocery store and the car in front of me just stopped. No warning. Just stopped."

Rashida glanced back at the street. Both cars rested in the intersection, underneath a traffic signal. Her gaze swung back and connected with the officer's. She gave him credit. His eyes didn't betray his thoughts.

"Insurance and license, ma'am," he repeated.

As her grandmother dug around in her large purse, Rashida looked for the driver of the Porsche. A young thirtyish-looking guy was having his neck examined by a paramedic on the tailgate of the ambulance.

Her grandmother was still digging in her purse.

"Grammy, let me—"

"Hush." She batted Rashida's hands away then finally produced the two items and presented them to the officer.

"Are you sure you're okay?" Rashida asked again as the officer walked back to his vehicle with the license and insurance card. Her gaze ran over her grandmother's plump body, looking for any sign of injury. She was as sturdy as the bomber she drove.

"I'm fine," her grandmother snapped in an undertone.

"Why were you driving? I told you I'd pick you up."

"I wanted to get there early, and you were taking too long. I sent you a note."

A note. "You texted me? Grammy, I was driving. It's illegal to text and drive."

The officer returned her grandmother's license and insurance card. He then tore off a sheet and passed it to Rashida's grandmother.

Grammy studied the sheet, a frown twisting her brown face in confusion. "What is this?" she demanded, her island accent now more pronounced. She held up the sheet like a piece of dirty linen.

"A ticket," the officer said as he snapped his notebook closed. "For following too closely. *And* driving with a suspended license, which is usually an arresting offense. But due to your age—"

"Wait, what?" Rashida blurted. How had that slipped by her? She or Karla took care of bureaucratic things for their grandmother.

The officer turned and walked toward the crash scene.

"Me, following too closely?" Her grandmother's voice rose in a screech. "He stopped his little car too quickly. No warning." Grammy trailed after the officer.

Rashida grabbed her by the arm. "Grammy, no."

She turned on Rashida. "What do you mean, no?" She waved the sheet in the air. "I have to give this back to him."

"Let's go."

The Porsche was being loaded onto the flatbed of a tow truck. Rashida looked around for her grandmother's car. "Is the Cadillac still drivable?"

"Of course it is. Nothing happened. I don't know why the big fuss."

"The big fuss is the officer could have arrested you."

Grammy huffed. "No way—"

"They take driving with a suspended license very seriously. Let's get out of here before he changes his mind."

The officer was now directing traffic around the tow truck and Grammy's Cadillac Eldorado.

"Are the keys still in the car?"

Grammy patted the pockets of her house dress. When she didn't feel them, she started to dig through her purse again.

Rashida resisted the urge to sigh. Her grammy would never admit to being flustered.

"Wait here," she said, giving her grandmother's arm a pat.

Rashida walked to the Cadillac then slid behind the wheel. The keys still dangled from the ignition. When she turned the key, the engine roared to life. Gingerly, hoping to avoid the glass and car parts, Rashida moved the car around the corner and parked it in front of her Toyota.

Now the dilemma. She didn't want her grammy to drive, but she couldn't leave the tank on the street too long. Who could she call? If she called her sister, then her mother would know about the accident. The fender bender would provide more fuel for the ever-burning battle between Grammy and Rashida's mother, Essie, who wanted Grammy to sell her home and move in with her.

Rashida went back to her grandmother. "We're going to leave your car here, and I'll come back for it later."

"Will it be okay?" Grammy cast a worried look toward her pride and joy.

"It will be fine." Car thieves were not looking to steal an almost fifty-year-old car. Well, maybe they might take the tires, but Rashida was not going to tell Grammy that. She ushered her into the Toyota.

"You're so busy these days. I thought I'd just go to the store on my own."

Rashida's heart twisted in her chest. What had given her grandmother the idea she was too busy to help her? *How about you being late to pick her up?*

"I was just driving, minding my own business, when that car just stopped. I barely tapped it."

Rashida held back a snort as she maneuvered the car away

from the curb and into traffic.

The Porsche's bumper in the street told a different story. Plastic didn't come out on the winning side against Detroit steel.

"I'm sorry I was late."

Her grandmother patted her knee. "Don't worry about it. I'll manage. I always have."

Rashida shot her a side glance. Was Grammy trying to make her feel guilty? If so, she was doing a good job of it.

After parking in the grocery lot, Rashida pointed at the sheet of paper still clutched in her grandmother's hand. "You can pay online."

Grammy crushed the slip of paper to her chest. "I'm not paying this ticket. I'm going in front of the judge."

Rashida groaned. "When is the court date?"

Her grandmother smoothed out the sheet. "In three weeks. But I'm not waiting until then. I'm going this Monday and telling the judge what I think about this ticket."

"Grammy, you can't go in front of the judge if it's not your day."

Her grandmother snorted. "Watch me."

Rashida's stomach sank. She'd planned to go back to Quinn Enterprises to speak with Marcus Quinn on Monday. She couldn't be in two places at once, but no way would she allow her grammy to go to court by herself. The old woman might get herself arrested.

Seeing Marcus Quinn before Tuesday just got more complicated.

CHAPTER FOUR

On Monday before heading to his father's Buckhead office, Elliott stopped by his own business, Luxury Designs, Inc., to strategize for the week with his business partner, Chris Hollins. Their company specialized in designing high-end custom homes.

He and Chris had clicked right away as freshmen at Georgia Tech, and both had graduated from the school of architecture. When Elliott decided to leave Quinn Enterprises and form his own company, he could think of no better partner than Chris.

Elliott had done a year of post-graduate study in Columbia, South Carolina. He'd worked for a firm that specialized in historic restoration. From time to time, he took on projects around the state, restoring old nineteenth-century homes. So, when a rundown bungalow in the Inman Park area of Atlanta became available, Elliott had renovated it for their office.

He poked his head into Chris's space. "How's it going, man?"

Chris swiveled in his stool in front of his draft board. "Going great. Came to work to rest."

At Elliott's raised eyebrow, Chris said, "Took the kids to Six Flags." He rotated his neck, making the vertebrae pop.

"The highlight of my weekend."

Elliott chuckled. He'd been on outings with Chris and his wife, Crystal, and their two small sons. Pure pandemonium. Made Elliott glad he was single and childless.

"How about you?" Chris walked over to the Keurig. "Celebrate with lots of chicks and champagne?"

Chris, who'd married straight out of college, lived vicariously through Elliott.

Elliott held up one finger.

Chris scrunched up his bearded face. "One girl?"

At Elliott's nod, Chris asked, "How'd that happen?"

"Met someone at a bar downtown on Friday." Elliott knew he was smiling too much but couldn't dim the wattage.

Chris stirred sugar into his black coffee. "Let me guess. Sexy, blond, and—" He pantomimed curving his hand over his chest. "I know you, man. You've got a type. She had big ones. Right?"

Elliott laughed. "You've got a one-track mind. She was sexy."

"Well, that was a given." Chris placed his coffee in the drink holder next to the draft board. "How long you planning on wining and dining this one? A week? Two?"

When Elliott didn't comment, Chris studied him. "What's wrong?"

"Nothing." Elliott swung a chair over to Chris's desk. "Let's get started."

"Oh, no, you don't. Spill." Chris moved from the drafting table to his desk and peered into Elliott's face "Wait. You struck out?"

"Are we going to get some work done?"

"Whoa. You *did* strike out. And it's bothering you." Chris

leaned back in his chair, grinning.

Elliott didn't say anything. Any words he might utter would only add fuel to the flame.

"It never bothered you before, so you must like this woman. I need to meet her." Chris's white-toothed smile flashed in his dark face.

"I didn't strike out." Elliott clamped his lips shut. "She just didn't leave her number."

"But that's good, right?" Chris took a sip of his coffee.

"Let's get to work." He settled back in his chair, and Chris took the not-so-subtle hint to drop it. "What's up for the week?"

An hour and a half later, Elliott was in his father's massive office, unsuccessfully trying to make headway on his father's active projects. But he couldn't concentrate. His thoughts kept drifting back to Friday night. To Rashida. The scent of her skin, the huskiness of her moan, the taste of her honey.

The landline rang.

Irritation buzzed up his spine like a chainsaw. "Yes?" The word came out sharper than he intended.

"Mr. Erickson is here," Ms. Silverman's disembodied voice informed him.

"Send him in." Elliott rose to greet his father's financial lawyer. Hopefully, Erickson had some good news.

White-haired and dressed in a blue pinstriped suit, Robert Erickson was Marcus Quinn's contemporary. But unlike Elliott's father, Erickson appeared to be in good health. Erickson walked through the office door with a brisk step but a somber expression.

Elliott perched on the edge of his father's desk and

indicated that Erickson should take a seat.

The lawyer didn't smile, which made Elliott's jaw tighten in anticipation of bad news. "Hit me with it."

The older man crossed his leg over one knee. "You know a couple of months before your father's heart attack he purchased some land in the Millhouse area."

Elliott nodded. "I saw the sales contract. Was that a wise decision based on the company's finances?"

"No," the lawyer said, "but your dad was adamant about buying the land."

Just as Elliott suspected. His father could be a headstrong businessman, but in the past his decisions had been sound.

"What attracted Dad to this property?"

Erickson shrugged. "Price. The land had been on the market for a long time. Marcus thought he could buy it cheap, put up a commercial building, and make money from the rent. The area is on the cusp of changing. Marcus thought if he held on to the property long enough, he'd make a large profit when he sold it."

Land speculation was not Elliott's area of expertise. "Did you agree with him?"

The lawyer unbuttoned his suit jacket and seemed to relax into the subject. "The area is definitely about to change. I've seen the signs. His plan could work, but he's got to find the capital to build. Right now, no bank will lend him the funds he needs."

Elliott ran a hand through his hair. "What type of commercial building did he have in mind?"

"He drew up plans." Erickson straightened and looked around the office.

"I'll look for them. Just give me the highlights."

"He had the idea of making the building large enough to house three retail stores. A high-end grocery and two other businesses that would appeal to Millennials. But as I said, Marcus was overextended. I warned him about some of the riskier projects he took on, but he didn't listen. His business hasn't been the same since the 2008 recession."

"What's your suggestion?" Elliott asked.

Erickson scratched his beardless chin. "We could try a third-party investor."

"You have someone in mind?"

"I might. Haven't talked to him in a while, and there's no guarantee."

Elliott looked over at the papers spread across the desk. A throb started at the base of his skull. "He would be willing to take on all this?"

Erickson rose then buttoned his jacket. "All we can do is ask."

"I appreciate it." Elliott walked the older man toward the door. "By the way, I've been receiving calls from Garrett Thompkins. Do you know him?"

Erickson grimaced. "Corporate raider. He's called me also. Wants to pick apart your father's company like the vulture he is." The lawyer paused before stepping through the door. "Heard the zoning meeting is tonight. Your dad was—is quite a salesperson. Are you ready to step into his shoes?"

"Got it under control." *Liar.*

Erickson studied him for a long, weighty moment then shook Elliott's hand. Once the door had closed, he stared at the chaos on his father's desk.

This shit was as much under control as a brush fire.

• • •

"**O**kay, if we can get started." Reverend Clemmons stood at a makeshift podium.

The noise level fell to a whisper. Rashida stood in the middle of the aisle, with no seat.

She'd been so absorbed with completing an article on West African cuisine for her blog that she'd lost track of time. When she'd arrived late to pick up Grammy, her car wasn't in her drive.

So now Rashida stood in the middle of a packed church, searching for her.

"I'd like to introduce the architect for the proposed construction. Mr. Quinn," Reverend Clemmons said, lifting an arm.

She was still miffed Mr. Quinn hadn't returned her calls, but she'd get a chance to have her say after he finished speaking tonight.

The chairs were so tightly packed that everyone in his row had to stand to let Mr. Quinn pass. When he stepped into the aisle and headed for the podium, she frowned in confusion. His hair...that walk...that build...

She shook her head to clear it. Every male was not Elliott. She needed to get him out of her system.

When Mr. Quinn turned to face the crowd, Rashida's world turned upside down.

Her Elliot was a Quinn of Quinn Enterprises?

Elliott glanced out over the crowd. As he reached inside his jacket pocket, his gaze connected with hers. A quizzical frown lined his face. His lips silently mouthed her name.

"Rashida," someone stage-whispered then pulled on her arm. She glanced to her right. Grammy motioned for her to take the empty seat next to her.

Rashida stumbled across feet and stepped on a few toes before plopping into the waiting chair. Her brain was like a hamster on a wheel, going in endless circles and getting nowhere.

Her grandmother leaned close. "Close your mouth."

Rashida obeyed. Her teeth came together with a snap. The man who'd made her come so many times she almost blacked out was the same man who planned to destroy her grandmother's neighborhood.

Elliott finished what he'd come here to say and took his seat. The minister opened the floor for others to speak. He twisted in his chair, hoping to get a glimpse of Rashida, but there were too many people.

For a moment, standing at the microphone, he'd thought he'd conjured her up out of his dreams.

He stuffed the notes into his jacket. Thank God he'd had enough foresight to jot some key points down on cards, because the moment he saw her, every coherent thought had flown out of his head.

Why was she here?

Her voice brought him back to the here and now. She stood at the microphone. He thought he'd imagined her allure, but his body tightened, and his hands flexed, both wanting to touch her again.

"I'm Rashida Howard, and as most of you know, I was raised here in the Millhouse neighborhood."

Elliott groaned as the ramifications of those words hit home. *Great. Just great.* He'd planned to find her again. It would have taken time for his brain to catch up to his heart, but there was no way he could let a woman like that get away. A woman who'd redefined pleasure for him. A woman who'd made him forget everyone else he'd ever had sex with. Now the possibility of rekindling Friday night looked as remote as snow in July.

"I skinned my knees, sold my lemonade—" Here, people chuckled. She had a human quality. He could feel her pull on the crowd.

"—hounded Ricky Thompson until he said he'd be in my club." More laughter.

"I'll be in your club now, Rashida," a male voice shouted from somewhere deep in the crowd. More laughter.

Elliott could barely refrain from turning to catch a glimpse of the male who wanted to stake claim to the woman *he* wanted.

Her face lit up when she smiled. He couldn't take his eyes off her.

"But seriously..." Her features had lost their animation. "This is our neighborhood. A place where you raised your children, where we as children fought our battles and made lasting friendships. This is a battle to save our neighborhood. Mr. Quinn's words were eloquent, but he doesn't know the memories formed here. The dreams forged here. He has no connection to this place. It's about profit for him and his company."

Elliott's body tensed, and heat flushed his face. She didn't know anything about him or his father. She didn't know what his father's goals were for the neighborhood. *But it is about profit*, a little voice in his head reminded him.

Your father needs this project to be successful or his whole business goes down the drain.

"I recommend the Zoning Commission say 'no' to Quinn Enterprises' application for changing the Millhouse area from residential to mixed-use."

A round of loud applause reverberated in the room. After Rashida took her seat, speaker after speaker took the floor. Some for the change and some against.

After Erickson had left this morning, Elliott had done some serious thinking and intensive research about the area and its potential.

It was all about attracting young families into the area, and building his father's market complex would be just the start. Eventually, this would raise the tax base and bring needed income into the city's coffers, which in turn would give more money to the schools and the infrastructure. The mayor couldn't help but stand behind such a project. Information Elliott had outlined in his speech.

"It's after nine," the minister said. "We'll have to end our remarks. Remember the Community Council meets next month. See everyone there. Drive safely and God bless."

Elliott focused his attention on finding Rashida. He thought he spotted her in the crowd, but before he could reach her, a group of citizens surrounded him with their questions. He couldn't ignore them, even though his desire to find Rashida pulled at him. This project needed his patience and the support of the community.

Finally, he managed to extricate himself and went in search of her. Would she even talk to him? What was the chance they could move beyond this and see each other occasionally?

He found her outside, surrounded by her own small group of supporters. He took a seat on the church steps and listened as she spoke.

The security lights in the parking lot had flickered on, creating a hazy amber backdrop for her stage as she gestured wildly with her hands. When people laughed at something she said, he laughed also, having no idea why he laughed, just happy to see her again and be in her presence.

When the last person faded away and just a few cars remained in the lot, it was only the two of them. She eyed him but made no attempt to close the distance between them. He was going to have to make the first move, which was okay with him. He would do whatever it took.

"I didn't know this was your neighborhood," he said, moving closer to her.

"I didn't know you were a money-hungry interloper. I thought you were an architect."

Ouch.

The sun was beginning to set. Its rays cast her body in a golden halo. An angel. An angel with a bite.

"I am an architect."

"And your father's errand boy?" Hands on her hips, her body sent out waves of hostility. He remembered the sexual desire she could also send out with that wickedly sexy body.

"I'm just trying to improve the community," he said in his defense.

She leaned toward him. "Improve the community for who? Definitely not for the poor and the elderly you're trying to displace."

Her anger excited him. He stepped closer. "I'm not trying to displace anyone."

They were so close now he could see the gold specks in her brown irises.

"Well, either you haven't done your research or you're

delusional." Her chest rose and fell with her agitation. Her breasts were definitely one of her best features. Along with her mouth, her eyes...

If he leaned a little more, he could capture those plump lips with his. He wet his lips. He could almost taste her.

"Rashida."

He blinked. A sprite stood at Rashida's shoulder.

"Rashida Joanna Howard." Out of that small body came the bellow of a Marine sergeant.

Rashida gave a little shake of her head as though she were clearing water from her ears. It pleased him to know she was feeling him like he was feeling her.

The sprite pulled Rashida away then stepped into Elliott's space. He glanced down at her. She glared up at him with goldish-brown eyes eerily familiar. "Stay away from my granddaughter."

"Grammy." Rashida pulled her away and toward the rear corner of the lot.

The grandmother gestured toward another part of the lot. "My car."

"No." Rashida shook her head. "You're not supposed to be driving."

Elliott didn't understand what was going on, but obviously Rashida had a problem. Two cars and one driver. Which left someone's car here in the church parking lot.

"Can I help?" This might be his only opportunity to talk with her.

"No, we've got it covered," Rashida snapped.

"I can drive you back here to pick up your car."

"Thanks for the offer, but I think you've done enough." She rushed after her grandmother.

A minute later, an old Cadillac belched and chugged its way out of the church's parking lot.

Elliott watched until the brake lights faded away.

"The women in that family are a force to be reckoned with, aren't they?" Reverend Clemmons stood a few feet away beside a dark sedan.

"Yes, they are." *But worth it*, Elliott thought.

"Good luck." The minister climbed into his vehicle. Just before he exited the lot, he pulled up in front of Elliott. "I'll bring Rashida back to get her car, so you don't have to worry."

Elliott propped himself on the hood of the only car besides his left in the church's lot. He had no way of contacting her, so he'd wait all night if need be. The desire to clear the air between them was that strong.

An hour later, the glare of headlights signaled a vehicle coming up the church's driveway. He slid off the hood.

Rashida opened the passenger-side door and stepped out.

"Rashida, would you like me to wait?" The minister leaned his head out of the driver's window.

She waved to him. "I'm okay."

The minister must have had his doubts because he didn't drive away.

She stopped just short of touching distance. "What do you want, Elliott?"

In all the time he'd been waiting for her to return, he hadn't perfected what he wanted to say. "Can we go somewhere and have a drink and talk?"

"I'm not thirsty. Plus, I don't have anything to say to you."

He blew a hard breath out through his nose. "I'm sorry. I had no idea this was your grandmother's neighborhood."

She didn't look at him but stared at the dark church. "Does

it matter? It would have been someone else's grandmother's neighborhood."

He threw up his hands. "I'm not trying to destroy the community."

"Then what are you trying to do?"

They were obviously going to have their say right out here in the parking lot.

"My father wants to revitalize the community by bringing business into the area." His father's plan was not as altruistic as Elliott made it sound. But he couldn't very well say his father needed the money to bring his business back from the brink of bankruptcy.

"And what would happen to the current residents' homes? Are you going to revitalize them also?"

Elliott sighed. "My father's plan doesn't focus on residential real estate, just the commercial aspects of the neighborhood."

"I don't think we have anything more to say." She moved around him and climbed into her car.

Elliott gripped the window frame before she could drive away. "Wait."

He had to find a way of staying in touch with her. "When we met the other night, we liked each other." He tried to inject a hint of lightness in his tone. "And don't say you didn't." The words fell flat. Sounded desperate.

She didn't blink an eye.

Sweat sprung out on his brow. He ran a hand over his damp face, staring at the church for a bit of divine intervention. Nothing.

Boy, he'd never had to work so hard at this. Never wanted to work so hard.

"That was before I knew who you really were."

"I'm the same guy." *The same guy who buried himself in your pussy until we both were satisfied.* But he was smart enough not to mention that little detail, standing out here on holy ground with her holding his balls in a vice.

"Why don't we sit on the church steps and talk like we did over dinner? Remember?" He wasn't good with flowery language. He was a technical guy, not a poet. But if it meant getting on his knees and quoting the little bit of Shakespeare that he knew, he'd do it.

"Is your father withdrawing his application?" Rashida asked.

"He can't."

Her lips tightened into a stubborn line. "Then we really don't have anything more to talk about."

She raised the window and sped out of the parking lot, coming within a hairsbreadth of crushing his feet under the car's tires.

CHAPTER FIVE

The Uber deposited Rashida, two evenings later, in front of a building with flashing lights, a marquee with champagne flowing from a slipper, and a crowd of people.

She adjusted the spaghetti straps of her black slit dress and resisted the urge to touch her thick, coarse hair. The air was as humid at ten p.m. as it had been at eight a.m. If she lost any of her hair pins, she'd look a hot mess.

According to her best friend, Monique, the grand opening of Synchronicity, a new Midtown nightclub, was the most anticipated opening of the year. A freelance writer, Monique covered all social events from nightclubs to flea markets.

Rashida, who wasn't into the club scene, had promised her friend she'd hang with her tonight. It gave Rashida the opportunity to enlist Monique's help with an article about the changes in the Millhouse district. It would take a couple of drinks and some coaxing to get her friend to agree. Monique shied away from social commentary articles.

But Rashida planned to pitch this article as a chance for her friend to move beyond the fluff pieces—something Monique had been trying to do for a while, without much success.

"Rashida!"

She scanned the crowd, waiting to enter the club. Monique waved both her arms over her head to get Rashida's attention. Not that she had to, since she was taller than most of the women and nearly as tall as some of the guys.

She slipped in line next to her friend, earning her some glares from the couples who'd probably been in line for an hour or two.

"You look hot," her friend said. Always ready to hype someone else up, Monique was actually the hot one. With her smooth ebony skin and toned body, she had a come-hither smile when men were in the vicinity.

Maybe she should get out and jog with her one morning. *When pigs fly.*

Her friend peered down at Rashida's feet. "What are those, six-inch heels?"

The thigh-high slit in her dress allowed Rashida to stick out her leg so Monique could get a better look at the Valentinos. "I found them at a thrift store. A steal."

"I have to give it to you," Monique said. "You'll hunt down a sale."

Rashida noticed she was getting some not-so-discreet check-outs. If she was looking for a man—which she wasn't, especially after all the drama with Elliott—there were some definite prospects here in line. But damn, thinking about Elliott ruined the pleasure of checking out the eye candy surrounding her.

"How'd the zoning meeting go?" Monique asked the question, but she was busy scanning the crowd and taking pictures of the partiers to catch a response.

On the street was not the place to tell her friend about the disaster that was her life. "Let's get inside and have a drink.

I'll tell you about it."

Two heavy teak doors and two The Rock-wannabees guarded the entrance. Rashida and Monique entered the club to the chest-thumping bass of Jamaican house music and the smell of new leather.

A wide spiral staircase led down to a ballroom-sized dance floor. Three bars formed a *U* and lined the walls. Strobe lights flashed, music blared, so Rashida knew she and her friend wouldn't be able to talk.

It took almost twenty minutes to get her margarita, but the bartender did a great job. She blended the right amount of tequila with the sweet-and-sour mix, and the salt around the rim was thick the way Rashida liked it.

She and Monique sipped their drinks as they toured the outer edges of the dance floor. The place was packed, and this was a Thursday night. Rashida couldn't imagine what Friday and Saturday would look like.

She touched her friend's arm and leaned forward to shout in her ear. "Where can we talk?"

Monique held up a finger then proceeded to text into her phone. A minute later, she led Rashida to an almost invisible door in the wall behind one of the bars. A young lady waited for them. As soon as the doors closed, a wall of silence cocooned them. The carpeted corridor muffled even the *click-clack* of their heels.

The young woman's braids swung from side to side as she walked in front of them down a short hall and into an office. She indicated they should take a seat before she left, closing the door behind her.

"Whose office is this?" Rashida asked as she looked around. They sat in contemporary orange leather lounge chairs in front of a space-age-styled desk of glass and chrome. A cream-colored leather chair sat behind the desk.

"McAllister's. He owns the place." She glanced at the door. "He'll be here in a minute, so spill."

This wasn't exactly how Rashida wanted to tell her friend of the fiasco of the last few days, but sometimes...

"I slept with a guy."

Monique patted her mouth to hold in a mock yawn.

"I fucked a stranger who turned out to be the architect attached to this zoning project."

Monique's eyes widened, then she grinned. "Was he good?"

"Was he good?! Did you hear what I said?"

Monique lifted a shoulder. "Okay. You got complications."

"You're crazy. I've got more than complications. His family has money, and with money comes clout. That could buy this vote. I need your help."

Monique took another sip of her drink. "I'm all ears."

Rashida told her about the proposed article she wanted her friend to write.

"I can't—"

"Yes, you can." Rashida leaned forward in her seat. "This is your chance to step out—"

When the door to the office opened, a tall guy with a five o'clock shadow and close-cropped hair swept into the room on a wave of citrusy cologne.

"Monique?" He looked from Rashida to Monique.

Rashida had to give her friend a nudge to get her speaking. "Hmm...yes?"

Rashida hid a smile. She'd never seen her friend so flustered.

"I'm Monique...Simmons."

They shook hands. "Malcolm McAllister." He took a seat on the edge of his desk. "You called about doing an interview on the club?"

McAllister was dressed in a light gray suit with a black pullover underneath. From the name, Rashida would have thought he was Scots-Irish, but this man had a mixture of African and European cultures in his face. He was attractive but had nothing on Elliott.

Stop.

As Monique stammered through her interview, Rashida plotted her strategy for getting her friend to do the article.

"You okay?" Rashida asked as they made their way back to the pulsing bass heart of the club.

"Yeah. Yes."

Rashida smothered a laugh. Her friend's eyes had gone vacant, while a dopey, bordering on dreamy smile hovered around her generous lips.

No surprise that Monique wanted to have another drink before they left. Probably hoping for another run-in with Malcolm McAllister.

It had been a long haul between men for Monique, so Rashida didn't begrudge her this fantasy. They strolled, dodged dancers, and peered into the dimly lit VIP section to see if they could spot any celebrities.

When they passed one of the booths, she almost choked on a sip on her second margarita.

"What?" Monique asked.

Rashida moved closer so she could get a better view of its occupants.

The guy was bald, tall, and ripped. It was hard to see the woman he was with, because the guy, even sitting, dwarfed her.

Monique sidled up beside Rashida. "What are you doing?"

"Trying to make out who this dude is." Rashida worked her way around two women who blocked her view.

The guy's hand gripped the woman's ass, kneading it like a piece of dough as his tongue appeared to search for her tonsils.

"He's enjoying himself," Monique said in a loud whisper. She leaned into Rashida to get a better view and started videoing the couple.

Rashida was too shocked by the action on the sofa to pay her friend much attention.

The guy came up for air, wiping his lips with the back of his hand, then reached for his drink.

Rashida's stomach churned, threatening to bring up the sour margarita.

"Isn't that—"

"Yeah. My brother-in-law."

F riday morning traffic was light as Rashida maneuvered through the streets from the farmers market back to her grandmother's house.

Preoccupied during the shopping trip, she'd followed like a zombie behind her grandmother as she'd squeezed the melons. Rashida shuddered. The image of Kenneth's big hands squeezing the ass of a woman who wasn't Karla made Rashida gag. Okay. Even Kenneth squeezing Karla's ass was disgusting. He'd never been good enough for her sister. He'd even tried to hit on Rashida when he and Karla were first dating.

What should she do? Tell her sister about what she'd seen in the club? Would Karla even believe her? Thank God

Monique had a video. If it came to that.

Rashida shied away from inflicting that much pain. But if it had been Alex feeling up some woman in a club when they were together, wouldn't she have wanted to know?

"You never told me you knew him." Grammy side-eyed Rashida from the passenger seat of the Eldorado.

Kenneth? Alex? She blinked, trying to bring her attention back to the here and now.

"If by *him*, you mean Elliott Quinn, I don't." *Not really.* Rashida took her eyes off the road for a moment and focused on her grandmother, who sat with her mouth tight and her hand clutched around her purse.

"I met him for the first time a few days ago." *And we screwed each other's brains out.* She couldn't say those words to her grandmother. She also couldn't tell the woman who'd practically raised her that she had planned to have carnal knowledge of his body again. But that was before she'd found out who he was. Now that would never happen. Never in a thousand years.

"Well, he looked like he wanted to know you even better. *Know you* like in the biblical sense."

Already does. He practically designed a roadmap on my body. "You're imagining things." But the idea he still hungered after her sent delicious chills over her skin. *Girl, get a grip.*

Grammy only grunted. "Like I imagined how your daddy pursued my Essie."

Rashida's interest quickened. Neither her grandmother nor her mother had spoken very much about the early courtship of her parents. Rashida didn't know what had happened between them. Just that their relationship ended when she and Karla were babies, and his name was never to be spoken again. She didn't remember very much about him, just vague memories of a slender, brown-skinned man who smelled of mangoes.

She glanced over at her grandmother. "Do you think he's still alive?"

"Probably. That kind of man you can't kill easily."

She shot her grandmother a sharp glance. "Kill?"

Her grandmother's lips tightened, an indication she'd said all she was going to say on the subject.

They drove in silence for the next few minutes. Just before they reached the house, her grandmother said, "I thought you'd forgotten about me Tuesday."

Rashida's throat threatened to close, and tears pricked the back of her eyelids. She loved this woman, and the idea her grammy felt she didn't care made her immensely sad.

"I'm sorry." She reached across the seat and touched her small hand. "I had an article to write and I got tied up with it. You could have called, you know."

"I didn't want to be a burden."

Rashida had to swallow before she could speak. "You are never a burden."

Grammy turned in the passenger seat to face her. "I am quite capable of getting myself around this city."

Rashida blew out a harsh breath through her nose. "Your license is suspended. If they catch you on the road, they'd throw you in jail."

"First, they'd have to catch me."

Rashida groaned. She could see it now on the evening news. The police chasing her grandmother down I-285, lights and sirens blaring. She shuddered.

"Grammy, please, don't get on the road until we can get your license renewed." She glanced over at her grandmother.

"Where are your glasses?"

Grammy pulled her purse tighter into her body and feigned interest at the houses and people they passed. Rashida knew that fake preoccupation. Her grandmother didn't want to talk about the glasses because she hadn't the slightest idea where they were. Rashida wanted to put her mind at rest.

"It's time for a new prescription. Maybe we can find you some of those large-frame glasses. You could look like Diahann Carroll."

Grammy humphed. "I don't need a new prescription. I see just fine. So fine, in fact, I could see how shook up that Quinn fellow was when he saw you standing in the aisle." She looked over at her granddaughter. "With your mouth hanging open."

Luckily, they pulled up to her grandmother's house, putting an end to her observations about Rashida and Elliott.

"I've lived here for almost thirty years." Grammy examined her home as if she'd never see it again. "It's the only house I've lived in since I left Tobago."

"And you'll be in your house a few more years," Rashida said.

"How are we going to win against that boy? He has money. Money always wins."

At that moment, Rashida would have promised her grandmother anything. Lied if she had to. She wrapped her arms around her grammy's shoulders. "Don't worry about it. I've got this under control. Quinn Enterprises may have money, but I've got a few tricks of my own."

Her grandmother's face relaxed for the first time in days. Rashida was determined to do whatever was necessary to keep that hope in her eyes.

• • •

Rashida and twenty other picketers marched at eight a.m. in front of the Quinn Enterprises tower. Sweat ran down her face, between her breasts, and caused her sleeveless shirt to stick to her skin.

In the second hour of their picket, her co-conspirators started wilting from the heat like sun-scorched plants. She put down her placard and started distributing water from the cooler.

"You don't have to do this."

Her heart pole-vaulted into her throat. Elliott stood within touching distance. When had he arrived? She'd watched for him, planning to up the volume of their protest when he showed up.

"Are you withdrawing your application?"

His green eyes searched her face. What was he looking for? A sign of weakness? He wouldn't find it.

"You know I can't."

"Then we protest."

She distributed the ice-cold bottles of water. The last bottle she saved for herself, which she opened and poured over her hands. Her skin tingled from the coldness. She trailed her wet fingers over her forehead and then around her neck. She wanted to upend the bottle down the front of her shirt but thought better of it, especially when she caught Elliott watching.

She drank the rest of the contents. The cold liquid refreshed her strained vocal cords.

She and the others had been shouting "Save the Millhouse District" and "Stop Quinn Enterprises" since they'd arrived.

Slipping back into position in the circle, she continued the chant, looking pointedly at Elliott whenever she rotated around his way.

An older gentleman stepped out of the building and stalked over to Elliott. The two carried on a whispered but animated conversation. A conversation about the demonstrators, because several glances and hand gestures were thrown in their direction.

Rashida knew from her search on the Quinn Enterprises website this wasn't Marcus Quinn.

The older man studied the picketers, his face screwed up in a massive display of displeasure. He said something else to Elliott. By the time Rashida rotated around the circuit again, both men had disappeared.

Her group was to demonstrate for two hours, then the second wave of picketers would relieve the first group. When her two hours were up, she took a quick bathroom break. When she returned outside, the picketers weren't marching. They stood huddled near the door. Two police officers were questioning Marty Hollis, a Millhouse resident, who lived one street over from Grammy.

"What's the problem?" Rashida asked when she reached Marty.

"Says we have to disperse," he said, a worried frown creasing his dark brown skin.

Rashida studied the two officers. They studied her back— their expressions flat. One was a female cop about thirty, short and stocky. The other officer was male with short, cropped hair and an expression that said, "I have a few years on the job, and I don't give a rat's ass what you're going to say."

"Officers, I have a permit." Rashida dug in her backpack and produce the required paperwork.

The female officer gave it a cursory once-over. "You can't

march here. You're disrupting business."

"How are we disrupting business?" Rashida asked, flinging her arm back in the direction of the front door. "We're not stopping anyone from going into the building."

"We can move to the sidewalk," Marty mumbled to Rashida. "That's public property."

Rashida wanted to argue, but some of the protesters were older citizens. No way did she want anything to happen to them.

"Okay. We'll take to the sidewalk," Rashida agreed.

"Won't work, either," Officer Crew Cut said. "You'll have to disband."

She could feel the heat rise in her face until her head felt ready to explode.

"We have the right to assemble," she said to the officers. "Would you deny us our constitutional rights?" American history was not her strongest subject, but she did remember the First Amendment.

Silent communication passed between the two officers. The female cop spoke into her collar. "We need a police van at—" She turned away as she gave the address.

Rashida's pulse hammered in her ears. Her reflexes seemed to slow down.

"Tell everyone to go home," she instructed Marty.

"No. You stay," Officer Crew Cut said to Marty. He pulled out handcuffs and proceeded to pull Marty's hands behind his back.

Her mouth went dry as a Georgia summer. Her mind seemed to move in slo-mo. Her gaze locked on the handcuffs. *Think.* She turned and made a shooing motion to the protesters.

They scattered like leaves in a good strong wind. Thankfully, the police didn't appear to be interested in pursuing them.

She glanced around for Elliott. There was no doubt in her mind he was responsible for calling the police. It didn't seem like his style, but who else could have done it? Her anger spiked when the cold metal of the handcuffs snapped over her wrists.

Elliott ended the cell call from his dad, who just happened to be watching the midday news. First Erickson and now his old man both giving him an earful about this protest and how it reflected poorly on Quinn Enterprises.

He refocused his attention on the blueprint on the computer screen.

The intercom buzzed.

Elliott ran his hand through his hair. He might as well go home for all the work he was getting done.

"Yes, Mrs. Silverman?"

"The coast is clear if you want to go out to lunch. Those people are gone."

"Those people?" he asked. He leaned back against the chair's headrest and closed his eyes.

"The protesters," she said. "A couple of them were arrested. The others dispersed."

His eyes sprung open. "What?" He leaned forward, hoping he'd misheard.

"A couple of the protesters were arrested."

"Why?"

"I don't know. The police just carted a couple of them away."

When he jerked open the door that separated him from

his father's secretary, she jumped like she'd been scalded.

She placed a hand to her heart.

"Did you actually see the police arrest someone or is this just office gossip?"

Mrs. Silverman drew her thin body up so straight he could run a ruler from the top of her head to her heels without bending it. "I don't listen to idle gossip. I saw this with my own eyes. They arrested an older Black gentleman and a young lady."

An iron band clenched around Elliott's chest. *Rashida?* "Describe?"

"Well, he looked to be—"

"Not him. *Her.*"

His father's secretary scowled at him. "I guess you could call her curvy. Springy hair. She seemed like the ringleader."

"Why do you say that?"

"Because she told the rest of the protesters to run, and they ran."

Definitely Rashida. Elliott was halfway back in his office before he drew another breath. He shouted over his shoulder. "Find out what precinct the police took those two."

When Mrs. Silverman found the police location, he called Robert Erickson. "Meet me at the Hemphill Avenue police station."

Twenty minutes later, Elliott and the attorney stood in front of the booking sergeant. "Do you have a Rashida Howard here?"

The policeman tapped on his computer keys. A minute later, he glanced up. "She's here."

"I'd like to post bail for her and the gentleman arrested with her. I don't know his name."

"Give me a moment," the officer said. "Have a seat."

Elliott and Erickson took seats on hard plastic chairs.

"Is this wise?" the lawyer asked. "I mean, she was protesting against Quinn Enterprises. How is this going to look?"

Elliott gave him a grim smile. "I'm sure you'll know how to spin it so the company comes out smelling sweet."

"Rashida Howard?"

At her name, Elliott looked toward the information desk. The sergeant motioned to him.

"She's being booked for disturbing the peace. When she appears before the judge, he'll set bail."

"How long will that be?" Elliott asked.

The policeman glanced at his watch. "The judge has court around three p.m. But I don't know where she'll be on his docket."

It was now one thirty p.m.

Elliott motioned for Erickson. "This is her lawyer. Can he see her before the hearing?"

Elliott sensed rather than saw Erickson's resistance.

"I'll call him when he can go back," the sergeant said.

Back at their seats, Elliott propped his arms on his thighs. He studied the floor. "Did you call the police?" He turned his head so he could examine the lawyer's face.

"You of all people know your father needs no blight on his reputation."

Elliott gritted his teeth to keep in the expletive that wanted to charge out of his mouth. "Did you call the police on the protesters?" he asked again.

"I did."

The old man didn't even look remorseful.

Blood pounded through Elliot's body like a runaway train

going through a tunnel. "We have to make this right. You have to do whatever it takes to make sure she isn't charged. And if there's a fine, we have to pay it."

"Your father's account can't—"

"You should have thought about that before you called the police." Elliott ran his hands through his hair. This was not what he wanted. He never wanted to cause her any distress. And being jailed was a major stressor. How had this gotten so out of control?

At two thirty, the sergeant allowed Erickson to meet with Rashida. At four p.m., she walked out of the detaining cell and out into the corridor.

The spring was gone from her step but not the fire in her eyes. She didn't say a word to Elliott when she passed but nearly scorched him with a look.

He caught up with her on the sidewalk. "Can I drive you home?"

"I'd walk before accepting a ride from you." She moved to the end of the sidewalk, scrolled through her phone, typed in some information, and then slid the phone into the back pocket of her jeans.

Elliott approached her warily. "Listen, I'm sorry about what happened. Having you arrested was not my doing."

She turned on him, her eyes hot and her face distorted. "That's your problem. You don't think about how this affects other people's lives. You just make your money and move on. You see this?" She held up both hands, palms turned toward him. Ink stained her fingertips.

"I'm fighting to help people keep a roof over their heads. I'm fighting so they can hold on to the only thing of value they have. And what are you fighting for, Elliott? To build on a piece of land that will bring your family more money?"

He wanted to defend himself. Tell her this project would put his father's business back in the black, but it was a weak defense after she'd been jailed trying to protect her grandmother's property. His father might lose his business, but he'd still have a place to call home.

"You okay, Rashida?" A fortyish Black male walked toward them, his eyes hard and suspicious as they took in Elliott. "Vera's here with the car. Can we drop you off somewhere?"

Her face relaxed. "Thanks, Marty. I've called an Uber. I'm so sorry about this." She waved her hand toward the jail. "I never—"

"Don't worry about it." He gathered her in his arms, and she patted his shoulder. The guy whispered something in her ear. She nodded.

A knife twisted in Elliott's chest. He should have been the one offering her comfort. Now, she'd never give him a second chance. And it bothered him more than he wanted to admit. He cared what she thought of him.

Marty threw another dark look in Elliott's direction before walking to the car that had pulled up to the curb.

Somehow Elliott's life had gotten intertwined with this woman, and he couldn't—didn't—want to walk away.

Rashida had the Uber drop her off at her grandmother's house instead of her apartment.

Bees buzzed in and around the wildflowers that grew in Grammy's front yard. The yellows, oranges, and wild pink blossoms were a contrast against the storm-darkened sky. A sky that reflected her spirit.

When she'd gotten up this morning, no way could she have predicted the day would turn out the way it did. Her heart ached for the protesters who had put their trust in her enough to come down to the Quinn building. She hadn't kept them safe.

Grammy waited for her at the front door. "I was worried about you." She enfolded Rashida in her arms like she used to do when Rashida was little.

It didn't matter that Rashida was several inches taller. She needed the comfort her grammy provided.

"Come on inside and eat something."

The last thing on her mind was putting food in her mouth, but she followed her grandmother to the kitchen. But when her grammy served up fish broth, Rashida cleaned her bowl.

"So, tell me what happened."

Thunder rumbled.

The lights flickered. They held their breath. The utilities were above ground, and sometimes when bad storms moved through the area, her grandmother's house lost power.

Rashida shrugged, hoping the gesture would downplay the trauma associated with being arrested. "Not much to tell. We marched. Marty and I got arrested. Here I am."

A frown creased her grandmother's brown face. "I'm not sure how these things work. Did they throw the book at you?"

Rashida couldn't keep the grin off her face. Leave it to her grandmother to bring her out of her funk. "Grammy, you've been watching too many of those old cop shows. No, they didn't throw the book at me. The judge said it was a misdemeanor and set a fine. End of story."

"I'll help you get the money for the fine." She pushed a step ladder up to the cabinet, hefted herself up, and pulled a jar from the top shelf. Inside, dollar bills along with some coins were crammed to the top of the container.

A queer pang almost like heartburn surged through Rashida's chest. Tears stung her eyes. Grammy didn't trust banks.

Rashida took the jar from her grandmother's hands and replaced it on the shelf. "Thank you for the offer, but the fine's been paid."

"By who? You?" Her grandmother scoffed. "If you had the money, you'd have been out of that place you call an apartment."

Her grandmother was always passing judgment on Rashida's place. Yes, it was small, but it suited her purposes.

"Not me. Quinn Enterprises." Something bitter coated her tongue when she said the name.

Slack jawed, her grandmother stared at her. "Wonder why? Probably 'cause it served their purposes. Otherwise, you would have rotted in jail." She shuffled to her chair at the kitchen table.

Why had their lawyer represented her in court? Grammy was probably right. It would have been bad press if he hadn't. She'd recognized him as the old guy who'd argued with Elliott earlier that morning. She believed Elliott when he'd said he hadn't called the police. So, it didn't take a genius to figure out the old lawyer had pulled some strings and gotten the protesters removed from the site.

"Don't mention you were arrested to your mother," Grammy said. "It'll just be fuel on the fire to get me out of here."

"Don't worry, I won't. And Grammy...?"

Her grandmother's head lifted.

"They have money, and if today was any indication, they know some powerful people. Let me handle this."

Rashida knew how feisty the old woman could be. Her grammy would go after Quinn Enterprises with a pitchfork if she thought she could change their minds. And Eula Mae Robinson did not look good in orange.

CHAPTER SIX

Wind whipped at Elliott's pants legs and practically lifted his hard hat off his head. His phone buzzed in his pocket, but he ignored it. His cell had been buzzing for the last thirty minutes. He was on the fourteenth floor of an unfinished highrise, and between the metal studs, the city spread out before him. Stone Mountain, a prehistoric landmark of granite some twenty miles east of downtown Atlanta, reared its monadnock head through the clouds. But now was not the time to let his focus shift.

"When is the concrete pour scheduled?" Elliott raised his voice to be heard over the wind and the whine of power tools.

The project manager consulted his watch. "Oh seven hundred tomorrow."

"Everything else okay?"

The manager nodded. "You've taken care of our problem with the concrete company, so everything is fine."

With Erickson's help, Elliott had moved around some funds to pay for the next concrete delivery. Quinn Enterprises needed an infusion of capital quickly.

"Good."

He rode the buck hoist down to street level. Once on solid ground, he maneuvered his way past steel girders, wheel barrels, and through the chain-linked fence to reach his vehicle. Inside, he pulled out his cell.

Three missed calls from his father. Elliott's pulse rose.

"What's up, Dad?"

"Where the hell have you been?"

Elliott took a deep breath. His father might be on medical leave, but he was still trying to micromanage a business he'd put Elliott in charge of.

"Consulting on the Pryor Street construction. Fourteen stories up."

"Oh. How's it looking?" The bluster had faded from his father's voice.

"Going well." He didn't mention the money shortage and how he'd robbed Peter to pay Paul. If he hadn't, the building would have fallen seriously behind schedule. Telling his father about the money concerns would do nothing good for his recuperation.

"What was so urgent?" Elliott stared out the windshield. The sun had risen. Its rays bounced off the steel girders, creating rings of rainbows around parts of the unfinished building.

"Have you seen the paper this morning?"

"Dad, I had to be here early. I didn't have time to read the paper. What's in it?" Elliott closed his eyes and massaged the tension building at the back of his neck.

"An article in the *AJC* about the disappearance of the Millhouse area. Claims another part of Atlanta culture will disappear to make way for Starbucks and other yuppie institutions, all courtesy of Quinn Enterprises. Claims the flavor of the community will be destroyed. What the hell is the flavor of the community?"

"First Amendment rights, Dad. People can voice their opinions."

"Then I can voice mine. I want you to write a rebuttal."

Elliott's headache only got worse. "Dad, I can't run your company and put out literary fires. Ignore it. The more you call attention to these attacks, the bigger they get. If *you* want to write a rebuttal, then fine, but I don't have the time. I need to let you go. I have two companies to run."

Elliott disconnected the call before his father could say more.

Did Rashida know something about the article? Even if he wanted to ask, he had no way of contacting her. Why hadn't he gotten her number the first night in the bar or even later at the Ritz? Hell, why hadn't he gotten her number after bailing her out of jail?

Yeah. Like she'd have given it to him. She'd have probably cut off his cock first.

He couldn't understand this crazy need to explain himself to her. Nothing like this had ever happened with his other hookups. They'd mutually parted ways. Why this woman? How had she burrowed her way under his skin?

He tapped his phone on the steering wheel. Traffic sped around the construction site.

He knew so little about her. She had a grandmother she cared deeply about, and she worked for *Atlanta Magazine* as a food critic. He stopped tapping his phone and stared at it a moment. Since she was a critic, she might have an online presence and a way for her followers to contact her.

A wealth of information about Rashida appeared after he typed her name into a search engine. He hit pay dirt when he found her food blog. Scrolling through the posts, he found one she'd written a few days earlier where she mentioned eateries in the Millhouse area. One had a great breakfast menu.

He glanced at his watch. Seven thirty. If he was lucky, he might catch her there.

E very other Friday morning, Rashida joined her mother, Essie, at the food bank run by their church. They sorted food donated by organizations into boxes to give to families who came to the church for help. Her mother had been doing work with families in need since she'd gotten on her feet almost twenty years ago. Rashida had started volunteering before she was a preteen.

She wanted to talk to her mother about Karla and Kenneth. What better way to ease into this touchy topic than with great pastries and coffee from one of their favorite little restaurants in Millhouse? Her mother was always in a rush to get to the church and rarely took time for herself on the one morning she had off from the hospital.

When Rashida stepped into Mama Mambo's, two teenage girls stood behind the pastry counter, giggling and shooting glances into the dining area. Rashida didn't bother to turn around. When she'd worked concessions at the movie theater as a teen and one of the popular football or basketball players showed up, all the female employees became a giggling gaggle of hormonal geese.

Leni Monroe, known affectionately as Mama Mambo, came out of the back, wiping the flour off her hands. She glanced at her teenage employees, one of whom had the stamp of Leni in her widow's peak and her large black eyes. "Ladies, we have a customer."

Both girls moved toward Rashida. "Can I help you?" both asked. Neither of them made eye contact with her but threw glances toward the dining room instead.

Leni shook her head and wandered back to whatever she had going on in the rear of the bakery.

Rashida had a serious sugar addiction. When she came into Mama Mambo's pastry shop, it was as if she'd died and gone to heaven. And like all the other times she'd come into the store, she couldn't decide what she wanted.

"The pecan cinnamon buns are particularly tasty," a familiar male voice said from behind her.

Rashida whirled so quickly she almost fell off her platform sandals.

Elliott caught her elbow to keep her from pitching into a display of packaged dinner rolls. "Careful." His hand on her arm was firm, steadying. His touch sent a jolt through her body, which did nothing to help her rocky balance. It was only after she righted herself that she realized both her hands were on his hard, ripped biceps. She dropped her hands like she'd touched a hot wok.

Excited twitters of girlish conversation broke out behind Rashida. So that's what all the giggling was about.

"What are you doing here?" Her voice sounded as if she had a frog lodged in her throat.

"Buying cinnamon buns." Green eyes sparkling with humor, he tilted his head and gave her a wolfish grin. Sunlight glittered off the red highlights in his dark hair. The man was too handsome for anyone's good. She gave herself a mental shake. What in the world was she doing? She was as moon-eyed as those girls behind the counter.

Counter? God, she was here to buy pastries and coffee and get to the church. She turned and stared down at the pastry shelves. Everything was a blur. She couldn't think. Why was he here? It couldn't be a coincidence. This area was far from Buckhead.

"Two cinnamon buns and two large coffees with hazelnut creamer," Rashida said to the girls.

Like a vaudeville act, the two sprang into action, colliding off each other, giggling then moving around the other to package and pour.

Rashida rummaged around in her purse for her debit card. Maybe if she ignored him, he'd go away. Finding her card, she slapped it down on the pastry case top.

"Can we talk?" Elliott asked.

The whisper of his breath on her neck made goose bumps break out like hives.

Rashida threw a panicked glance in the girls' direction. They were busy making a mess of her order.

"Go away. We have nothing to talk about," she whispered. Why had he shown up today? Today, when she wanted to have a serious conversation with her mother about relationships. About how the Howard women had a bad track record with men. How in all honesty could she have that conversation when all she wanted to do was fall into bed with Elliott and never get out?

"No pressure," he said. "I'll wait at the table outside. I have something serious I want to talk to you about. I just need a minute of your time."

Rashida turned her head to stare at the tables, even though she'd passed them numerous times on her way into the store. She nodded. "But only for a minute."

He made his way toward the exit.

The girls pulled the order together quickly once Elliott left the bakery.

Juggling her purchases and her purse, Rashida backed out of the store then took a seat across from him at one of the bistro tables.

"What do you want?" she asked.

"The article in the *AJC*." His eyes had lost their usual twinkle.

"What about it?"

He cocked his head. "Since you didn't ask which one, I assume you had something to do with writing it."

Monique had finally come through and written the article. She'd done a good job. Rashida hoped this would be one of many articles that her friend could use to build her writing portfolio.

When she didn't respond, he continued, "My father suffered a heart attack seven weeks ago. He's at home recuperating. He read the article and was upset at how it portrayed his company."

Well, now she knew why Marcus Quinn had never returned any of her calls.

Her heart went out to Elliott. She could only imagine the anguish he must be feeling. "I'm sorry to hear your father is ill."

"But…" he prompted.

"But I have to worry about my grandmother also. She would lose everything she and my grandfather worked for."

Elliott frowned then nodded his head as though he understood. He couldn't possibly understand.

And no way could she admit to him she would lose the only refuge she'd known all her life. She wasn't ready for him to know how vulnerable that made her. And since they weren't and never would be a couple, there was no reason for him to know.

Without looking into those seductive green irises, she picked up her pastries and practically ran for the car.

Rashida's pulse was still elevated when she rushed into the church basement. She was so off-kilter from seeing Elliott, she'd almost left the coffee in the car.

"What's wrong?" her mother asked when Rashida barreled into the room.

"Nothing. Why do you think something is wrong?" Her voice sounded like she'd inhaled helium. "Here." She handed her the coffee and pastry.

Her mother's eyes lit up with pleasure. "Thank you. This is so sweet."

While she sipped her coffee and took bites of the cinnamon bun, Rashida eyed the cans of food and fresh fruit, trying to buy time for her emotions to level off. But thinking about what she wanted to discuss with her mother only made her blood rush even faster through her veins. "I hope everyone likes bananas. There's sure a lot of them."

Her mother mumbled her agreement as she chewed.

Rashida set to work, going over in her head how she'd broach this subject with her mother.

"Is there any more fruit?" The Tobago accent lingered in her mother's voice, even after thirty years in the States. Her "there" came out more like "dare."

Rashida took a deep breath, readying herself to meet the task she wanted to accomplish.

She and her mother worked the morning shift at the church

alone, which made it a great place for a private conversation.
Her mother was very sensitive about her eldest daughter and
her marriage. Translation: her mom wanted to pretend her
daughter and son-in-law were lovebirds living in marital bliss.

"Mom?"

"Hmmm..." She sorted cans of vegetables into the boxes.

"How does Karla seem to you?"

Her mother peered over her glasses. "Fine. Why?"

Rashida shrugged. How should she proceed? Might as well
jump in with both feet. "Kenneth's cheating on her."

There, she'd said it.

Like a frame of film put on pause, her mother didn't move.

Rashida never knew the story of her parents' marriage.
Had her father cheated on her mother? Had the marriage at
one time been a loving one?

"And how do you know?"

"Because I've seen him around town with other women.
Lots of different women."

"He could be entertaining clients." Her mother went back
to sorting food, but Rashida knew she'd gotten her attention.

"From the way he was feeling them up—"

Her mother's head jerked in Rashida's direction, a look
of disgust on her face.

"—they may have once been clients, but they've graduated
to much more."

"Have you mentioned this to your sister?"

"No." Rashida didn't know what she should do. Maybe the
two of them could stage an intervention.

Her mother gave up the pretense of sorting. "Good. Don't."

Rashida's stomach free fell. So much for the intervention.

"Why not?" This was so not how she'd hoped her mother would

respond. She'd expected some reluctance, but this...?

"Because it will break her heart."

Like yours was broken?

"Mom, it will break her heart more if she finds out we knew and didn't tell her. Listen—" Rashida reached for her cell with Monique's video that had been burning a hole in her back pocket. "I've got this video that will prove—"

"Ladies, how's it going?" Reverend Clemmons advanced on them. For such a big man, he moved as silently as a cat.

Broad as he was tall, the minister reminded her mother of the ex-football player, Roosevelt Grier. He'd been one of her father's favorite players.

"Did I come at a bad time?" He glanced between Rashida and her mother, maybe sensing the tension between them.

Her mother recovered first. "No, Reverend. We've finished this conversation."

Rashida didn't agree but wisely kept her mouth shut.

The reverend turned his soulful gaze on her mother. Rashida side-eyed him. He'd been widowed five years, and she believed the reverend was now on the hunt for a wife. Plenty of the church women wanted to be in line for the position, but he had his attention fixed on her mom. Except her mother seemed to be as oblivious to the reverend's feelings as she was to what was going on in her older daughter's marriage.

Was it possible for one of the Howard women to find true love? It would be wonderful if it could be her mother. She'd been alone far too long. If anyone deserved love, it was her.

Her mother would never ask the minister out, though, and he was either too shy or too intimidated to say more than hello.

"Mom and I are planning a cookout at Grammy's two weekends from now and wondered if you'd be interested in coming?" Rashida said. She could almost feel the scorch marks on the sides of her head from her mother's intense displeasure.

"I would be honored to come," the reverend replied brightly. "What should I bring?"

"Just your appetite." And judging by the man's girth, his appetite would be pretty healthy.

The reverend rubbed his massive hands together. "Am I gonna finally get a chance to try your cooking? I've heard so much about it."

"Yes, you will," her mother said. "Rashida loves to cook. She just wants me and her sister to entertain the guests while she prepares all the food."

Judging by the minister's crestfallen expression, he'd been referring to her mother's cooking. Probably wanted to take her for a test run before he bought the product.

Rashida gave herself a mental slap. She had to stop being so cynical about marriage. Somewhere out in the world, there were happy unions. She just didn't know any. And for that reason, marriage wasn't on her list of things to experience before she died. But maybe her mother would be happy, because the reverend beamed down on Essie Howard like she was the moon, the sun, and the stars.

And for just a moment, Rashida wondered what it would be like to have a successful union with Elliott.

CHAPTER SEVEN

Elliott knew there was a problem the moment the Land Rover turned onto Millhouse Road.

Traffic had slowed, and people filled the street.

"Probably an accident," Elliott said to his passenger.

Monroe Redding grunted.

A nondescript man in a well-tailored suit with thinning brown hair, Redding, the venture capitalist Erickson had spoken of, had said little in the fifteen-minute drive over.

With only a one-day layover in Atlanta before he headed back to Los Angeles, he'd agreed to meet with Elliott about the project. Except he'd asked few questions. A bad sign.

Elliott had done some research on the guy. He wasn't on the same scale as Warren Buffett, but who was? Elliott just hoped he'd be interested in investing some of his considerable wealth into his father's business.

"This is the beginning of the neighborhood," Elliott said. "At the turn of the twentieth century, attempts were made to bring light industry into the area, since it was half a day's wagon ride from downtown Atlanta.

"The property we've purchased is on this main street. It borders the neighborhood. Records indicate a couple of brothers operated a gristmill on the site."

"Interesting."

The man's tone indicated he was less than enthralled by the recital. Two women carrying placards dashed between Elliott's vehicle and the one in front of his. He decided to can the history lesson and concentrate on not hitting any of the pedestrians.

A news van entered the main road from a side street.

Redding leaned forward to peer out the window. "Whatever's happening must be newsworthy."

"Usually, the area is pretty quiet. A busy day is a fender bender."

"Is the property close by?" Redding asked.

"Just up ahead." Elliott studied the banker who'd said more words in the last minute than he'd uttered on the drive over. "How about we park the car and walk? By the time you finish looking over the building and the surrounding land, the traffic problem should be cleared."

Redding nodded his agreement.

After Elliott found a parking spot, they moved in the direction of the property his father had acquired. His pulse kicked up as they neared the destination. It appeared to be the epicenter of the traffic problem.

A small group of protesters carried signs and moved in a circle in front of the dilapidated building Elliott's father had purchased. A white news van was parked on the street. A reporter and cameraman stood off to the side, watching the protesters and setting up their equipment.

A small crowd had gathered on the sidewalks, spilling over into the street.

A drum beat at the base of Elliott's skull. The placards read:

Save Millhouse!

Stop gentrification!

"Is this the property?" Redding asked.

Elliott nodded. Of all the days to have a protest.

"Sounds like your project doesn't have the approval of the residents."

Redding stood at Elliott's elbow as they observed the group walking in a circle and shouting, "Don't destroy Millhouse!"

"It would seem that way," Elliott remarked, trying to figure out how he could turn this around. Luckily, Redding hadn't been in town when Rashida and her crew had protested at the building in Buckhead and been arrested. Today's protest would seem like a minor blip rather than a recurring issue.

The reporter and her cameraman finished a live segment. She walked toward the protesters, looking for someone to question. She headed straight for an elderly woman with a mop of gray curls.

Elliott couldn't believe his bad luck. Rashida's grandmother.

"They just don't understand what the project can do for the neighborhood," he said.

He could feel Redding's gaze on him. "Oh, I think they understand."

"Excuse me a moment," Elliott said.

He threaded his way through the crowd, wanting to get closer to the interview being conducted.

"It's the rich against the poor and the elderly," Rashida's grandmother said into the microphone.

Elliott's collar tightened. This complex his father wanted to build would only help the neighborhood. Why couldn't the protesters see the benefit?

"What is your name?" the reporter asked.

"Eula Mae Robinson."

"So, Mrs. Robinson, you think Quinn Enterprises is trying to drive the existing residents out of their homes?"

"That's exactly what I think." Her vigorous nod made her curls bounce.

Elliott couldn't let this get out of hand. He had to defuse this situation. He moved through the crowd and up onto the sidewalk. "I'm Elliott Quinn."

The reporter moved with the speed of a raptor. She stuck the microphone in his face with an unholy gleam in her eye. "Mr. Quinn, will you tell our viewers what your plans are for the area?"

He had the attention of the group in the street, including Monroe Redding, who stood on the edge of the gathering. He could feel the animosity from the protesters at his back.

"My father bought this property"—he gestured to the building behind him—"to build a commercial space that would bring business into the Millhouse area. Money generated by these companies would revitalize the area. Quinn Enterprises is not in the residential real estate business. Buying homes is not our intent."

"Do you have any businesses that have already leased the proposed space?" the reporter asked.

"A national grocery chain has shown some interest."

"But that's dependent on the zoning application being approved. Correct?"

She'd done her homework.

"Yes," Elliott said. "When the zoning application is approved."

From the corner of his eye, he could see Mrs. Robinson advancing on him. "Who's going to shop in this fancy, expensive store, hmmm?" She poked him in the side with her placard. She didn't wait for a reply. "Not any of us."

The reporter stepped back but stayed close enough to hear every word they said.

"I won't let you drive us out of our neighborhood." Rashida's grandmother took another step in Elliott's direction, jabbing the stick into his side again.

He decided to take the high road and stepped off the curb, out of her reach, which seemed to calm her.

Flashing lights indicated the arrival of a police car. Two officers stepped out of their patrol vehicle right in the thick of the bystanders.

"Do you people have a permit for this protest?" an officer said.

All eyes focused on Rashida's grandmother. She must have been the organizer.

"We have a right to protest," someone shouted.

"Not if it turns disorderly or causes traffic delays," one of the officers said. "Disband or I will have you all arrested."

Mrs. Robinson gave Elliott the evil eye then said something to the other protesters. They lowered their placards and slowly moved off.

Situation defused. Elliott exhaled a sigh of relief.

"Ready to go?" Redding asked.

"Yeah." Elliott hesitated. Remembering the grandmother's license had been suspended, he looked around for Rashida. She had to be here somewhere.

He followed the old lady's progress from the sidewalk to a rusted-out car that belched black fumes and appeared to take up a city block. An elderly woman with steel-gray hair whose head barely cleared the steering wheel sat in the driver's seat.

Shaking his head at the thought of the two old ladies on the road, Elliott turned to Redding. "Ready to check out more of the area?"

"Lead on."

They crossed the street.

Brakes screeched.

"Watch out!"

Pain exploded in Elliott's left hip. A feeling of weightlessness. Then blackness.

Rashida pushed through the masses waiting in the Emory University Hospital's emergency room like a scythe cutting through grain. She'd caught part of the midday news and seen her grandmother and some of her cronies marching on Millhouse Road and then caught the report of the pedestrian struck by a car at the scene of the protest.

The television commentator hadn't released the pedestrian's name.

Her grandmother's frantic call filled in the rest. Mrs. McClain, her grandmother's neighbor, had hit Elliott with her car. The two women had driven to the protest together.

Why was Mrs. McClain still driving? She was half blind. Surely her license had been revoked years ago.

Rashida made it to the information desk, ignoring the protests and curses aimed at her for cutting the line.

"Elliott Quinn. Is he here?"

The person manning the front desk pointed her toward another window, where she repeated her question.

A petite redhead in scrubs studied her. "Mr. Quinn is here,

but only next of kin can go back."

"I'm next of kin." The lie slipped easily from Rashida's lips. "I'm Mrs. Quinn."

Rashida's anxiety must have communicated itself to the redhead. She lifted an eyebrow, but whether she was about to ask for identification, Rashida would never know. "Go around the corner and I'll buzz you in. He's in cubicle sixteen."

When she pushed through the double doors, the sharp anesthetic smell of pine cleaner hit her in the face but couldn't completely mask the copper smell of blood and the acrid stench of urine.

The emergency room consisted of small, individual glass-walled rooms. She walked up and down the corridor without finding Elliott then finally stopped a male with a stethoscope around his neck. "I'm looking for Elliott Quinn."

"Hold on." He walked back to a center desk and spoke with someone Rashida couldn't see then came back to her. "Mr. Quinn is having an MRI. Are you family?"

At Rashida's nod, he indicated the room with an open door and no bed. "Have a seat. It may be about forty-five minutes."

Inside the cubicle, she plopped down on an uncomfortable plastic chair and bowed her head. Because her grandmother and one of her friends had been the cause of Elliott's accident, she'd rushed here to do damage control.

Okay, it had been more than damage control.

She wanted to make sure he wasn't seriously hurt. Yes, she could have called, but she had this unexplained need to put her hands on him. And to do that, you had to come in person. Right?

So her grandmother had barely hung up the phone before

Rashida was flying down North Decatur Road toward the hospital.

Although Grammy hadn't driven the car that hit Elliott, Rashida hadn't missed on the televised replay of the protest that her grandmother poked him with her sign. What had possessed Grammy? She was always the voice of reason when Rashida and Karla fought.

At eighty-three years old, Grammy and Mrs. McClain were the same age. Neither woman would do well behind bars.

The time crawled with Rashida alternating between pacing and handwringing.

Finally, a male employee pushed Elliott's hospital bed back into his cubicle.

He was awake. And by the climb of his eyebrows into his hairline when he saw her, he was also alert. "What are you—"

"Listen, I'm so—"

A nurse appeared in the open door. "He's doing fine, Mrs. Quinn," she said as she flipped through Elliott's chart.

Rashida shot him a quick glance to see if he'd caught how she'd been addressed. He had. Humor flashed in his eyes, and he grinned then mouthed, "Mrs. Quinn?"

Her face flooded with color. The room was suddenly overheated. She glued her attention to the nurse and tried to ignore Elliott.

"Blood pressure is stable. No nausea. The doctor will review the MRI and come in to talk to you two in a few." She patted Elliott's arm then left, enclosing them in a vacuum.

Rashida moved toward the bed. "I'm so sorry." She gripped her hands together to refrain from touching him.

When he didn't speak, she rambled on. "Grammy's not violent. You must have done something to set her off. And...

and I'm sure Mrs. McClain didn't mean to hit you."

He only tilted his head and lifted his eyebrow in a sardonic gesture.

"Say something." She hated that silent treatment. It made her want to ramble on to fill the void.

"Something."

She growled, irritated at him and herself. "You're fine. I don't know why I rushed down here."

"Why did you...rush down here?"

"I..." Should she tell him the truth? That she'd been scared shitless he'd been seriously injured. "I—"

The door opened, and three people in scrubs entered. A Black female separated from the group. She had what Rashida assumed was Elliott's chart.

"Mr. Quinn." She glanced over at Rashida and nodded then shifted her attention back to Elliott. "I'm Dr. Gardner. How are you feeling?"

"Fine. A little shaky and my head hurts."

The doctor handed the chart to one of the two standing silently behind her. She pulled a penlight from her breast pocket and leaned over the bed to look into his eyes.

"Your MRI showed no damage to the brain. No swelling. No indication of a bleed." She straightened, placing the instrument back in her pocket. "You've suffered a mild concussion but no broken bones. If you want, we could keep you overnight for observation, or we could send you home if someone—" She glanced at Rashida. "If someone will be there with you for at least the next twenty-four hours."

"My wife will be there with me."

Rashida opened her mouth to say she wasn't his wife, but Elliott spoke first.

"How are your grandmother and her friend doing?"

Why was he asking about Grammy and her friend now? Was this some type of emotional blackmail?

Since Grammy hadn't mentioned anything about an arrest when she'd called, Rashida had to assume Mrs. McClain was at home also. "They're okay."

The doctor waited not so patiently for Rashida's response to her question.

Right. I'm his wife. "He'll be fine at home. I'll be there all evening."

"Good," the doctor said. "I'll send the nurse in with prescriptions for pain and nausea. If you're unable to rouse him, call an ambulance."

She patted Elliott on the arm. "Take care, Mr. Quinn."

The doctor left the room with her entourage following closely behind.

Elliott turned his gaze on Rashida's fuming one. There was an unholy light in his eyes. "My place or yours?"

E lliott had lied to the doctor. As he and Rashida rode up the elevator to his apartment, the ding for each floor rang in his head like the bell tied to the bars of an overactive three-year-old's first tricycle.

But if given the opportunity to spend the night in the hospital or spend the night with Rashida, he'd lie again.

With Rashida at his side, he stumbled out of the elevator and down the hall toward his apartment like an old man who'd had one too many drinks.

At the door, he patted his pockets for his keys.

"I have them." She jangled the keys in her free hand.

He didn't remember how she'd gotten the keys but was glad she was in control, because he sure wasn't. His head had started to pound on the drive over in her small car. The drugs he'd received in the hospital had worn off.

Once inside his apartment, he sprawled on the sofa and cursed the sunlight pouring in the floor-to-ceiling windows. At night, the windows provided a beautiful glimpse of downtown Atlanta. But now the sunlight was like a shiv to his brain.

"Do you want me to get this filled?" She rattled paper under his nose. It might have been two sheets or twenty. They swam in and out of focus.

"I'm fine."

"Suit yourself." Her voice had the long-suffering tone of an overtaxed mother.

He drifted in and out of sleep, half-aware of her moving around his apartment.

"Take this." She shoved two tablets under his nose and held out a glass of water. He obeyed without complaint. He just hoped it wasn't cyanide.

Hours or days later, he woke, and the pain had subsided to a dull ache. She must have found the remote to lower the shade, because the room was in shadow even though his watch told him it was only six p.m.

He could hear her puttering around the kitchen, and he smelled eggs. He forced himself off the sofa and made his way to the kitchen. No way did he want her waiting on him. He'd gotten a bump on the head, not a bullet to the brain. ·

He slid onto one of the bar stools that surrounded the island. The Carrara marble felt cool against his fingers.

"Sorry there was no food," he said. "I usually eat out."

"No problem." She didn't face him but continued to stir the eggs. When she finished, she divided the food between two plates and added a twist of lime for decoration.

He chuckled, imagining her dismay when she opened the refrigerator to find a few eggs, bottles of champagne, and dried-up limes.

She stood on the opposite side of the island. "I'm sorry about"—her hands fluttered around her head, her curls bobbing with the motion—"about your injury." She lifted her gaze briefly to catch his. "I'm sure Mrs. McClain didn't mean to hit you with her car."

"And your grandmother?" he asked. "What's her excuse?"

"You must have said something that upset her."

She must have known how weak that sounded, because she bit her lip and wouldn't meet his eyes.

"I'm sure I've made lots of people upset, but they don't stab me."

She placed her hands on her hips. As she leaned toward him, her face contorted in frustrated anguish. "She doesn't usually attack people."

"So, we do agree she attacked me?"

She didn't answer but instead took her plate of uneaten eggs to the sink and scraped them down the garbage disposal.

He pushed his own plate away. This was not how he'd envisioned the evening going.

"Listen." He got up and carried his plate to the sink. "I'm not going to press charges against Mrs. McClain. And your grandmother… She would have made a wicked pirate a few hundred years ago."

Rashida's mouth quivered in the first sign of humor he'd seen from her all day. He hated to see that levity disappear.

And disappear it would when she found out the police would probably press charges against Mrs. McClain.

He decided to change the subject. "Let's order in."

With deadpan delivery, she asked, "You don't like my cooking?" Her eyes gave her away. They'd warmed to a rich honey-gold.

"I'm sure your cooking is wonderful. I'm just not in the mood for eggs." He opened one of the island's drawers and pulled out takeout menus from a half dozen restaurants.

"What are you in the mood for?" he asked. He was in the mood for a lot more than food.

Later, after consuming gyros, rice pilaf, and a Greek salad from the Mediterranean restaurant around the corner, they relaxed on the sofa.

She was a foodie. Dinner seemed to loosen her up, because she entertained him with stories of her grandmother's antics and of the family meals they'd shared and of her favorite food blogs she'd written.

When she talked, her eyes sparkled and her hands flew in wilder and wilder gestures. He drank in her words, her enthusiasm. Caught in her whirlwind, he'd become drunk on the champagne of her presence. But for all she'd told him about her family, she hadn't once mentioned her father. When they'd dined at the Ritz, he'd gotten the impression there wasn't any contact with her dad.

"It's just you, your mother, and sister…"

"And Grammy," Rashida finished for him.

"Aw, yes, Grammy."

She chuckled.

"Do you miss your dad?" he asked.

The humor in her face faded. "You can't miss what you've

never had."

She'd shut down. He had an important question to ask. Would she open up and be honest? Regardless, he couldn't waste this opportunity. The way their relationship was going, he might never have another chance. "Why'd you leave that morning after we'd made love?"

She started to gather up their leftover food. He touched her arm. "You're running away again."

She stared into his face then flopped down on the sofa. "I didn't see any reason to stay. We had sex. It was good. Why drag it out?"

"I wanted more. Still do." He'd said his piece. The ball was in her court.

When she didn't respond, he said, "We made a connection. Don't say we didn't."

She bit the corner of her lip. "The sex was good," she repeated. "But—but we're so different."

"I'm not proposing marriage. Let's enjoy each other and see where it goes." He held his breath.

She shook her head then rose. "I can't." Picking up the plates, she headed for the kitchen.

"Okay." She'd have to come to him. He'd never force his desire on her. But he could maybe help things along. Her phone lay face down on the coffee table. "What's your cell's password?"

She immediately appeared in the opening between the two rooms. "Put that down."

"I just want to give you my contact information. You know, in case I fall into a coma in the middle of the night. You can give 9-1-1 this address."

"I already have your address, remember? I drove you here."

He smiled up at her. "Oh, yeah." He tossed the phone lightly in the air. "Humor me. I just want you to be able to call me in the middle of the night in case you need anything."

Her eyebrows shot up. "Like a booty call?"

He couldn't stop his grin. "I wouldn't hold it against you if you wanted to use me."

She slid onto the cushion next to him and snatched the phone from his grasp. After punching some numbers into the cell, she handed the phone to him. "Only because you might fall into a coma."

His pulse sped up at her confession.

After he entered his contact information, he dialed his number as she gathered up more items for the kitchen.

"Your phone, ma'am."

She pocketed her cell then headed to the kitchen. Meanwhile, his cell buzzed in his pocket with her incoming call. Whistling, he picked up the rest of the food and followed her. One step forward. A start.

They made short work of the cleanup. When they finished, she turned to him. "Do you want me to go?"

Hell no. He shook his head. Mistake. A bell bonged from one corner of his skull to the other.

"Not unless you want to. I have a guest bedroom." He wouldn't suggest his bed. She might take off and leave him, not caring about his concussion.

"Okay. I'll stay."

He relaxed. At least she'd be near.

Elliott tossed and turned most of the night and was just drifting off to sleep when he smelled lavender. She stood at the door watching him. He held his breath, willing her to come to him.

But she didn't. She turned and disappeared as quietly as she'd appeared.

Dawn was seeping between the blinds by the time he fell asleep.

CHAPTER EIGHT

When Elliott returned to the Quinn Enterprises' office the next morning, there'd been no messages from Monroe Redding. The venture capitalist had vanished like Houdini.

Elliott spoke into the intercom. "Mrs. Silverman, would you get Mr. Redding on the line?"

While he waited for his father's secretary to contact Redding, Elliott walked to the window to stare down at the cars moving like ants along Peachtree Road. When Rashida had stepped out of the Uber in front of his building the evening they'd met, he'd had no idea she would change his life. He'd had his share of gorgeous women. One or two had been serious, but he'd spent the last five years building his business, and none of those relationships had survived.

Rashida had blown in like a hurricane and disrupted his quiet existence.

The intercom buzzed.

"Mr. Redding's on the line."

Elliott picked up the desk phone and connected with the call. "Mr. Redding? Elliott Quinn here."

"Ah, Mr. Quinn. How are you?"

"Doing fine. Back in the office." Elliott focused his attention on one of the pictures on the wall. His father shaking hands with one of Atlanta's past mayors.

"So soon? That clunker gave you a smart tap. You went down hard. Scared the bejesus out of me."

Elliott had little memory of it. Just weightlessness then for a second a sharp pain. "My father always said I had a thick skull."

Redding chuckled. "I'm glad you're okay. What did the police do with the old ladies?"

"I'm not sure. I won't press charges." He made a mental note to check on Mrs. McClain's case.

"Good to hear. Your goodwill will go a long way in establishing rapport with the community. Interesting to see the elderly on the front lines."

Elliott didn't want to dwell on the protest or the accident. He needed to find a backer for the project, and quick. "I know we didn't get to see much of the property. I'd like to remedy—"

"I walked the neighborhood after you were whisked away. Lovely old homes. Most in need of repair but good bones. I could see the area turning into a showplace."

A weight lifted off Elliott's chest. Maybe things would be okay.

"But you're sitting on a powder keg," Redding continued. "You're also sitting on an opportunity that could be very profitable for both of us if handled correctly."

"My father would be happy to hear you say that."

"No. I mean profitable for *you* and me, Elliott. I took the opportunity to look at your company's website and was very impressed with your home designs."

"Thank you." This conversation was veering off track. "I appreciate—"

"Your father is financially in the red, and frankly, I wouldn't think of partnering with someone who is so overextended."

A vise started to tighten around Elliott's chest. Redding was bringing back yesterday's headache.

"But I see potential in the neighborhood. Your father's building would be the anchor drawing young professionals into the area."

The pressure on Elliott's chest eased.

"But your designs would make them want to call the community home."

Elliott forced the scrunched-up muscles in his face to relax. Where was this going?

"I want you to design a community for me," Redding said. "A community that would appeal to young urban professionals."

Elliott's head spun. How did they get from funding his father's project to him rebranding a community? "Mr. Redding, I'm flattered, but..."

"My interest would be in the whole community, not just the market arena your father wants to build. If you get approval from the zoning board and get the community on board, I'd be willing to invest. But based on the opposition I saw yesterday, I think it's doubtful you'll get community approval."

Elliott smoothed his hand across the grains of the old desk. It had belonged to his great grandfather and then to his grandfather. "I'm confident the zoning committee will approve my father's application. By this time next month, we'll be breaking ground." From his lips to God's ears.

Getting the community on board was another matter and would be a hard sell. To make room for Luxury Designs' floor plans, some of the existing homes would have to be torn down. Would homeowners be willing to sell?

"I hope so, Mr. Quinn. With your background, we could be

a dynamic duo. Me buying the properties and you designing the homes. Keep me posted. Until then." A *click* indicated Redding had ended the call.

Elliott sank into his office chair. The call with Redding had taken a left turn and headed down a path he hadn't foreseen. Although confused, he couldn't deny his excitement. His and Chris's business had been plodding along, paying for itself but not growing as they'd hoped. Now Redding offered them the chance to put their company on the map.

Elliott's eyes drifted back to the photo hanging on the wall—his father in his former glory. Of course, Elliott had to do everything he could to make sure his father returned to a functioning, productive business. The venture capitalist made it quite clear the community had to be on board with the changes or no millions of dollars for his dad.

Elliott returned to the window, his sights on the cars and people moving below. He needed to smooth over the rough waters with the community.

He needed Rashida. She was the key.

Rashida stepped into Buckley Real Estate's foyer. Two large ferns dominated the room, but the receptionist wasn't behind her desk. Rashida checked the time on her cell—lunchtime. Good. If luck held, her brother-in-law would also be out of the office.

She walked through the large, open space until she spotted her sister at her desk. Karla waved her over. "What's up?"

"Hi." Rashida knew her smile was too bright and her voice too perky. "Where's Kenneth?" She jerked her thumb toward his office.

"Out," Karla said. She glanced at the clock on her desk. "He should be back any moment."

Rashida had no desire to see the man. He brought out a primitive rage in her. And since his performance at Synchronicity—a performance she was sure he didn't know she'd seen—she thought it better if they didn't meet face to face. She wouldn't be held accountable for what would come flying out of her mouth. "Do you want to grab lunch?"

Karla's pencil-thin eyebrows lifted. "Didn't we just have lunch the other week?"

"What can I say? I enjoy your company."

"Riiight." Karla looked down at her desk.

"Forget the paperwork," Rashida said. "You need some time out of the office." She gripped her sister's arm and pulled her toward the front door. "Trust me. The paperwork will be here when you get back."

Rashida had a sneaky suspicion her sister did Kenneth's paperwork as well as her own. He thought of her as a glorified administrative assistant, even though Karla probably had the greater number of closings each month.

"Are you driving?" her sister asked.

"Of course."

Ten minutes later, Rashida pulled her Toyota into a spot at the entrance to a park close to Karla's office. Rose bushes lined the walk, and massive hardwoods provided plenty of shade. They'd need it because the day was hot as Hades and just as humid. Here and there a few puddles remained from an early morning thundershower.

Near the park's entrance, the smell of tomatoes, onions, peppers, and meat floated from an enchilada food truck. They grabbed food and drinks then headed for a bench in the shade.

"There was a little problem yesterday," Rashida said.

Her sister, who'd taken a dainty bite of her food, finished chewing then swallowed. "What problem?"

"Grammy participated in a protest." Rashida dropped her head then glanced up at her sister through her lashes. "Actually, Grammy organized the protest."

Karla's eyebrows shot up. "What is it with you two?"

"What do you mean?" Rashida had a feeling she was in for a lecture. Karla took being the oldest quite seriously.

Karla's mouth tightened, and her eyes narrowed. "It didn't escape my notice that your friend, Monique, just happened to write an article on the Millhouse area. And don't tell me it was a coincidence."

"Well, I might have had something to do with it."

"Maybe a lot to do with it." Karla took another nibble of her enchilada.

"But that's not the half of it," Rashida said.

Her sister side-eyed her then took a deep breath. "Do I want to know the rest?"

"Grammy was in Mrs. McClain's car when they struck someone."

Her sister placed her plate down on the stone. "Is the person okay?"

Rashida had to be careful. She didn't want her sister to know she knew Elliott Quinn. She didn't want to stir up a hornet's nest. "They took him to the hospital for observation."

"I knew this would eventually happen. Both of them should have had their license suspended a long time ago." Karla blew out a breath. "Who did Mrs. McClain hit?"

Damn. Why couldn't her sister be satisfied with knowing

the guy was okay? "Elliott Quinn." She rushed on, "But he's fine."

"And you know this because?"

"I went to the hospital to check on him and he'd been released." That was technically not a lie. The hospital did release him. They'd just discharged him into her care. Something her sister didn't need to know.

Karla closed her eyes briefly. "Was it an accident?"

"Of course. Why would you—"

"Because it was Elliott Quinn, of all people. I assume the protest was over the new plans for the Millhouse building."

"Yes. He's not going to press charges."

"How do you know?"

"I asked him."

Karla took her half-eaten enchilada to the trash. "Why did you bring me out here to tell me this? You could have raised my blood pressure back at the office."

"We need your help."

"Who is *we*?"

"Grammy and the folks from the neighborhood. I have to figure out a way to get Quinn Enterprises to listen to reason. And you know how these real estate things work. What can we do?"

"What do you mean, 'listen to reason'?"

Why did her sister have to be so dense? She knew what Rashida meant. She just wanted her to spell it out.

"Abandon the project."

Karla rubbed her forehead. "Have you been smoking?"

Rashida let out an exasperated sigh. "Of course not. You know I don't fool with that stuff."

"If they've already purchased the property, they won't walk

away," Karla said. "They would lose too much money."

"Okay, I didn't think it through. How about sell the land?"

"Doubt it. Too much money tied up while they wait for a buyer. Your best bet," Karla said, "is for the community to come together and suggest some other options for the land. Options that benefit both parties."

Rashida nodded. "Sounds good. What do I have to do?"

"Poll the community. Determine what they'd like to see built in the neighborhood. Maybe you and some of the community leaders could decide on two or three of those suggestions then present those to Quinn Enterprises."

"You're wonderful," Rashida said.

"Yeah. Yeah. Now just get me back to the office."

Rashida allowed herself to hope for the first time in ages.

Elliott pulled into the driveway of a two-story home in Dunwoody. Before he could get out of the car, a Nerf gun was plastered against the driver's side window.

"You are under derrest."

A smile tugged at Elliott's lips. "Oh, I am, am I? Do you think you're tough enough to arrest me?"

Big brown eyes stared at him through the slits of a black space helmet. "Get out with your hands up."

Elliott complied. With the gun pointed at his knees, since the holder was too short to reach his back, Elliott marched to the front door of the house.

The storm door offered a view straight through to the kitchen. Crystal tossed a salad at the end of the island. A slender woman with smooth skin and braided hair, she brought order to Chris's chaos.

Elliott rang the doorbell. He must have looked comical standing with his hands raised.

"Elijah, how'd you get out again?" Crystal said when she opened the door to allow Elliott to enter. "What did I tell you about pointing a gun at people? Do you want me to take it away?"

Elijah dropped his head. "No, Mommy."

"Apologize to Uncle Elliott."

"Sorry."

Elijah scampered off, leaving his mother and Elliott standing in the entry.

"Come on back," Crystal said. "Chris is starting the grill. We're going high cuisine tonight. Hot dogs and hamburgers."

"Sounds good." Elliott had called his partner to ask if he could stop by after work. Chris had no idea what Elliott wanted to discuss. Out of respect for Crystal and the kids, if Elliott needed his partner after hours and it was necessary to meet in person, he came to Chris's house.

"Beer in the refrigerator," Crystal said. "And be careful. Wyatt has a new rubber snake, and it shows up in the strangest places."

Elliott chuckled and pulled two beers out of the refrigerator. "I'll guard my beer. Never a dull moment around here, huh?"

"Never," she said drily.

Out on the patio, Chris arranged wood chips in his new smoker. "Bring your appetite?"

Elliott handed him a bottle of beer. "Sorry to intrude on your family time."

Chris waved him off. "After all this time, you're family, too."

Elliott leaned on the end of the picnic table, watching Chris make love to his grill. Elliott smiled then took a swallow. The brew slid down his throat, the coolness easing the tension that had built after visiting his dad. He breathed in the scent of grass cuttings, wild onions, meat cooking from someone else's yard, and roses from Crystal's flower beds. "Where's Wyatt?"

"In his room," Chris said. "He's giving thought to his actions. His brother woke from his nap to find a snake in his bed. Scared the kid to death. The neighbors probably thought we were killing him."

Elliott grinned. "I heard about the snake. Is that why Elijah is walking around armed?"

Chris shook his head. "Don't be in a hurry to have kids."

"First I'd have to find a wife." He thought about soft tendrils of hair falling on smooth almond-colored skin. He looked up to find Chris watching him.

"This woman…Rashida, you like her, don't you?"

Elliott rubbed his forehead. "Am I that obvious?"

"She was with you all day after the accident. I didn't see you calling up…" Chris snapped his fingers. "What's her name? Mia?"

Mia was the last woman Elliott had seriously dated before meeting Rashida. He smiled to himself. "No, I had no interest in calling Mia. Rashida showed up at the hospital, and I took advantage of the situation."

Chris cocked his head and wiggled his thick eyebrows. A tell-all gesture.

"Forget it." Elliott finished off his beer. "Plus, there's nothing to tell." He tossed the bottle from hand to hand. "Got in touch with Monroe Redding."

Chris straightened from his crouch over the grill. "Bad news?"

"Yes and no." Elliott tore at the label on the empty beer bottle.

The sliding glass door opened, and Crystal stepped out with a tray of hot dogs and hamburger patties.

"We can discuss it after dinner."

Chris locked eyes with Elliott for a moment then nodded. "Right. Let me light the grill and get this masterpiece of a meal on the road."

Wyatt, the snake charmer, barreled out of the house a moment later.

"My man." Elliott grinned.

"Uncle Elliott." Small arms wrapped around his legs.

Chris's oldest by thirteen months beamed up at Elliott. He had the same mischievous brown eyes as his brother. The boys were so close in age they were often mistaken for twins.

As Chris cooked the dogs and hamburgers, Elliott set out paper plates and juice boxes. Later, he lounged in a deck chair as the boys ate their dinner. Chris offered Elliott a dog.

He shook his head. "No appetite."

Chris nodded. "Okay. I assumed you didn't come over just to eat with us. Even though my new grill cooks some superb dogs."

He turned to his wife, who sat beside her sons, munching a burger. "Do you mind taking over bathing and bed duty after we eat? I'll come up and say good night."

"This once." She glanced over at Elliott. "And only because it's you." The sternness of her words carried little weight because of the twinkle in her eyes.

"Thanks." Elliott smiled. He hated intruding on their

evening, but Redding's interest in Luxury Designs' floor plans might be the step up the company needed.

Once the boys had left for their baths, Chris grabbed two beers from the refrigerator and he and Chris sat in the lounge chairs and stared up at the sky. It was almost completely dark, and the stars were beginning to make their appearance.

"Monroe Redding," Chris prompted, breaking the silence.

"He's offered to fund Dad's project, but only if the community is happy with the changes coming to the neighborhood."

Chris frowned. "How do you make them happy?"

"Hell, if I know."

"Did your dad ever talk to the community about his plans for the land?"

Elliott wiped at the condensation on the beer bottle. "I don't know. He only talked to me about his projects in passing, and sometimes I knew nothing about them until they were completed."

"Is it too late to get the community involved in what's going to be built?"

Elliott gave his friend a sour look. "We're talking about Marcus Quinn. He's the mastermind, and there's rarely any other input."

"It sounds like if he wants this money, he may have to change his tactics."

"That's not all," Elliott said. "Redding offered our company a chance to design the new homes in the Millhouse area. Says he likes our floor plans."

Chris's face went blank for a moment as he processed the news. "Holy f—" He cut off his expletive. "Wait. What?"

Elliott nodded. "It appears Mr. Redding is interested in gentrifying the area."

Chris turned his lawn chair so he faced Elliott. "Let me make sure I understand this. Redding is going to give your father the money—with strings attached—then he's going to start buying up property in the area and putting up new homes."

"That about wraps it up."

"But our houses don't fit in that neighborhood. Not unless we tear down everything and start from scratch."

"No joke," Elliott agreed. "Before, all the residents had to worry about was Dad's commercial building. Now…"

"The bulldozers are coming, and the residents will be blindsided," Chris said.

"Not all of them," Elliott said. "I think Rashida and her grandmother have a good idea of what's coming. I think that's been the reason for the protests."

Chris looked at Elliott in surprise. "There's been more than one protest?"

Elliott explained about the staged protest outside Quinn Tower and about the magazine article. "Rashida didn't write it, but I think she had something to do with it."

He glanced over at Chris. "It doesn't sound like such a great opportunity, does it?"

"We've got to make it work. This might be the break we need for the business," Chris said. "And if we don't do it, some other company will."

"We just have to make it work for both sides," Elliott agreed. "And we have to design homes that fit with the existing neighborhood. Not all the residents will want to sell."

"Agreed. You think your girlfriend can help?"

"Let's hope." Since Elliott had ended the call with Redding, he'd thought of nothing else but how he could get Rashida on his side.

ashida wiped a bead of sweat from her forehead. The window A/C unit whined and rattled but couldn't put out enough cool air to make the place comfortable. Grammy's small bungalow was a sweatbox.

"You need another unit," Rashida stated for the hundredth time. She plopped onto one of the kitchen chairs.

"It's not hot," Grammy said. "We didn't have the luxury of air conditioning where I grew up."

"You had the benefit of the ocean breezes." Rashida wished she could be there now. Sitting on the beach, waves lapping at her feet.

Grammy grew up poor on Tobago, a small island just a short ferry ride from its neighbor, Trinidad. Rashida's mother had grown up there, also, before leaving for Miami when she was twenty.

"Plus, the electricity man said poof." When Grammy's hands flew up pantomiming an explosion, flour from the bake she'd been kneading showered the kitchen.

Rashida and her mother had wanted to buy another unit for Grammy's bedroom, but Karla, having dealt with old homes before, suggested they consult an electrician first. Sure enough, the guy said the wiring couldn't support another unit.

The house might go up in flames.

"Well, at least let's go out to dinner," Rashida demanded.

"Tsk." Grammy nodded toward some plantains. "Peel and slice those."

Rashida exhaled a breath of frustration out through her nose.

"None of that, young lady." Grammy pointed a floured finger at Rashida. "You spend too much money on me as it is. Save your money so you can get out of that cracker box of an apartment."

"It's not small, it's cozy."

Grammy rolled her eyes.

Rashida started to separate the darkened skin of the plantain from its flesh. Her fingers immediately became sticky. "The zoning committee meets in a couple of weeks. We need them in our corner."

She glanced over to make sure she had her grandmother's complete attention. "It will look better if you and Mrs. McClain make some type of restitution to Mr. Quinn—"

"I did nothing to him. And he stepped in front of Mamie's car."

Rashida had seen the footage from the local television station. Elliott had practically done a tap dance to elude her grandmother's poking. She couldn't speak to Mrs. McClain striking him with her car, but from the police report, Elliott had stepped out onto a crosswalk and had the right of way.

Rashida's phone buzzed in her pocket. She ignored it. "Mr. Quinn isn't going to press charges."

"He shouldn't. It wasn't our fault." Her grandmother paused with her hands in the dough. "He's okay, isn't he?"

Rashida nodded. "Yeah." Sighing, she rinsed her hands.

Grammy would dig in her heels, and there'd never be an apology if Rashida pushed her.

She dug the phone out of her dress pocket. Elliott had left a voicemail. "It's Elliott. Call me when you get this message."

She wanted to ignore the call, but she needed to know what the enemy was doing. And it didn't matter if her body said otherwise. Elliott *was* the enemy.

Reluctantly, she called him back.

"Are you interested in grabbing a bite to eat?" he asked.

She turned her back to her grandmother. Wouldn't do for Grammy to overhear her conversation. "Why?"

"We didn't finish our discussion."

"About?"

"You remember me saying I'd come if you called?"

Rashida's face flooded with heat. "Is this a bo—" She was about to ask if this was a booty call, but Grammy was kneading the hell out of the bake in her attempt to listen to Rashida's conversation.

She could invite him over and force the issue of the apology but thought better of it.

She lowered her voice then hunched over her cell to create some privacy. "I'm at my grandmother's house, and we're about to have dinner."

"Invite him to dinner," Grammy said. The woman had bionic hearing.

Rashida muted the call. "You don't know who—"

"Hello." Her mother's voice rang out from the direction of the front door.

Crap.

"We're in the kitchen," her grandmother called.

Realizing she still had Elliott on mute, she unmuted the

call. "Maybe this isn't—"

"Come to dinner!" her grandmother shouted.

"Who's coming to dinner?" Essie asked as she breezed into the kitchen.

"Rashida's young man."

She muted the call again. "He's not my *young man*."

Her mother turned to Rashida with a raised eyebrow. "Are you ashamed of us? Invite him." Curiosity made her mother's body almost vibrate.

Rashida hadn't brought anyone around since she and Alex had gone their separate ways almost eleven months ago. She'd gone out for a drink with a few guys, but she hadn't introduced anyone to her family. They probably feared Alex's leaving had permanently scarred her. She could see it in their faces when they asked about her weekends from time to time.

Grammy had given up all pretense of cooking. Stubborn woman.

Rashida took in a deep breath and let it out slowly. God. She hoped she was doing the right thing. Keeping an eye on her mother and grandmother, she unmuted the call. "Do you want to come over for dinner?" *Say no.*

"I'd love to," Elliott said. "Text me the address."

She walked into the living room for a little privacy. "How did you get my number?"

He chuckled. "After I programmed my number into your cell, I called myself."

Drat. How had she missed that?

There was a pause on his end. "Are you going to send me the address?"

"I'll text it to you."

As she sent him the information, she wondered about her

motives. Was she inviting him over because of Grammy or because she missed him?

It had been torture being in the same apartment with him. She'd watched him sleep and had to fight the urge to crawl into bed and curl her body around his.

"Is he coming?"

Her mother's voice made her jump. How long had she been there? Had she heard any of their conversation?

"He's coming." She avoided her mother's gaze, because Essie Howard always saw too much.

Her mother trailed her back into the kitchen. Grammy glanced up from slicing the plantains Rashida had abandoned. She didn't speak, just gave Rashida the eye. What was with these women? A man called and they were already planning her wedding.

"Look," Rashida started off, "this might get a little awkward. This guy is—"

"Hey." Her sister's voice called out from the front room.

Rashida groaned. "Jesus." Was the whole family going to be here?

"Do not take the Lord's name in vain," her grandmother admonished.

Karla stepped into the kitchen.

Her mother shrugged. "I forgot to mention your sister might stop by."

Rashida's head popped up. Was this God's way of intervening? They were all here. Could telling Karla be this easy with her surrounded by the women who loved her?

Rashida traced the edges of her phone. She sent her mother a pleading, heartfelt message. *Please, Mommy.* They needed to get this Kenneth thing out in the open.

She opened her phone to the video. "Karla, I need to—"

Essie's face instantly transformed into a mask of horror. "No. No, Rashida. Not now."

"What's up?" Karla looked from one face to another. When no one spoke, she walked over to the counter and dug a fork out of the drawer and dove into the Chicken Pelau. Grammy smacked her hand.

Behind her daughter's back, Essie pleaded silently with Rashida. "Don't do this," she mouthed.

Jesus. We are so messed up. How do we ever get out of this cycle of loving a man then suffering the pain when they mess up and leave us?

"Rashida has invited her young man over for dinner," Essie interjected.

Rashida's stomach churned and burned as if a vat of acid sloshed inside it. But she caved. She couldn't stand the anguish in her mother's expression.

She took a deep breath, submerging the need to get what she'd seen in the club off her conscience. "He's *not* my young man, and it's not a relationship. He's just…he's just…" She gave up. They would know soon enough. What a fiasco.

Elliott parked his car on the street and hiked up to Rashida's grandmother's door. A profusion of wildflowers surrounded the Craftsman cottage and an old-fashioned swing hung from hooks in the porch ceiling.

As he waited for someone to answer his knock, he studied the surrounding homes—a mixture of 1950s ranches, small cottages, and bungalows that sat back from the street on probably half-acre lots. He did a mental catalog of the floor plans he'd designed that could fit on that size property.

The door screeched. Rashida floated out in a strapless yellow daffodil of a dress. Her face glowed and her thick hair rested on top of her head, leaving her long neck exposed. Like a bird drawn to honey, he moved toward her, wanting to press his lips to the spot where her neck met her shoulder.

She put out her arms to hold him off. "Listen. This isn't a good time."

Her words jarred him back to reality. *Isn't a good time?* He tore his gaze away from her neck. Had she changed her mind about dinner?

Before she could explain, the screen door opened again. Two women stepped out.

The older one moved toward Elliott, smiling with such warmth it made him forget Rashida's lack of welcome.

She put out a hand. "You must be Rashida's—"

"Friend," Rashida interjected.

"I'm Essie, her mother. It's so wonderful to meet you."

Elliott took her hand, pleased he was getting to meet the people close to Rashida. "Elliott Quinn. And now I see where she gets her beauty."

Rashida's mom ducked her head, but he didn't miss the pleased expression on her face.

Beside him, Rashida said something that sounded suspiciously like "full of it." He suppressed a grin.

"I'm Karla, her sister. It's a pleasure to meet you, Mr. *Quinn.*" Taller than the other two women, she also had dark eyes.

Elliott glanced at Rashida. Something about the emphasis that Karla had placed on his last name made him wonder if he was missing something.

Rashida only shrugged, a resigned weariness in her eyes.

"Come inside," Ms. Howard said. "I want you to meet my mother."

Elliott threw Rashida a questioning look. Guess Mom didn't know he'd already had the pleasure of meeting Eula Robinson.

Rashida shrugged. A gesture that made the fabric of her sunny dress rise and fall over her breasts. Elliott lost his train of thought.

She nudged him toward the open screen door.

Inside, he followed Rashida's mom through rooms with dark wood and built-in cabinets.

The farther he traveled from the front room, the warmer and more humid the rooms became. By the time they reached the kitchen, sweat coated his skin and he'd entered Hell. The heat in the room dried the spit in his mouth.

"Mom, this is Elliott, Rashida's friend."

The woman Rashida called Grammy turned from the stove. An array of emotions from surprise to anger to resignation flitted across her face. He could have sworn the meat fork in her hand lifted. Was she going to skewer him? She had a thing for poking him with sharp objects.

Her gaze moved from her daughter back to Elliott before giving him a tight smile. "Nice to meet you."

So, she was going to pretend they didn't know each other. Fine with him. He wiped an escaping bead of sweat from his temple.

"Take Elliott to the living room. It's cooler," Mrs. Howard said to Rashida. "I'll bring some lemonade."

In the front room, the window unit put out a blast of tepid air. Elliott wanted to prostrate himself before it. The house must be at least eighty years old. Maybe older. "I love these old homes."

"I could tell," Rashida said. "Your face lit up like a kid at Christmas." She studied the room, probably trying to see what held his attention. "Don't let your excitement show around my grandmother. She's convinced you're out to get her house and everyone else's in the neighborhood."

If Redding had his way, this neighborhood would look different in three years. Large McMansions that all looked the same would be barely contained on the small lots that made up the neighborhood.

And what part would he and Chris have in the change? It was a lovely neighborhood. He'd hate to lose the historic feel. Maybe they could design homes that didn't destroy the current look of the community. But what if that didn't fit Redding's vision? Would he and Chris still accept the venture capitalist's offer?

How was he to have a future with Rashida if he accepted Redding's offer? And how was his father's company supposed to survive if Elliott didn't accept Redding's offer? He was caught between a rock and a hard place, to use an old proverbial phrase.

"Dinner is ready," Rashida's mom called.

In the dining room, a buffet table sagged under the weight of a mountain of food. Rashida, her signature scent competing with the heavenly aroma wafting off the food, stood at his elbow, naming the dishes.

"Macaroni pie, stewed chicken, callaloo, plantains, stewed pigeon peas, chicken pelau, and for dessert black rum cake and soursop ice cream."

"Soursop?" he asked.

"It's a tropical fruit. The taste is like a mixture of strawberries and apples."

"Sounds good."

"Try the chicken pelau. Rice, chicken, spices, and what we call pigeon peas." She pointed to the dish.

He filled his plate.

"Elliott, what do you do?" Rashida's mom asked when he took a seat at the table across from her.

"I'm an architect, ma'am." He was ready to dig into the delicious smelling food.

Grammy passed him a dish of diced fruit in some type of sauce. At his raised eyebrow, she said, "Mango chutney."

He liked mangoes, so he took a generous helping.

"Are you responsible for the new high-rises going up downtown?" Rashida's mom asked as she added a few shakes of red sauce from a bottle. She offered the bottle to him with a lift of her eyebrow.

"Better not." The food on his plate would be spicy enough. He took a forkful of the chicken dish. Wonderful. Spicy but wonderful. He followed that forkful with a bite of chutney. He chewed once…twice…then heat exploded on his tongue and spread down his throat like an out-of-control house fire.

He grabbed his water glass and guzzled the liquid so fast some of it leaked from the corner of his mouth.

"Are you all right?" Karla, who sat on his right, leaned toward him.

His eyes watered, and he couldn't speak. He could trace the mango chutney as it burned a path to his stomach.

Rashida took a forkful of the chutney, tasted it, then glanced at her grandmother. "New recipe, Grammy?"

Her grandmother shrugged. "Maybe." Her lips twitched.

Grammy's image wavered in front of him. *So, she isn't*

ready to play nice.

"Try this." Rashida handed him a platter of flat bread. "It's called bake." She took a bite. "It's safe."

He bit into the bread tentatively. No explosions. He devoured it, then, not sure if he wanted to try any more of Rashida's grandmother's cooking. *Is this how she plans to get rid of me?*

He tried to continue the conversation with as much aplomb as he could manage. "I design new homes," he croaked. "My father is the one that designs high-rises."

"When he isn't trying to destroy neighborhoods," Rashida's grandmother said.

Essie looked from her mother to Elliott, clearly confused. "Okay, I'll bite. What's going on?"

"His daddy bought the old factory on Millhouse Road and the land that surrounds it." Grammy tossed that out like a bomb into a crowded room.

"What does your father plan to do with the property?" Essie asked.

Elliott pushed his plate away. He'd lost his appetite. "He plans to build a shopping complex that he hopes will attract stores like Whole Foods and Starbucks."

Essie frowned. "Whole Foods is rather pricey. How will stores of its ilk help the community?"

"It won't," Rashida's grandmother interjected. "It will destroy our little area."

Rashida and Karla had been silent during this tennis match between him and their grandmother. Rashida had been open about her opposition. What about her sister? She was a realtor. In the long run, this would bring her a wealth of clients. He couldn't close his eyes to the fact that the new clients could push the old residents out of their homes. But an inner voice reminded him that the old residents would be pushed out only if they were willing to sell.

"We hope it will bring revenue and other businesses into the Millhouse area. Those revenues would be used for better schools and infrastructure," he said.

"The population around here is past the childbearing age. Better schools would only help if there was a younger population," Essie said.

"Exactly," the grandmother said. "Out with the old. In with the new."

"But only if they want to sell." Elliott was getting tired of being the villain.

Rashida's grandmother turned an angry face on her granddaughter. "Why did you invite him here? Are you in with this plan?"

Rashida dropped her fork onto her plate. It hit with a *ping*. "First of all, I didn't invite him. You did."

"What?" Her grandmother looked as confused as Elliott.

"Secondly, I'm not in on the plan. I lived here, too. Why would I want to destroy it?"

Elliott's head started to pound. This was not how he'd hoped the evening would go. He didn't want to pit family members against each other. Yes, the building his father wanted to construct would put much-needed money back into his failing company, but the new project didn't have to destroy the community.

"Why can't younger and senior homeowners live in the same community?" he asked.

Her mouth tight and fire in her eyes, Grammy leaned over the table. "That can only happen if people sell?"

"That's right." He looked around the table. First at Rashida then the other women. "But that doesn't have to be a bad thing. Those people who want to sell would sell."

"And you think they'd get a fair price for their property?" Grammy looked about ready to leap across the table.

"Of course they would," he said. "They should have a realtor"—he looked at Karla—"to make sure they get what their property is worth."

He'd walked into a hornet's nest. Why in his arrogance did he think coming here and rubbing elbows with Rashida's family would smooth over everything and they'd be happy with the changes to the community?

"Karla," Essie said. "What does this mean?"

Rashida's sister took a deep breath. "If the zoning committee approves Mr. Quinn's application, he'll be able to build his shopping complex. If the complex draws people here to spend money, it will attract other businesses." She held Elliott's gaze. "Homebuyers will want to live in the area because the stores they shop at are here."

Karla shrugged, but Elliott knew it was far from an indifferent gesture.

"The community will become more desirable, and where there's demand, property taxes increase. The community as we know it will change. Very few of the current residents will be able to pay the higher property taxes." She looked at her grandmother. "But that will be a few years down the road."

Rashida's grandmother pushed her chair back from the table and rose. "Meaning I'll be dead, so it doesn't matter?" Her voice cracked.

"No, Grammy. That's not what I meant," Karla called after her fleeing grandmother.

From somewhere in the house, a door slammed.

"I didn't mean to upset her," Elliott said.

Essie sank her forehead into her palm and sighed. "Selling the house has been an ongoing discussion between me and my mother. The house is old and needs to be updated. No one in the family has the money for repairs. Maybe your father's building will be a good thing. She can sell the house at top dollar and come and live with me."

Rashida stood. "You know that's not what she wants." She threw her napkin down on the table and stalked out. Presumably to check on her grandmother.

Essie turned to Elliott. "I'm sorry. We've spoiled the meal for you. You have to forgive those two. My mother has been here for thirty years. This is the last place she and my father lived. For Rashida...well, this was a sanctuary when her father left the family. The neighborhood has special memories."

He nodded, because he didn't know what else to do. "I should go. Thank you for dinner."

As he made for the front door, he heard weeping. He paused, wondering if he should seek out Rashida's grandmother and apologize.

He didn't know how to ease her fears. If his father's application was approved, things would change in the community. Maybe, as Karla said, not right away but soon.

This evening's conversation had given him new insight into how the child Rashida had been shaped into the woman she was now. Her confidence and boldness masked a little girl who could always come back to this area for comfort. And he and his father were about to take that all away from her.

He was going to have to decide, and he feared that decision would cost him the woman he was coming to care for deeply.

CHAPTER
TEN

Rashida waited in the church lobby for Reverend Clemmons to finish his meeting with the deacons.

Why had she let her mother and grandmother push her into inviting Elliott to dinner? She could have said no.

Because you wanted to see him.

Like a sign from God, corroborating her mental thought, sunlight beamed through one of the stained-glass windows in the main chapel, producing a prism of color that spread across the wooden benches. *Don't lie. You're in church.*

The dinner had not resulted in Grammy apologizing to Elliott and, in fact, had made the situation between the two worse.

"Sister Howard, how are you?"

The minister had snuck up on her again. The man needed bells on his shoes to announce his presence.

"I'm fine, Reverend. I need a few minutes of your time."

"Come to my office." He touched her arm to direct her toward the back of the church.

Today instead of his usual suit he wore slacks, a blue shirt, and a pair of Air Jordan sneakers.

Once in his office, he settled his bulk behind his desk. She took the seat opposite.

"What's on your mind?"

"I want to present some alternatives to Quinn Enterprises' current plans to build on Millhouse Road. Something the neighborhood *and* the company could live with. I'd like your suggestions, since you know what's happening in the community."

He waved away her comment. "You think too highly of me."

"No, I don't." She shook her head. "That came out wrong. I mean, it's well deserved. Your status."

He bobbed his head and gave her a humble smile. "Thank you."

"So, whatever we come up with has to be good," Rashida said. "I have a feeling the approval of this project is a done deal."

"Meaning what?"

"Meaning the Quinn family probably has the zoning committee in their pocket."

The springs in his chair protested when he shifted his weight. He held up a thick finger. "Now—"

She rushed on, "I'm not certain. It's just a feeling I have. Well, based on the research I've done on the firm and the family."

He gave her a curious look. "The family's well-connected and has been a part of Atlanta society for a long time. But don't count out the zoning committee. They're good people. And I'd like to believe they'll return an impartial decision. One that is the best for the community and the city."

"Call me cynical, but I'm not as optimistic."

Spreading his large hands out in an expansive gesture, he asked, "What do you need from me?"

"Some ideas." She hated this helplessness. She lifted her gaze to his. "I don't want to think it might already be too late."

"Have you thought of anything?" he asked.

"Just a community center. The problem is it benefits the neighborhood, but I don't see how it helps Quinn Enterprises."

"Hmmm." The minister steepled his fingers under his chin and stared over her head at the wall behind her. "How about a nursing home? The median age in the area is about fifty-five. It could benefit the community and make money for Quinn Enterprises."

"You mean if they retain ownership of the nursing home?"

"Yes, exactly."

Rashida's heart rate sped up at the idea. "I like it."

"You can present both options and see which one is more acceptable."

Rashida hoped Elliott's father would find one of them to his liking.

On Monday afternoon, Rashida exited the elevator on the twentieth floor for the Quinn Enterprises suite. As she'd mentioned to Reverend Clemmons, she'd investigated the Quinn architectural firm. Being on staff at *Atlanta Magazine* meant she had unlimited research resources at her fingertips. What she'd found spiked her anxiety.

Elliott was from old money. He'd given her clues of his family's prominence, but now it stared her in the face. There were pictures going back seventy years of a Quinn in the company of a mayor or a governor or a U.S. senator. She'd studied the pictures of Marcus Quinn and noticed a strong family resemblance between father and son. The same dark hair with hints of copper, the same height, but she couldn't tell from the picture if they had the same green eyes.

They had influence. Influence the residents of Millhouse didn't have. So, she'd come to the office, waving a white flag. Of sorts. She wasn't going to lie down and bare her belly, but she would push the compromise she and Reverend Clemmons had agreed on. Her goal would be to get Elliott on board and, through him, his father.

She needed to strike the right note to let Elliott know this was a business appointment, so she'd toned down her usual bold colors for a dark suit, pearl earrings instead of loops, and sensible pumps instead of her five-inch Christian Louboutin heels. And she'd made an appointment. No more unscheduled visits.

She glanced at her watch. Right on time.

"Have a seat. Mr. Quinn will be right with you." Elliott's ancient secretary directed Rashida to a chair, eyeing her as if she expected Rashida to explode at any moment.

Five minutes later, the door directly behind the secretary's desk opened. A twenty-something blonde dressed like a sixties model, right down to the sheath dress that hit her mid-thigh, waltzed out, followed by Elliott.

"I can't believe you don't have sixty minutes to grab lunch with me. We can go downstairs to the little bar in the lobby."

"Sorry, Mia. I have an appointment." He glanced over at Rashida. "And here she is now."

Mia turned her attention on Rashida. Her eyes narrowed as her gaze flickered over Rashida's body. She glanced back at Elliott. "I don't mind waiting until you're finished. What's it going to take? Ten? Fifteen minutes?"

Heat rose in Rashida's face.

Don't do it. Her inner voice cautioned. But her blood boiled. No one dissed her that way. She strolled over to Elliott and placed her hand on his chest. "We'd better hurry, baby, before they give our room away." She said the words on an exaggerated purr and leaned her body into his.

She'd caught him off guard. His eyes widened then darkened with some emotion she couldn't name.

Leaning down, he covered her lips with an open-mouthed kiss.

Air left her body in a whoosh. She grabbed handfuls of his shirt and closed her eyes to combat the dizziness.

Sound receded. Time expanded. She inhaled sandalwood and male musk and felt the warmth of his skin and the hardness of his body pressing into hers.

Someone coughed, and reality intruded.

Rashida's eyes sprung open. Awareness returned. With it came the realization they had an audience. Both the secretary and the young woman stared with open mouths. Rashida regained her composure enough to give the woman who'd attempted to diss her a cat-ate-the-canary smile.

"Let me grab my phone and keys," Elliott whispered. He rushed back into his office.

The young woman turned on her heel and huffed off. Rashida lost the smile but couldn't shake the dizziness. That was their first kiss since the one at the Ritz. If she thought she'd imagined their attraction to each other before, that kiss told her she hadn't.

"Nice performance," the secretary said.

Rashida lifted her chin. "Who said it was a performance?"

The secretary glanced at an old-fashioned appointment

book open on her desk. "Because he has a meeting in forty-five minutes. If the plan was to go off with you, he'd never have scheduled the appointment."

Rashida's face heated.

Elliott returned, gripped her elbow, and said, "Let's go."

"Don't forget you have Mr. Erickson at two," the secretary called after them.

"Uh-huh," Elliott said.

Rashida had to double step to keep up with his long strides. "Where are we going in such a hurry?"

"To the hotel."

She dug her heels in then turned and faced him. "You know I wasn't serious, don't you?"

He pulled her close, his hand firm on her lower back, almost grazing her ass. He leaned in and whispered in her ear, "That kiss felt serious to me."

She swallowed, losing focus for a moment as her breasts brushed his chest. The ding of a distant elevator brought her out of her sex-induced fog. "You have an appointment."

"And if I didn't?"

Rashida's heart ping ponged off her rib cage. He couldn't be serious? Could he?

A slight flush stained his skin, and a vein throbbed in his forehead. The same vein had throbbed as he strained and thrust into her body.

She shook her head to get rid of the vision. *Get a grip.* She couldn't be waylaid by this physical attraction that existed between them. "I have something important to talk to you about. Is there somewhere we can have a private conversation?"

He lifted his eyebrow in a suggestive manner.

"Not that private."

His large hand guided her into the elevator. "Okay. Let's grab a drink at the bar downstairs."

The bar, a semi-dark space off the lobby, had very few customers—a couple eating at the counter and three guys gobbling down burgers at a front table. A talk show played on a television mounted in the corner. Closed captioning ran across the bottom of the screen.

Elliott led her to a table out of sight of the door.

"Are you hungry?" he asked.

She shook her head. Too keyed up to eat.

"Drink?"

"Ginger ale." She needed to keep her wits about her, so no alcohol.

He moved off toward the bartender.

Whatever had possessed her to come to his office? When she'd devised the plan, it had seemed like a safer bet than going to his apartment. But that kiss…

Her impulsiveness would be the death of her.

"Why didn't you just call me?" Elliott asked when he returned with the drinks. "You have my number."

She moved the straw, creating more bubbles in her ginger ale. She'd practiced all evening. Now none of the words seemed strong enough. Persuasive enough. "After all the drama the other night at dinner, I needed to speak with you in person and in a neutral setting."

He took a sip of his drink, eyeing her over the rim of the glass before placing it on the napkin. "I didn't thank you for dinner. I had a good time."

"Liar."

He chuckled. Crinkle lines appeared around his eyes. "Okay. I thought my organs were going to fry."

"I'm sorry." In her mind, she could still see his eyes widening and his mouth forming a perfect *O* of surprise.

He waved away her apology.

She took another draw of ginger ale through her straw. The fizz from the drink bubbled up her nose. When the urge to sneeze had passed, she faced Elliott squarely. "I spoke with Reverend Clemmons, and we came up with a couple of alternatives that might work instead of the marketplace."

Elliott cocked his head. "Alternatives?"

"Something that would benefit both Quinn Enterprises and the neighborhood."

He stroked the side of the glass. For one wild moment, Rashida could have sworn she felt his touch stroking her body. She shook her head, trying to rid herself of the sensation. But the throbbing in her lower abdomen couldn't be willed away. *Damn that kiss.*

"You know this is my father's project, don't you?" he finally said. "I'm just holding things down until he returns. Any changes would have to be approved by him."

"Don't you have legal power of attorney?"

"For some things, but nothing big."

"You could talk to him, right? Present these alternatives to him." Panic built in her chest like a caged bird trying to break free. The next zoning meeting was in ten days. If they didn't present an alternative before then, the committee would make its recommendations based on the original application. And the residents would lose their chance of having some input into what would be built in their community.

"What are the alternatives?" he asked.

"A community center or a nursing home."

He twirled his glass around in a circle, his forehead creased in thought. He refocused his attention back on her and not his drink. "Honestly, I don't think my father will find either one acceptable."

Her stomach cramped, causing the bubbles from the ginger ale to float into her throat. She rubbed her cold hands on her pants. "Why not?"

"It comes down to money. My father needs to make a significant amount of money right away from this project, and I don't think he can from either the community center or the nursing home. Frankly, the nursing home requires a lot of bureaucracy. Bureaucracy my dad's not going to want to be involved in."

She wished she'd ordered a stiff drink. "Will you at least present it to him?"

"Sure. I'll present it. But don't get your hopes up."

Her grandmother would be mortified to learn Rashida had felt the need to compromise with Quinn Enterprises. Good thing Grammy didn't know, because the plan had failed. Rashida needed to do something big. Something bold to get Marcus Quinn's attention.

CHAPTER ELEVEN

Elliott moved deeper into the room full of Atlanta Symphony donors. Classical music provided background to the cacophony of voices that filled the space. He shook his head at a passing waiter with a tray of champagne flutes. He needed something stronger. Smiling and nodding to people in his path, he made his way to the bar.

Once armed with his whiskey, he searched the room for his hostess. He found Deidra Cloyd holding court at the French doors that led outside. He could have waited for her to make the circuit of the room, but he wanted to do what he'd come to do and get the hell out.

And what he'd come to do was meet Zoning Commissioner James Hartwell. Erickson called in favors and learned Hartwell planned to attend this fundraiser. Elliott's dad had asked him to seek out Hartwell and put a plug in the man's ear about their project. It was not how Elliott liked to do business, but he was doing this for his father. No matter how distasteful.

Deidra Cloyd had been a friend of his mother's. She'd tried to keep in touch after his mother's death, but his father's briskness had severed that connection.

When he reached Mrs. Cloyd's side, she presented her cheek for a kiss. "Elliott, when I heard you were coming, I was beside myself."

"It's great to see you." The warm, spicy scent of her perfume brought back memories of sitting at his mother's feet, playing as she and Deidra laughed and gossiped together. He realized those were the only carefree memories he had of his mother with someone other than himself.

Deidra placed a bejeweled hand on his arm. "It's wonderful to see *you*."

He could have sworn she had tears in her eyes. *Damn*. A knife twisted in his gut. He hated using her and her gala this way.

"I heard Marcus had a heart attack. I'm so sorry." Her hand fluttered to her throat. The light from a multitude of chandeliers reflected off an emerald-cut diamond ring. "How is he?"

"Getting better every day," Elliott lied. "And as cantankerous as always."

"And you? You're well?"

"Doing great." Another lie.

"Have you seen Lissa?" Lissa was Mrs. Cloyd's only child. She and Elliott had played together as children. He remembered a dark-haired, serious girl with knobby knees and gaps between her teeth.

Deidre gripped his arm. "Come." She practically dragged him through the crowd.

Their journey ended in front of a small group whose conversation halted abruptly with their hostess' appearance.

"Guess who this is?" she said.

The music had stopped—Elliott learned it was a live quartet playing in the other room—and Mrs. Cloyd's question filtered out and above those talking around them.

The three women and one man's attention shifted to Elliott. "Hi." He raised his glass in greeting.

The women smiled politely. The guy didn't acknowledge Elliott but stared into his glass of champagne.

A tall, slender brunette separated from the three women then angled her body toward Mrs. Cloyd. "I haven't a clue."

"It's Elliott. You remember little Elliott." Mrs. Cloyd extended her arm toward the brunette, and the young woman, dark hair swinging, moved to Deidre's side.

This was Lissa?

"It's good to see you again," he said, covering his shock with a smile.

Her dark blue-eyed gaze swept over Elliott. "You've changed."

He couldn't help but respond to her teasing tone. "So have you." And she had. She'd turned into a beauty.

"I'll leave you two to talk," Mrs. Cloyd said.

Before she could drift away, Elliott touched her arm. "Do you know James Hartwell?"

"Yes, I do."

She searched his face. What did she see? His duplicitousness? Would she know the only reason he'd accepted her invitation was the possibility of meeting Hartwell?

Her gaze swept the crowd. "I don't see him. Is he a friend of yours?"

"Never met him."

If his interest struck her as odd, she didn't mention it. She moved in circles where people attended these functions to see and be seen and to network. "Would you like to meet him if he shows up?"

Elliott stared into his hostess's earnest eyes. This was the whole reason for coming tonight. But something about her happiness in seeing him after so many years tugged at his conscience. He wouldn't use her event to further his father's goals. Maybe he could find another way to meet Hartwell. "No. Don't bother."

She studied his face for a long moment. "If you're sure." She waved to the other three and hurried off.

Lissa introduced him to the group. He tried to look interested as he sipped on his drink. They continued their conversation, and his mind drifted to his dilemma with Hartwell. He rejoined their conversation to learn they were lawyers, but only the guy worked in Lissa's firm. When he touched Lissa's back, Elliott smiled. This guy thought Elliott was competition. Little did he know that Elliott's attention and affection had already been captured by someone else.

Lissa turned to Elliott and asked, "Do you want to walk around the grounds?"

"Sounds great."

Elliott grabbed another whiskey, and she picked up another champagne flute from a passing waiter.

"Is this going to be okay with your boyfriend?" Elliott couldn't remember the man's name.

"He's not my boyfriend."

"You might want to give him the heads up. He's ready to murder me with his Brooks Brother's tie clip."

Lissa lifted her gaze to the ceiling then gave a little shake of her head. "He has as much chance of being my boyfriend as he has of flying to the moon without a shuttle."

They stepped through a floor-to-ceiling French door, onto a balcony. From the balcony a long series of steps led to an expanse of grass. Strategically lit lanterns allowed people to walk in safety around the grounds.

Elliott followed Lissa to the edge of the balcony where she leaned against the stone and watched the guests mingling out on the lawn. He placed his drink on the ledge.

Hidden from the road behind hedges and a large black iron gate, the Cloyd's house was one of the large estates near the Chattahoochee River.

"Mother says you're an architect," Lissa said. "Do you love your job?"

"Most days. How about you?"

She smiled ruefully. "Some days."

Elliott had been surprised and impressed to learn she was a lawyer. With the Cloyd money, she could have been a socialite, jetting from one country to another.

Her finger rimmed her champagne glass. "Married, engaged?"

He shook his head. "Neither." From the glances she was sending him from beneath her lashes, she was coming on to him. Under other circumstances, he would welcome the interest.

"Dating someone special?"

He took a moment to reflect on her question. Rashida was definitely his someone special.

"You're taking too long," she said with a smile. "Who is she?"

"Elliott? Is that you?" A slender Black woman walked toward them. With her was one of the guys who'd checked Lissa out when they'd stepped onto the balcony.

What were the chances? "Karla?"

The woman nodded. She turned to Lissa. "I'm Karla Buckley, and this is my husband, Kenneth."

"Lissa Cloyd." She extended her hand to Karla.

The women shook hands. Lissa nodded coolly at Kenneth. She must have been aware of Kenneth's interest.

"Elliott is a friend of Rashida's," Karla explained to her husband. "His father bought the old building and land on Millhouse Road."

Kenneth, a tall man with a shaved head, nodded. "Nice property." He directed the statement at Elliott, but his attention kept drifting in Lissa's direction.

An awkward silence developed.

"I'll tell Rashida we ran into you," Karla said to Elliott. "Ms. Cloyd." She lifted her fingers in a farewell gesture to Lissa.

Lissa inclined her head. "Nice meeting you."

Elliott watched Rashida's sister walk away. She took her husband's arm, and they strolled back inside.

"Is Rashida the one you're dating?" Lissa regarded him, her eyes probing.

"Why would you think that?"

"Just by the way your body tensed when Karla said her name."

She must be a great lawyer. Caught everything. "We're not dating."

"But you'd like to be?"

Elliott shrugged. "I'd like to be, but we're on opposite sides of an issue."

"And if you weren't?"

Elliott stared down at the inch or so of whiskey left at the bottom of his tumbler before meeting Lissa's inquisitive stare. "I'd be hers in a heartbeat."

"Too bad for me." She finished off her champagne and placed her empty glass on the balustrade.

She was a lovely woman, and under other circumstances he might have asked her out, but now, Rashida occupied his mind and ruled his heart. He hadn't given up on the chance that they could find a solution to their real estate dilemma, one beneficial to both her family and his father.

"You mentioned James Hartwell?" Lissa leaned against the stone railing, her gaze on a group of people to their left.

"Yes."

"He's over there with Mother."

Elliott casually turned his head. Mrs. Cloyd had her hand on the elbow of a middle-aged man who was just a few inches taller than her, which probably put the guy around five foot six inches. Laughter broke out among the group of five people at something this guy had just said.

Mrs. Cloyd caught Elliott's eye. She turned and said something to the group then, with a hand on Hartwell's elbow, moved them in Elliott and Lissa's direction.

The residue of the drink in Elliott's mouth turned sour. Deidra Cloyd was coming toward them with not only who Elliott presumed was James Hartwell but also a man that Elliott wouldn't piss on if he were on fire—Garrett Thompkins.

Thompkins had been blowing up Elliott's cell the night he'd met Rashida in the bar. The saints had turned their back on Marcus Quinn to bring both salvation in the form of James Hartwell and destruction in the form of corporate raider Garrett Thompkins in the same night.

"Elliott, I want you to meet James Hartwell," Mrs. Cloyd said. "He's a Dekalb County commissioner."

"Nice to meet you." Elliott shook the older man's hand, acutely aware of Thompkins hanging on the periphery and taking it all in.

Mrs. Cloyd turned to Thompkins. "And this is—"

"Elliott and I are old buds." Thompkins reached out a hand, and Elliott reluctantly shook it.

"And this is my daughter, Lissa." Mrs. Cloyd beamed.

Prominent teeth showed as Hartwell acknowledged Lissa. "A pleasure."

Unfortunately, Thompkins' social graces weren't as refined as Hartwell's. The corporate raider tried to bring Lissa's hand up to his lips, but she gracefully slid her fingers out of his grasp.

Mrs. Cloyd, a consummate hostess, pretended not to notice. Turning to Hartwell, she said, "Elliott and his father own an architectural firm."

"Actually, Dad and I haven't worked together in over five years. I have my own company now."

Mrs. Cloyd laughed, a sound like tinkling glass. "Oh my goodness. I guess it's been a while."

There was a moment of awkward silence before Hartwell asked Elliott, "So, what projects are you working on?"

Elliott definitely wouldn't bring up the Millhouse project in Thompkins's presence. The corporate raider would waste no time in questioning the viability of Elliott's father's company now that he was in poor health. That would be the kiss of death to their zoning application.

"My business partner and I are working on some floor plans for a new subdivision north of the city," Elliott said.

"What about your dad?" Thompkins asked. "I heard—"

A vise-like pressure clamped around his chest. He could see his father's business going down the toilet.

"Mr. Thompkins." Lissa slid in between Elliott and the corporate raider. "Why don't you tell me about your company over something to eat?"

Thompkins looked like a dog salivating over two bones. Elliott imagined he wanted to keep the business conversation going, but he wouldn't turn down an invitation to be in Lissa's company. He beamed down at her as she led him back inside to the party.

Should he leave Hartwell to speculate about his father or should he bring up the subject? He hoped honesty would work for him. "I'm running my father's company until he's back on his feet. Which will be in a few weeks." *Hopefully.*

Hartwell nodded in what Elliott interpreted as a sympathetic gesture. "So, you've taken on the task of two companies?"

"I have a great business partner who's holding down the fort."

Hartwell turned to his hostess. "These young people have more energy than I ever had at their age."

Mrs. Cloyd laughed. "James, at our age, wisdom trumps energy." She glanced around the balcony. "Oh, there are the Sharps. Let me introduce you."

"Good meeting you, Elliott," Hartwell said. They shook hands, then the commissioner trailed after Mrs. Cloyd.

Elliott felt like he'd dodged a bullet. He hadn't brought up the Millhouse application, but at least Hartwell knew his name, and hopefully Mrs. Cloyd's unofficial endorsement of Elliott would stay with the commissioner.

Rashida worked all Saturday morning trying to complete an article for her blog before she had to meet Elliott. She was giving him a personal tour of the Millhouse area.

Her cell buzzed at her elbow. Karla. Rashida groaned and for one second debated not answering the call.

"What's up?" She studied a word, trying to decide if she'd spelled it correctly. She was such a horrible speller. Spell check said, *I got nothing.*

"Do you remember the Atlanta Symphony event I mentioned a couple of days ago?" her sister asked.

"Yeah." Rashida changed a letter but still couldn't get rid of the red squiggly line from the word processing software.

"Well, it was last night, and you'll never guess who I ran into."

Rashida suppressed an aggravated sigh. She didn't really care. Karla and Kenneth moved in a different stratosphere from her. "You're right. I couldn't guess."

"Elliott Quinn."

Her fingers froze on the keyboard. "Really. That's nice." She was all ears.

"He was there with his girlfriend."

A grain of rice couldn't have passed down Rashida's throat. *A girlfriend?* She gave up all pretense of writing.

Elliott had a girlfriend. Why should she be surprised? They weren't an item. Hell, they weren't even dating. But it didn't stop her blood from boiling in her veins, remembering his attempts to get her back in bed.

"I thought you and he—"

"Nothing happening there." Rashida strove for an air of indifference, even as she strained to draw breath through her narrowed windpipe.

"Good. Because Lissa Cloyd couldn't keep her eyes off Elliott, and I suspect her hands. Even Kenneth noticed."

Karla didn't know Rashida and Elliott had hooked up, so

she rambled on about Lissa Cloyd, her money, her parents, and the gorgeous Cloyd mansion. Rashida usually tuned out when her sister described these boring events, but now, she hung on every word.

"Glad you had a good time," she said. "Look, I've got to get back to this article. It's due in a couple of hours." It was due on Monday, but Karla didn't need to know that.

Long after they'd ended the call, Rashida stared at the computer screen, not seeing anything. She'd almost given in and slipped into his bed that night at his apartment. A flush of heat made her cheeks burn. Thank God she hadn't. She'd preserved some of her dignity.

She tried to continue with the food piece, but her attempts made the article dry and uninteresting, like a drumstick left too long on the grill.

The timer on her phone buzzed. She'd set it so she would have plenty of time to get ready to meet Elliott. Now she wanted to hurl the phone to the other side of the room or, better yet, tell Elliott to stick it up his ass. But that would be a waste of a good phone.

Her finger hovered over his number. There was no way she could meet him today. Or any other day.

But this tour wasn't about her. It was about her grammy and the residents of Millhouse. Her goal today had been to help Elliott see the folly in letting the neighborhood be destroyed. Just because Elliott was a two-timing, low-life womanizer—

Rashida stood up abruptly. *Breathe.* She took five deep breaths then hurried to get ready. Her feelings for Elliott wouldn't get in the way of her goal, which was saving the Millhouse district.

Twenty minutes later, she stared at the bottom of the cup

that had held two scoops of Rocky Road.

"You want another scoop, sweetie?" Mrs. Roberts, the owner, leaned over the counter, her fleshy hands making smudges on the glass top.

Rashida pulled the spoon out of her mouth. "Better not. I had a hard enough time getting into these jeans."

"Girl, you're skinny. You're a fine little thing."

Mrs. Roberts was probably the only one who thought it. "You're sweet," Rashida said.

"How's that young man Mrs. McClain hit with her car the other day? Mama says you knew him."

She thought she knew him. But she guessed she was mistaken. "He's okay. Had a mild concussion. No broken bones."

"That's good." Mrs. Roberts ambled out from behind the counter and began wiping down the ice cream parlor tables and chairs.

Too bad Mrs. McClain didn't break one of his legs. Rashida immediately felt contrite. *Admit it. You're jealous.*

Why was she getting twisted because Elliott had a girlfriend? He was free to date whomever he wanted. They'd made no commitment. And from Karla's description, this Lissa sounded more like his type of woman—attractive, thin, and rich. Not carrying an extra ten—okay, an extra twenty—pounds and barely making enough to hold on to her cracker box of an apartment.

"You want more ice cream?" Mrs. Roberts broke in on Rashida's mental tirade.

She shook her head then threw her cup and spoon in the trash. The thought of more ice cream made her stomach churn.

"See ya." She waved to Mrs. Roberts then stepped out into

the oven of a day.

In her car with the air blasting, she turned her cell phone end over end. The thought of him being with someone else was like a cancer eating at her soul.

Before she could stop herself, she dialed Elliott's number. She'd tell him she was ill and couldn't do the tour today.

"Hello?" The timbre of his voice sent shockwaves through her body, vibrating through her breasts and tightening her nipples into little buds.

God, give her strength. Let her be cool.

"Karla said she saw you with your girlfriend last night at the gala." She clapped a hand over her mouth then dropped her forehead onto the steering wheel. *What the fu—* What had just come out of her mouth?

There was silence on the other end of the phone. Then... "I don't have a girlfriend."

She lifted her head off the steering wheel and stared sightlessly out the windshield. "Oh? Really?"

"Really."

She could hear amusement running through that one word. She fumed. *Don't play with my feelings, buddy.*

"Are we still on for this afternoon?" he asked.

There was no way she could be in his company. "Something's come up. I can't meet." *Yeah, that something is rich, attractive, and better suited for you.*

"Lissa is not my girlfriend, Rashida."

"Riiight. I heard that song before. Let's skip to the chorus. In fact, let's skip the whole damn song." She groaned. Her mouth was a runaway train.

But she would not be pulled into the love song only to find out months down the line after she'd given him her heart that it was all a fantasy.

"She's not. We were childhood friends. Our mothers were best friends."

Rashida clamped her lips shut. She'd already given him too much ammunition to use against her.

"I'm not that kind of man."

A disbelieving laugh escaped her lips. All men were *that* kind of man if given the opportunity.

"I'm coming over," he said.

"Why?"

"If you're going to call me a liar and a cheater, you'll have to do it to my face."

"I'm not at home. Plus, we're not a couple, so why does it matter?"

"It matters to me that you think I cheated on you with her or cheated on her with you. Where are you?"

She could see Mrs. Roberts still bustling around the ice cream parlor. No way would she tell him she'd soothed her bruised heart with two scoops of Rocky Road. "I'm out."

"Meet me." He rattled off an address. "I'll text it to you. See you in thirty."

He hung up before she could agree.

When the text came in, she started her car. She had two traffic lights to decide whether she'd go home or meet him.

Rashida had only been to the Carter Center once. When she was ten years old, her fifth-grade class took a trip to the Jimmy Carter library and toured the Center. She hadn't been back since. Until now.

Except for two cars, the parking lot was empty. Before

she could cut the engine, Elliott stepped out of a Land Rover and was at her door.

Voice grave but eyes gentle, he grasped her hand when she opened her door. "Let's go inside. There's someone I want you to meet."

She studied his face, trying to figure out why he wanted her here. Outside the bedroom, she didn't know Elliott. She didn't know his hopes, his dreams. She didn't move in his circles of fundraisers and money. But the appeal in his eyes had her following him.

From the parking lot, they took a path that led to a long, rectangular pool. The white one-level complex spread out over several acres. At the end of the pool was the main library entrance. Before they reached the door, a slender woman in a blue tailored pantsuit stepped out. Her straight dark hair swung in a curtain behind her as she moved toward them.

"There she is," Elliott said. A smile hovered around his mouth. "How's it going, Lissa?"

Rashida's feet faltered. Elliott tightened his grip on her hand.

So this was the girlfriend who was not a girlfriend. The air of wealth and privilege wrapped around her like a well-fitted coat as she walked.

When they reached her, she patted Elliott's chest. Her blue eyes sparkled. "I don't see you for over twenty years then I see you twice in twenty-four hours."

Elliott chuckled. "I want you to meet someone." He pulled Rashida so she was slightly in front of him then placed his hands on her shoulders. "This is the woman I told you about. This is Rashida."

Lissa, whose eyes had shifted between Elliott and Rashida

as he spoke, now focused her full attention on Rashida.

"She's beautiful." She took Rashida's hand then glanced briefly at Elliott. "Now I understand why you turned down a date with me."

Rashida's breath caught in her throat at the admission. Was this woman to be believed? Rashida stepped back so she could see Elliott's face. Did he know her well enough to know she needed this proof? Did he care that much about her to provide that proof?

From the intense look in his eyes, he knew. And he cared.

One minute she felt a surge of exhilaration and the next a wave of dismay. What must he think of her that she needed such a dramatic display of his honesty?

"It's nice to meet you, Rashida." Lissa's voice was pleasant, cultured, and breathy.

"It's a pleasure to meet you also." Her words sounded stilted. She was thrilled but at a loss for words that Elliott would go to this extreme to reassure her of his sincerity.

Elliott looked around. "You work for the Carter Center?"

"I'm a lawyer—junior lawyer—at Jones, Baldwin, and Taylor. We are one of the attorneys for the Center."

"What are you doing here on a Saturday?" Elliott asked.

She shrugged. "Just trying to move up. I'd like to make partner in the next year."

Beautiful, rich, and ambitious. Rashida studied Elliott to see if he had second thoughts about choosing her over Lissa. He looked like a proud older brother. One whose younger sister had performed well in the school's string quartet.

Lissa took Rashida's arm. A gesture that caught her off guard. "We need to have a drink together. Just us girls." Lissa's spirit radiated warmth.

"I'd like that." And Rashida meant it. She sensed Lissa genuinely wanted to spend time with her, and wasn't just spouting the words because she thought it would score points with Elliott.

Rashida never had many girlfriends. Her family had been her confidants. The thought of having this woman along with Monique as a friend pleased her.

She liked Elliott's non-girlfriend.

As she and Elliott walked back to their cars, she wondered if she could trust him in *all* things. After he'd gone to the trouble of making sure that she and Lissa met, Rashida felt confident in where their relationship stood. But could she trust him to do the right thing for the Millhouse community?

CHAPTER TWELVE

Elliott, using an address Rashida had sent him, arrived at a mom-and-pop ice cream store in the heart of the Millhouse district.

"What flavor do you want?" Rashida asked as soon as he stepped into the air-conditioned space.

"I'm not much into ice cream."

She pouted. Elliott's gaze locked onto her kissable lips. He wanted to taste them, not ice cream. She looked good enough to lick in her blue jean shorts and hot pink shirt knotted under her breasts and bared abdomen.

"What's the purpose of being in an ice cream parlor without sampling the goods?"

He didn't remind her that she'd picked the spot. He'd have been quite content to spend the day at his place or hers as long as they were together.

"Mrs. Roberts, this is Elliott Quinn, the young man you were asking about. Let him sample the raspberry sorbet."

Mrs. Roberts handed him a miniature plastic spoon with a small serving of pink sorbet. "Glad to see you're doing okay."

"Thank you, ma'am." He knew she referred to his accident with Mrs. McClain's car. The community appeared to be tight-knit. News probably traveled faster than a MARTA rail car.

He stuck the spoon in his mouth. The confection was so sweet it tickled the area behind his jaw. "It's cold."

"You don't like it?" Rashida asked.

"Sorry." Sugar had never been his thing. Peanuts, olives, anything with salt, and an accompanying alcoholic drink would put him in heaven.

"Do you want to try something else? We have twenty-five flavors." Mrs. Roberts spread her arms wide. "Something to suit everyone."

He shook his head. "I'm sure it all tastes great, but it's wasted on me."

"Rashida, do you want a cup to go?" Mrs. Roberts asked, obviously considering him a lost cause.

Rashida backed away from the case. "Please don't tempt me. I'm weak. But we will take two bottles of water."

Outside, she handed him a bottle. "Thanks for introducing me to Lissa. She seems like a very nice person."

"I don't know her well, but if she's anything like her mother, she's a wonderful young lady." He glanced around. "My car or yours?"

"It's a beautiful day. Why don't we walk?"

"Walk?" He'd had visions of touring the neighborhood from the comfort of his air-conditioned vehicle, not sweating in Atlanta's ninety-degree-plus weather.

"It's only a couple of blocks," she said.

Dressed in slacks and loafers, it would be a couple of long, sweaty blocks. He took a deep pull on his water bottle. The cold liquid soothed a path down his throat. He'd be more visible to the neighbors if he walked. And he was there to be seen. To show them he cared about the community. "Lead on."

"This way."

He followed her, his eyes on her round, tight, jean-covered bottom.

"Mrs. Roberts and her husband ran the ice cream parlor together for twenty years until his death last year. Now she operates it by herself with some part-time help from a couple of high schoolers." Rashida glanced at Elliott. "It would be a shame for the place to go out of business because a brighter, shinier store moved in."

He guessed that was for his benefit.

His head swam as she pointed at one house after another and told him about the families that lived in each house.

"Come on." She grabbed his hand and tugged him around the side of a 1950s ranch. Behind the house was a worn path leading to a wooded area.

"We kids in the neighborhood used this as our personal shortcut between the two streets. The homeowners didn't mind."

She veered off the path. Later, he realized she'd approached the area with reverence. A hedge of stones guarded a small cemetery. Weathered by time, age, and rain, headstones slumped against each other, many of the names missing.

She dropped to her knees and started to pull weeds that had grown up between small stones almost buried in the soil. "These stones"—she pointed to the smaller ones—"belong to children. This was my favorite place as a child when I wanted to be alone. A few years back, I did some research. A hundred and twenty years ago, this land belonged to a family named Maier. I think this was the family cemetery." Her tone was respectful.

"If your father builds his commercial space and the area is destroyed by newer, bigger houses, do you think anyone will care about this cemetery? Care about the history behind this bit of land?"

She didn't wait for an answer before walking away.

He followed with her question ringing in his head. It really wasn't Quinn Enterprises' concern, since they wouldn't buy residential real estate. But did Redding have any qualms about destroying abandoned cemeteries? He hadn't struck Elliott as a sentimental man.

They walked out of the shaded woods onto another street. To the right, the street came to a dead end. They turned left.

"Yoo-hoo!"

"Oh, no," Rashida muttered.

Elliott glanced around, looking for the source of the voice. From her porch, a little old lady wrapped in a purple dress with yellow splotches waved her arms in greeting.

"Is that you, Rashida?" she called.

"Yes, ma'am," Rashida shouted back.

"Come on up. I've got some iced tea."

Elliott's shirt stuck to his back. The idea of a cold drink sounded wonderful. He'd finished his bottled water ten feet from the ice cream parlor.

"No, ma'am. We don't—"

But Elliott was already climbing the steps toward the promise of a cold drink.

"Mrs. McClain, this is Elliott Quinn. A friend," Rashida said as they settled in aluminum deck chairs.

"Quinn. Quinn. Why does that name sound familiar?" Mrs. McClain squinted at Elliott from behind glasses an inch thick.

"Would you like me to get the iced tea?" Rashida asked.

The elderly woman turned away from Elliott to stare quizzically at Rashida.

"The iced tea?" Rashida reminded her.

"Oh. Yes. Yes. Of course. I'll just be a moment." She turned and disappeared into the house.

"I was trying to turn down her invitation, but you didn't give me a chance."

Elliott grinned at her. "Sorry. The iced tea sounded wonderful."

She frowned and reached out a finger to touch the skin on his arm. "You're warm." She studied him. "Do you burn? Maybe we should have taken the car."

His arms did feel a little tingly where her finger lay. "I'm fine." In his attempts to see and be seen by the neighbors, it would be poetic justice if he got sunburned.

"I thought I'd bring out the brownies first," Mrs. McClain called from behind the screen door. "I didn't want to spill the tea."

Elliott jumped up, open the door, then took the plate of brownies from her.

"Mrs. McClain, let me get the tea," Rashida said.

"It's in the refrigerator. And you know where the glasses are." The words were directed at Rashida, but the old lady studied Elliott like a bug under a microscope.

"I just can't remember," she said, squinting behind the thick glasses.

"The brownies look good," he said, hoping to deflect her interest. She looked fragile enough for a stiff wind to blow her over. He didn't want her to remember she'd hit him with her car.

He bit into the chocolate dessert then paused in mid-chew. Something was off. Something was *very* off.

Rashida stepped out on the porch with three glasses of

iced tea on a tray. He reached blindly for one then hesitated. What had the old lady sweetened the tea with? Because she must have poured a cup of salt into the brownies.

These old ladies on Millhouse Road were trying to kill him.

"What's wrong?" Rashida asked.

Very aware of Mrs. McClain watching him, Elliott mumbled, "Nothing." He wanted desperately to spit out the mouthful of brownie, but with the old lady's gaze glued to his face, he couldn't spit or swallow.

Mrs. McClain squinted at him. "Is he having a heart attack?"

Rashida put the tray on the porch railing. "I think he may have bit his tongue. Why don't you get some napkins?"

"Of course. Of course." The elderly woman ambled away.

As soon as the screen door slammed shut behind her, Elliott leaned over the porch railing and spit out the brownie. He eyed the iced tea glass warily.

"What happened?" Rashida asked.

He took a sip. It was made with a ton of sugar, but it was palatable. "Salt."

One perfectly sculpted eyebrow rose to her hairline. "What?"

"She used salt instead of sugar in the brownies."

Rashida covered her mouth with her hand. At first, he thought she was horrified, but her stifled giggles couldn't be misinterpreted.

He picked up one of the brownies and approached her with it. "Try one."

Still giggling, she backed away, waving her hand to ward him off.

"Is everything okay?" Mrs. McClain stood in the open screen door.

Elliott straightened, tucking the brownie down by his side. "Everything is fine. Thank you so much for the delicious brownie. But we need to go. I have an appointment."

The elderly woman rushed toward him, a roll of paper towels in hand. She began placing several brownies onto a napkin. "Is your tongue okay?" Without waiting for him to respond, she rushed on, "Let me give you some to take with you."

"No. It isn't necessary." His tongue felt thick in his mouth. He needed copious amounts of water.

"I insist." She thrust the towel into his hand.

What else could he say but, "Thank you."

He tilted his head toward Rashida. "Ready?"

"You don't want more tea?" Rashida asked as she batted her lashes at him.

Smiling, Mrs. McClain looked from Rashida to Elliott. From her expression she knew something was off but couldn't figure out what.

"Thank you again for the refreshments." His mother would have been pleased with his manners. He interlaced his fingers with Rashida's and gently tugged her toward the steps.

"Come back again," Mrs. McClain called after them.

"We will," Rashida said.

"Speak for yourself," Elliott muttered. But he turned and waved to the old woman.

She stared after them with both hands clasped to her chest.

He and Rashida walked in silence, their fingers still intertwined.

"Mrs. McClain drove the car that hit you."

He thought about her squinting eyes behind the Coke-bottle glasses. "Yes, I recognized the name. She's vision-impaired?"

"That's my guess."

"Why is she still driving?"

Rashida shrugged. "No clue."

He glanced back the way they'd come. The sidewalk had taken a gentle turn, and he couldn't see the McClain house any longer. "Is it safe for her to live alone?"

"She doesn't have anyone she can live with. According to Grammy, she has a sister who's in a nursing home. Her only child—a son—was killed during the Gulf War."

"Maybe she also should be in a nursing home."

"Maybe." Rashida studied the houses they passed. "She'd probably die if she left her home, but it might ease her mind if she were in a nursing facility in her community." She glanced over at him. "Would you tell your father about Mrs. McClain? Maybe it would mean more if there was a face to go with the need."

Elliott didn't want to give her false hope. Erickson had had to talk his father into the idea of being a landlord of three self-sufficient stores. Owning a nursing home would entail too much work and an outlay of cash he just didn't have.

Rashida thought by changing his father's plan the community would stay the same. She didn't know Redding waited in the wings.

Elliott believed Redding was an honorable man and would offer a competitive price for the homes, but over time the scope and look of the neighborhood would change. The neighborhood she'd experienced as a child would no longer exist. And he and his father would open the door to that change by accepting Redding's money.

CHAPTER THIRTEEN

Rashida's cell buzzed and vibrated across the bathroom counter as she applied makeup.

Without looking at the phone, she knew it was Elliott. He'd started texting her once, sometimes twice a day with simple messages: *Hope you have a great day.* And at night: *Sleep tight.*

Sometimes she responded back. Sometimes she ignored him. Like now. She was so conflicted about their relationship. Yes, she'd been jealous when she thought he had a girlfriend, but that didn't mean there could ever be anything serious between them. There were too many complications in their lives.

She studied her face in the mirror. Too much mascara? She rarely wore makeup, so when she did, she always second-guessed herself.

She had a reservation at Southland, a mid-tier restaurant, not cheap but not an eatery that required a year's salary and a six-month reservation. It had been open for only four months, located near the Ansley Park area of Atlanta, and it was all the rage.

The phone buzzed again with an incoming text. Her hand jerked. *Damn.* Black gook smeared her eyelid.

She snatched up the phone, planning to send off a searing message to Elliott. The first message had been from him asking how her day had gone.

The second message had come from Renford Benefield, her dinner date and business associate. She read the text then groaned.

He'd gone to Mexico over the weekend with friends and now had Montezuma's revenge.

She sent him a reply saying she hoped he felt better soon. She'd have to go to the restaurant alone. No way could she cancel. Her review was due in her editor's inbox by tomorrow morning.

Yes, she tended to procrastinate. She didn't examine that weakness too closely.

After finishing her makeup, she went to her closet and picked out a pair of shoes to compliment her off-the-shoulder maxi dress.

After picking up her phone, she started to drop it in her clutch then remembered she hadn't returned Elliott's text. *On the way out. Have a good evening.*

He texted back immediately. *A date?*

Critiquing a restaurant. Alone.

Which one?

She didn't have time for twenty questions. *Southland.*

Always wanted to check it out. Want company?

She did—she wanted *his* company—and it irritated her that she did. Much to her annoyance, she found herself texting: *Sure.*

Forty minutes later, she stepped into the restaurant's waiting area. A group of women chatted around the hostess stand. A couple stood off to the side. Discreet conversation, the clatter of china, and the clink of glasses filtered out from the dining room. Frank Sinatra drifted softly from invisible speakers. The restaurant was decorated in black and white with splashes of purple—purple in the artwork, on the wall, and on the small pillows lining the back of the benches.

When she walked up to the hostess stand, the young woman gave her a polite smile. "Your name, please?"

"Rashida Howard."

The hostess glanced at the sheet in front of her. "Dinner for two?"

Where was Elliott? She turned and peered out the door, and she spotted him giving his keys to the valet. Her gut fluttered then immediately started churning. Was this a mistake?

Turning back, she pasted on a smile for the hostess. "Yes. Dinner for two."

She didn't want to appear too eager to see him, so she tracked his progress by watching the group of women. When their conversation halted, she knew he'd entered the lobby. Their gazes shifted as he made his way toward the hostess stand. She got a thrill from the appreciation in their eyes.

A slow smile transformed his rugged face when he saw her.

He wore a dark gray suit, a white shirt open at the collar, and no tie.

"Hey," he said.

He leaned in to kiss her cheek. His smooth skin rubbed against hers—he'd recently shaved. She inhaled deeply his signature scent. Sandalwood.

"You look beautiful," he said.

"You do, too."

His smile widened…and she realized her mistake. She'd

voiced her thought. His scent, the warmth of his skin, and his solidness had conspired against her.

"Follow me." The hostess led the way.

White linen covered small, intimate tables. Purple napkins graced the place settings. Their waiter stood at attention with a warm smile of greeting on his face.

When they were seated, he said, "I'll give you a moment to look at the wine list." He disappeared.

She fingered the wine list. "Are you a wine drinker?"

"Not if I can help it," he said. "Never developed a taste for it."

"Let me guess. You prefer scotch."

He grinned at her. "You remembered."

Heat flooded her face. She didn't want him to think she'd given that night any more thought after she'd walked out of the hotel room. The truth of the matter was she'd thought about every touch of his lips, every thrust of his hips, every orgasm. She shifted uncomfortably in her chair. The muscles in her lower abdomen felt heavy. Her dildo would be getting a workout tonight.

Needing to get back on track, she signaled for their waiter.

"Can you recommend a good white wine?" she asked when he appeared at their table. Wines were not her strong suit.

He pointed out several, commenting on their taste and aroma. She selected one.

"And you, sir?"

"Macallan 18 if you have it."

She remembered the smell of the scotch on his breath as he'd trailed kisses over her face...

Elliott stared at her strangely, and she realized he'd said something she'd missed.

"I'm sorry. What did you say?"

His lips twitched.

Could he figure out what she'd been thinking?

"I asked what's involved in critiquing a restaurant?"

Thank God, he'd gotten her back on track. She had a job to do.

"I start with the entrées." She moved her cutlery until everything lined up perfectly. His presence made her nervous. "Do they appeal to a wide selection of guests? Is the food well-seasoned and original? Are the flavors unique? Is the food under or overcooked? The price range is important. As is the wine list. Does it include a representation—"

He chuckled. "I had no idea so much was involved. You must be a connoisseur of all things edible."

"No. There's a lot I don't know. For example"—she fingered the wine list again—"I'm still working on becoming a wine expert."

She picked up a fork and examined it.

"Cleanliness of the flatware?" he asked.

"Of course."

"How about the bathrooms?"

She shuddered. "I leave that to the Board of Health."

Their waiter reappeared with their drinks. "Are we ready to order?"

"Can you give us a minute?" Rashida asked.

The waiter bowed and moved away.

"Listen." She leaned over the table toward him. "You have to share your meal."

"Why?"

"Because I have to sample as much of the menu as possible. If I taste your food, it keeps me from looking like a glutton."

He raised an eyebrow. "I don't know. You might hog the"—he glanced at the menu portfolio—"collard greens with smoked turkey. I'm a fiend for smoked turkey in my greens. Then I'll starve. I have a healthy…appetite." His eyes dropped to her breasts. Her nipples tightened into hard buds.

She pulled her mind back from the image of him laving each bud with his tongue. She cleared her throat and sat up straighter. "You'll survive. I only need a small sample of your meal. It allows me to get a taste of more of the entrees. I won't even eat it off your plate—you'll put it on a bread plate."

She realized how strange that sounded. When he didn't comment, she rushed on. "I know it might sound a little weird, so if you don't want to, I'll understand."

"Only if I can feed it to you," he said.

The words caught her off guard. Was he serious? "No. Not happening."

Only afterward did she see the humor twinkling in his eyes. She was so gullible.

The restaurant boasted a Southern cuisine with a flair. She studied the menu. All the Southern favorites: fried chicken, fried green tomatoes, salmon croquettes, steak, chicken and dumplings. Desserts included a pound cake with peach sauce, cherry pie, and a sweet potato tart.

When their meals arrived, she took pictures of the food. She'd ordered the trout coated in crushed pecans and pan-seared in a cast-iron skillet. Delicious. Never a fan of undercooked meat, she passed on Elliott's bloody steak. He enjoyed it, a plus she guessed. The fried green tomatoes were over-seasoned, but the sweet potato tart made her want to lick the dish.

While Elliott sipped an after-dinner drink and she drank

another glass of wine, they spoke of the beginning of their careers. He told her about the first years of working with his dad and she was in the process of telling him about trying to build an online presence when a shadow fell over their table.

"Elliott, I thought that was you." A tall male with sharp eyes had materialized at their table. He gave Rashida an appreciative once-over before turning his attention back to Elliott.

He stiffened. The gaiety that had been alive in his features earlier was now submerged under the guise of politeness. "Thompkins."

The man's gray-eyed gaze traveled from Elliott to Rashida, interest alive in his narrow face. "Quite a coincidence meeting a zoning commissioner at the symphony gala, wasn't it? Couldn't have worked out better for you than if it was planned."

Elliott didn't reply. An awkward silence filled the gap. His stony expression said more than any words could have. He didn't like this Thompkins guy and wasn't going to pretend he did.

Seemingly oblivious to Elliott's displeasure, Thompkins leaned across the table and extended his hand to Rashida. "Garrett Thompkins."

"Rashida Howard."

"A pleasure, Ms. Howard."

"Don't let us keep you from your dinner, Thompkins." Elliott's words were sharp as the steak knife he fingered.

Rashida studied the two men. The tension between them was thick as molasses. What was up?

Thompkins straightened to his full height, which must have been a few inches over six feet, and tugged on the hem of his suit coat. "Just wanted to drop by and pay my respects.

If I can help you with your father's business affairs, just give me a call."

When the man walked away, Elliott muttered, "When hell freezes over."

Rashida wondered what had just happened. She'd been privy to a side of Elliott she'd never seen. A side she hoped would never be turned on her.

Elliott's collar felt too tight, the skin at his neck hot and prickly. He picked up his water glass and took a big gulp.

What the hell was Thompkins doing here? The man was a jackal in a suit, preying on the weak. What he hadn't counted on was that Elliott would take over the reins of his father's company while he recuperated.

"I assume you two are not friends?" Rashida's soft voice reached through his fog of anger.

He released the death grip on his water glass and faced her. Her warm chocolate eyes radiated concern. He hoped he hadn't damaged the progress they'd made. "I'm sorry about that. And no, we are not friends."

"Who is he?"

Elliott wanted to forget he'd seen Thompkins, but he could tell that Rashida wanted into his world by the question she'd asked. He owned her explanation. "Thompkins is what we call a corporate raider."

At her frown, he said, "You saw the movie *Pretty Woman*?"

She nodded.

"Richard Gere's character was a corporate raider. Bought companies and sold them off in pieces."

"Oh." She gazed in the direction Thompkins had taken. "He wants to buy your father's company?"

"Yeah."

"But you won't let that happen."

The certainty in her voice made him cautious. She was a bright woman. She knew for his dad's company to stay whole all his projects would have to be a success. Including the Millhouse venture.

If he wanted to maintain the progress he'd made with Rashida, he couldn't let business intrude on their date. This dinner had been the way he wanted to spend his evenings. Laughing and joking with her across the table with nothing more pressing between them than where they wanted to cap the night off. His place or hers. He had to recapture that feeling.

"Enough about work. You were telling me about your social media attempts." He caught the waiter's eyes and lifted his whiskey glass.

As she talked, he was pulled in by how the light from the table lamp reflected in her dark eyes, the quiver of her lips, those soft, full lips he wanted to explore. Like before when she was animated, she talked with her hands. Those long, slender fingers he wanted touching him, stroking him. He shifted in his seat.

They needed time alone without the intrusion of their everyday world. A germ of an idea started to form.

He ran his finger down the sweating whiskey tumbler. "I have to go to Savannah this weekend to inspect acreage a client wants to build on. Do you want to drive down with me? Maybe make a weekend of it?"

She drained the last of her wine then stared down into the

empty stemware. "We've never—"

"Exactly," Elliott interrupted before she could voice an objection. He wanted her somewhere relaxing where they could talk about the next step in their relationship. Hell, to even admit that they were in a relationship. "We could have dinner. Stroll on the Riverwalk, or better yet, take a moonlight carriage ride around the historic area."

"The weekend is just two days away." A cute little frown had crunched up the area between her arched eyebrows.

"Low-key. Bring a bathing suit, some casual clothes, and sneakers in case we want to walk around." He reached out and covered her hand with his. "Please."

He wanted this to be the start of something permanent for them. No more being on opposite sides. He wanted her on his side. Always.

Once on the beach, he'd talk to her about Redding's offer. He had to put all his cards on the table.

Her gaze seemed to probe to the depths of his soul. Did she see the love he felt for her? He hoped so.

She slid her fingers from beneath his then began arranging her fork on her plate and the knife at the top of the white china. She worried her lip, then her head jerked up almost in defiance as if she'd made a life-changing decision.

Maybe she had. He hoped it was in his favor. Their favor.

CHAPTER FOURTEEN

Rashida sat in the passenger seat of Elliott's Range Rover as it sped along I-16 toward Savannah. The interior of the car was a cool sixty-eight degrees in contrast to the humid ninety-degree temperature outside. An eerie landscape of stunted leafless trees in murky water gave the area the feel of a place leveled by a tornado.

Inside, they rode in silence. Rashida couldn't shut off her brain. Her body was one tense ball of muscles. *Relax. Breathe.* God, what was she doing? Going away for a weekend with Elliott was big. They'd jumped over a few steps on the road to…what?

She gnawed at her cuticle, caught herself, then soothed the tortured finger. Had she made a mistake agreeing to this two-night trip? Someone was going to get hurt, and she didn't want it to be her. She couldn't take another relationship failure. "What are we doing once you finish with your client?"

"We're spending one night in Savannah. The rest is a surprise."

She hated surprises. "Your dad okay with you being away?"

"I have a phone. He has a nurse. If anything arises, she'll call me. Plus, he's doing better."

He took his attention off the flat expanse of highway and studied her. "How about some music? What do you like?"

Could he tell she was one step away from jumping from a moving car? "I'm easy. Anything but country."

"Hmmm…"

Rashida shifted to take in his expression. "Let me guess. Country is your favorite."

He shot her a sheepish grin. "Well, yes. But I do like other types of music."

"*What?*" she asked.

"Do you trust me?"

Did she trust him? Yes. After going to the trouble of introducing her to Lissa so she'd know he was an honorable man, his stock had gone up.

"It's not that serious," he said, throwing a grin in her direction. "I'm not asking for the president's nuclear launch codes."

"I trust you."

He touched a button on the dash, and the blare of a horn filled the car.

Jazz.

Elliott took his eyes off the road to judge her reception of his selection. "Do you recognize him?"

"*Him?*"

Elliott groaned. "Miles."

She put two and two together. "Davis."

He grinned over at her. "Of course. Who else?"

Who else indeed?

They were on the outskirts of Savannah when she realized she might like jazz. Or at least Miles Davis's version.

"Okay. He's good," she admitted.

"No," he said. "The man is brilliant."

Their hotel room looked out over the Savannah River. While Elliott visited his client, she treated herself to a spa treatment. Later that night, they sat out by the pool after dinner. He suggested they retire early so they could get an early start on the rest of the weekend.

She didn't question him. Maybe she should have.

"Time to get up," an annoying gnat whispered in her ear. She was not a morning person, so she ignored the voice, turned over and drifted...

"Rashida, it's time to leave."

She opened one eye and peered up at him. Elliott was dressed casually in cargo shorts.

"What time is it?"

"Seven thirty."

"Call me at nine."

"This is part of the surprise," he said with a laugh.

"I don't like surprises." She pulled the pillow over her head to drown out his voice.

He lifted a corner of the pillow, letting light leak in. "If you get up and get dressed, I promise you the best cup of coffee you've ever had."

She sat up, gave him an "I-hate-you" glare, then stumbled off to the shower.

An hour later, with a cup of coffee in her hand, they headed south down a two-lane road. When they reached the city of St. Marys, she looked over at him with suspicion that bordered on alarm.

"Where are we going?"

He opened the window, and the smell of water, dead fish, and seaweed floated into the car. He looked over at her. "Camping."

• • •

I hate camping. I hate camping. This refrain went through her head as she watched the city of St. Marys recede and Cumberland Island draw closer. Salt spray misted her face and made the deck of the ferry slippery.

A city girl, she liked sleeping on a mattress and taking hot showers. She hated bugs, cooking outside, and sleeping under the stars.

When her mother moved them from Miami to Georgia, they'd traveled frequently to the coast. She'd been three or four years old. Karla had been around six. They couldn't afford a hotel room, so they'd slept in their car and protected themselves from bugs by rolling up the windows.

Elliott had advised her to bring casual clothes, but she didn't know he'd meant hiking boots and shorts. She'd brought sandals and sundresses. They'd caught the very last ferry of the day because he'd insisted on buying her proper clothes. She eyed the backpacks. He'd hidden them under a tarp in the cargo area of the Range Rover so she wouldn't guess the surprise. Or maybe he didn't want her to turn around and go home.

He came up behind and put his arms around her. "You'll love the island."

"Uh-huh."

He chuckled. Placing his chin on the top of her head, he drew her closer. "The island is all wildness and freedom. You're an island girl. You'll love it."

"My mother and grandmother are island women. Except for a few visits to the ocean when I was very young, I've never been close to an island."

But on some elementary level, she could relate to that wildness. The minute she set foot on the ferry, the pulse and pull of the ocean infiltrated her spirit. She must have inherited that love from her mother and grandmother.

Twenty or so people left the boat with them and gathered around the Ranger's Station where they received instructions on the rules of the island. No cars, no pets, which sites had drinkable water, and the distance to each site. According to the ranger, each site became wilder the farther from the dock.

She hoped they weren't hiking to the campsite ten miles away. If they were, she'd go back with the ferry still docked and swaying on the ocean current.

"The hotel grounds are for guests only," the ranger said.

Rashida turned to Elliott, almost giddy with relief. "Hotel?" she whispered.

"Next time."

She rolled her eyes. He didn't fit a mold. She would have never thought camping was his thing. Exotic vacations—yes. Roughing it—no.

"Where are we staying?" she asked once the ranger finished his spiel and released them. She held her breath, waiting for his response.

"Stafford."

Three and a half miles from where they now stood. Crap. But it could have been worse. The most remote camp was ten miles away. Ten long hiking miles away.

Elliott picked up the heaviest of the packs, which contained the tent, food, and cooking utensils and slid it on his back. "Ready?"

She glanced wistfully at the ferry pulling away from the dock. "Yeah." Her pack contained blankets and her clothes for two days.

Considering she'd never hiked, it was the longest walk she'd ever taken.

Five other campers made the trek to Stafford. Elliott kept up a running dialogue with them. Rashida concentrated on breathing. She cursed every extra pound she'd put on in the last year.

By the time they made it to the Stafford site, her blisters had blisters, her legs were cooked linguine, and she needed to pee.

They set up camp in a spot farthest from the other sites and the farthest from the bathrooms. The facility only had cold water, which she discovered when she'd relieved herself and washed her hands.

When she wandered back to their site, Elliott had pitched the tent.

"Hungry?" he asked.

"Why?" She turned her head in the direction of the pounding surf. "Are we fishing for our dinner?"

He glanced at his watch. "I don't think we have time before dark."

"I was kidding," she said sourly.

He chuckled. "I know. You're being a good sport about this surprise. I honestly thought you'd love it."

"That's because you don't know much about me."

"I know more than you think." His gaze combed her features. "But I want to know more." His green eyes zeroed in on her mouth. "I want to know much more."

Would he be turned off when he learned there wasn't a whole lot more to her? She wasn't as complicated nor as sophisticated as his friend Lissa. Surprisingly, Rashida found she liked Lissa. They'd spoken a couple of times on the phone without bringing up Elliott. Outside of her family and Monique, she hadn't felt the need for lots of friends to talk to. Having these random conversations with Lissa had been fun.

"Let's walk down to the beach," Elliott said.

Waist-high palm ferns lined the sandy path that led to the ocean. The sound of the surf grew louder until the ocean spread out in a panoramic view from horizon to horizon.

She stopped. Memories of when she was young and she, her mother, and Karla had visited the beach assaulted her. It was a great time for her, but how had her mother felt? She was in a foreign land without her husband and without support. It must have been scary.

Elliott took her hand in his larger one and pulled her toward the beach. Sunlight beat down on her head, making her wish for a hat. The walk to the campsite had been shaded by tall palm trees and a few deciduous hardwoods. Here it was just water and sun.

She closed her eyes and breathed in brine. She remembered how peaceful the sound of the surf had made her feel when she was a child. The tension of the last several weeks rolled away.

When she opened her eyes, Elliott stared at her, not the ocean. Maybe sensing her need for privacy, he walked away and began picking up twigs and dried seaweed that had tangled in the low-lying sand scrub growing closer to the dunes. She joined him, and in a few minutes, they had two armfuls of twigs, small branches, and dried weeds.

Back at the camp, after dropping their wood next to the ring, Rashida surveyed their surroundings. She could hear the distant murmur of the other campers but couldn't see them through the dense foliage.

Each campsite had a fire ring, one table, and a steel vertical pole.

"What's this?" She waved her hand toward the pole, which had to be at least ten feet tall, with its base inserted into the sandy soil.

Pulling items from his pack, Elliott glanced up. "Keeps the raccoons away from the food at night."

She shuddered. She didn't relish sleeping in that thin canvas tent while outside large rats scurried helter skelter through their food.

"Speaking of food, what's for dinner?" She hadn't investigated his pack, so she hoped he wouldn't say canned beans or sardines. If she'd known this was their destination, she could have come up with some appetizing ideas for meals. But on the flip side, if she'd known they were going to go camping, she would have vetoed the idea.

Deciding to make the most of this adventure, she said, "Let's eat on the beach."

Elliott spread a blanket on the sand then held out his hand for Rashida to join him. She eased between his legs then rested her head against his chest.

He'd never taken the time for small pleasures like sunrises or sunsets. He'd been too busy as an adult either working with his father or building his own business. Now, with Rashida's back to his chest, the sun sinking below the water's horizon, and the smell of salt and fish, he was the most content he'd ever been.

Dinner hadn't been high cuisine, but it had been filling:

fruit, thin slices of Prosciutto, cheese and crackers. He'd found a small, insulated cooler guaranteed to keep food and drink chilled for up to twenty-four hours. He'd packed it with a bottle of her favorite wine.

"Tell me about your mother," she said.

"What would you like to know?"

"Was she like you?"

"How so?" He spoke into her hair.

"Confident, personable, warm."

"Thank you."

How did he describe his mother? "She was distant to everyone but me."

After a pause, she said, "How old were you when she died?"

His arms tightened around her. "Ten."

Rashida turned to stare into his eyes. "I'm sorry."

"It was a long time ago." Thinking about her still brought him pain. He hadn't protected her. Not that there was much he could have done at ten years old.

"She wasn't happy in her marriage to my father."

"Why not?"

Elliott could lie and say he didn't know, but he did. "I don't think she wanted to be married to my dad, but she couldn't leave him."

"Couldn't?" Rashida's intense gaze made him uncomfortable. He hadn't thought about his parents' marriage in a long time.

"She was unhappy, so she drank. A lot. If she'd left, my father wouldn't have let her take me. So she stayed. For me. I didn't realize how much she sacrificed for me until I was an adult."

Rashida stroked his arm. "Sounds like she loved you very

much. How did she die?"

"Car accident."

The anguish in her eyes made him reexamine the pain he'd carried for so long. Made him reexamine something he hadn't wanted to look at too closely—his father's role in his mother's death. Not the accident. She'd been alone in the car. But what had driven her to drink? And why hadn't his father helped her?

The ground vibrated. A herd of wild horses thundered onto the beach.

Rashida's body tensed, her gaze locked on the animals. "They're beautiful."

"From what I remember, a Spanish galleon sank off the island's shores about four or five hundred years ago. These horses are the descendants."

They watched the herd in silence until they galloped off the beach.

Darkness gathered. The pounding of the surf took the place of the blood rushing through his veins. He could stay here forever, but he didn't know how Rashida felt. "You want to go back to the campsite?"

"Not yet. It's so much cooler out here."

"We'll probably be able to stay for a while." He'd hoped that she'd want to stay here, so he'd place their blanket well back from the water and the high-tide mark.

"Good." She wriggled her derriere into his crotch. He closed his eyes and willed his body not to respond. His cock wasn't listening.

"Your dad is a hard man. Has he always been like that?" she asked.

"Yes. Which is one of the reasons my parents' marriage

didn't work. Work was his mistress. And now, he's determined to give himself another heart attack."

"Is work *your* mistress?" she asked.

"No." He didn't add that if she were his wife, he'd want to be with her as much as possible. He didn't say those words because he knew they'd scare her.

Elliot pulled her closer. A mistake. His cock throbbed. He glanced around, wondering if they could make love without someone walking out from the campsite. For some unknown reason, the chance of detection seemed to intensify the need to bury himself balls deep into her warm core.

Concentrate on something else.

"Have you thought about trying to find your father?"

Her body stiffened. "I'm not sure he's alive."

"You mother—"

"She hasn't had any contact with him since they divorced. She doesn't even know if he's still in the States. Probably not." Rashida shrugged. "Probably went back home, and for all I know, he has another family."

"You're not curious?"

"Why should I be? He didn't care enough about me and Karla to stay in touch."

Elliott heard the pain in her voice, a little girl's pain. He tightened his arms around her. He wanted to protect her from the world.

"I was engaged," she said bluntly.

The words kicked him in the gut. "What happened?"

She was silent so long he didn't think she'd answer.

"He left." She shifted in the sand. "No. That's a lie. I made him leave. I was too scared to follow him to San Francisco, so our relationship just…just ended."

"Maybe you didn't love him enough."

When she didn't respond, he wished he could get inside her head. Know her thoughts. Her heart.

"Maybe you're right." Her body trembled.

He wanted to tell her he was falling for her, hard. But the time wasn't right. He needed to be open and honest and tell her about Redding's offer first.

He opened his mouth, but the words wouldn't come. Once he told her about his role in the venture capitalist's plan, she'd hate him. He didn't want to lose her, so he kept his mouth shut. He was a coward.

He pulled her closer, wanting to pretend she was his for a few more hours, a few more days. The warmth of her lush body only made him want her more. He should not be thinking about making love to her when he hid something as detrimental to their relationship as his part in the upcoming demise of the Millhouse area.

"I want to make love. Out here." Her eyes dark with pain or lust, he couldn't tell which, roamed over his face.

He glanced toward the path that led to the campsites. "It's not very private."

"It's almost dark." Her hands clutched at his shirt.

The sun cast its last light through the clouds, making them purple streaked with orange. Anyone walking on the beach could still make out what they were doing. "We could go back to our tent—"

"Here."

She pulled his face down to hers. When her mouth touched his, he was lost. Gluing his lips to hers, he plundered her mouth like he wanted to plunder her soft, lush body.

Her fingers were busy, pulling at his shorts, then slipping

inside his boxers, grabbing his cock in her small hands even as her tongue fought for dominance with his.

Reluctantly, he pulled his mouth from hers. "Baby..." He glanced around the beach. No one. *Think*. It was hard to form a coherent thought. She dropped her head into his lap, then her tongue was teasing the hell out of the head of his cock. *Think. Blanket.*

He eased up on his knees, working the blanket out from beneath them, inch by inch. Her warm mouth slid farther down his cock. By the time he'd worked the blanket out and draped it over their bodies, he was in a full sweat.

"Rashida..."

She batted his hands away when he tried to lift her to her feet.

From somewhere in his sex-fried brain, the realization came that she needed to be in control. He dropped his hands and stopped protesting. He surrendered. She took him fully into her mouth. The warmth of her lips and tongue gliding along his length made his eyes roll back into his head. His skin tingled, his sac tightened. His mind short-circuited, lost in the heat of her mouth.

When the lights exploded behind his eyes, she was in command of his body and his heart. All he could do was ride the wave of pleasure.

CHAPTER FIFTEEN

When Elliott arrived at Rashida's grandmother's house, voices drifted out from the wooden privacy fence. The barbeque appeared to be in full swing. He reached into his car and pulled out a six-pack of beer and a bottle of wine, his contribution to the cookout.

Determined to win some people over to the idea of the marketplace, he opened the gate and stepped into the backyard. Voices muted out one by one until all he could hear were the cicadas.

He looked from one face to another. Maybe his quest was going to be harder than he thought. He waved in greeting and walked toward the back door.

Reverend Clemmons stepped out of the house. It took him just a moment to take in the situation. "Just give them time. Let's put that beer in the refrigerator." The minister held the door open, and Elliott stepped inside.

The kitchen was teeming with mostly women preparing food. He waved at Rashida's mom and grandmother. Grammy lifted her chin in a barely perceptible nod. Essie gave him a hug, holding a salad spoon away from his back as she squeezed him tight.

"Welcome. There's cold beer in coolers scattered around

the yard. Grab one and introduce yourself," she said.

Outside, Elliott found a beer. Conversation had restarted and people mingled in small groups. He strolled around the yard, waiting for the opportunity to invite himself into someone's circle.

Shouts of "that's mine" and "you can't draw" drew his attention to a bunch of noisy kids who occupied a picnic table a few steps from where he nursed his drink. Being an only child, he was never good with children. He guessed their ages to be around eight or nine. Four boys and one lone girl. Tears slid down her cheeks, but she practically vibrated with anger. Her arms were crossed, and her pointed chin stuck out.

"What's the problem?" Elliott asked as he moved toward the table.

They looked up at him with Stranger Danger suspicion in their eyes.

"Idris thinks he can draw. And he won't let anyone else have a turn," the little girl said. Her words floated out in a lisp caused by missing teeth.

Elliott studied the drawing Idris had made. As drawings went, it was pretty awful. The kids shared one sheet and one set of crayons.

"Give me a minute," Elliott said. "I'll be right back. Try not to kill each other before I get back." Someone giggled.

From his car, he pulled a sketch pad and drawing pencils. He'd wanted to be a cartoonist when he was a boy the way some kids wanted to be firemen.

When he returned, he gave each child a sheet of paper and one pencil. "Okay, go at it."

The girl with the missing teeth stared at her paper and made no move to draw. Since she'd been the only one comfortable enough to speak to him, he took a seat next to her. "What's wrong?"

She didn't look at him but stared down at her sheet of oversize paper. "I can't draw," she whispered.

"Of course you can," Elliott said. "Close your eyes." She did as he instructed. Her lids fluttered like the wings of a baby bird.

"What do you see?"

Her eyes flew open.

"Close your eyes again." Elliott kept the laughter out of his voice. "What do you see with your eyes closed."

"Nothing."

"Take a deep breath."

Her little chest expanded.

"And another breath."

She followed his directions.

Elliott wasn't sure this would work. He'd done it as a child when he couldn't escape into the fantasy world of his drawings. He'd needed that escape when the loneliness that overtook him after his mother died became too much.

"What do you see?" He could sense he had the attention of the other kids at the table.

"Fairies."

"Without opening your eyes, draw what you see." He positioned the paper in front of her then wrapped her small fingers around her pencil. He guided her hand to the paper.

She hesitated at first, making small tentative scratches on the paper.

"Fly," he whispered. "Let your fingers fly."

She looped across the paper with her pencil, creating something an abstract artist would be hard-pressed to interpret.

"Open your eyes."

When she opened her eyes, she stared at her drawing with a stricken expression.

"What did she draw?" One of the boys in the group crowded Elliott's shoulder trying to get a look at the girl's picture.

"The sky," another boy answered.

Someone scoffed. "Looks like chicken scratch."

Elliott ignored them. "You did a great job. What do you want to call it?"

She stared at her picture then up at Elliott with something like hope in her brown eyes. "For real?"

He nodded. "It has a lot of potential."

She might not know what the word potential meant, but she seemed to infer from Elliott's tone her drawing was good.

"The Blue Fairies."

"What's your name?" he asked her.

"Rissy," one of the boys answered for her.

"Charisse Hollins." She puffed out her chest. "I'm going to be an artist."

"You're on your way." Elliott flipped the drawing over then wrote with bold black strokes in cursive *The Blue Fairies* by Charisse Hollins.

Smiling, Rissy held the drawing between her fingertips and took off running. Elliott smiled after her.

He turned to find Rashida standing at the end of the table. She stared at him as though she'd never seen him before.

"Let me introduce you to some of Grammy's neighbors."

"Where did you meet Elliott?"

Rashida and her mother were in Grammy's kitchen,

cleaning up after the cookout. Grammy was sitting in the living room with Mrs. McClain and another neighbor.

"We met in a bar."

"Hmmm…" Her mother washed a serving bowl, rinsed it, and placed it in the draining rack. "Grammy said you seemed shocked when you saw him at the zoning meeting."

Rashida gaped at her mother in surprise. "Grammy told you she attended the zoning meeting?"

"She did."

"Wow."

"Does that surprise you?"

"Well, yes. I know you two are always butting heads about this house." Rashida studied her mother. "Grammy wants to stay in her home. I know you two have not seen eye to eye about it."

"She's getting older. I don't want her to fall with no one around."

"I know." Rashida didn't want to think about something happening to her grandmother.

Her mother crossed her arms and leaned against the sink. "We're getting off the subject. Why did Elliott's presence at the zoning meeting surprise you?"

"I met him a few days before the meeting. We had a drink but didn't exchange last names. It was a casual thing." She shrugged. "I didn't know he was connected to Quinn Enterprises and was surprised to see him at the church. That's all. Nothing else."

She went to the pantry, pulled out the broom, and started to sweep the kitchen floor. No way would she tell her mother she and Elliott had hooked up. Because her mother was a social worker, she'd probably heard everything, but Rashida didn't want to discuss her sexual liaisons with her parent.

"If it was so casual, why did you invite him to dinner?

You've never invited anyone over to meet us before. At least not since Alex."

Rashida paused and leaned on the broom handle. "That was your and Grammy's doing."

At her mother's raised eyebrow, Rashida explained the misunderstanding.

"You had plenty of time to tell us who was coming to dinner." Her mother smiled. "Pun intended. So why didn't you?"

"I wanted Grammy to apologize to him."

"To apologize for what?"

Guess Grammy didn't tell Rashida's mother everything. "She kinda got into a poking altercation with him at one of the protests."

"So you *hoped* she would apologize." Her mother started cleaning the countertops.

"Yeah. I hoped. We know how that turned out."

"Do you like him?"

Rashida wasn't sure how to answer. He was wickedly funny. Sexy. A great lover. And the biggest point in his favor, he listened when she talked and seemed to be genuinely interested in what she had to say even if he didn't agree with it. "I like him. But it's complicated."

"Relationships usually are."

Rashida closed her eyes in exasperation. "We're not in a relationship. We're on opposites sides of an important issue."

Her mother studied her like she was the biggest hot mess on a reality television show.

"Seriously, we're just…" *What? Frenemies?* "I don't know what we are."

What was with her mother and her sudden interest in her and Elliott? Would her mother be as forthcoming in a discussion about Rashida's father? They'd talked around it in the past. A comment here, a comment there. But nothing frank or in-depth.

Rashida barely remembered him. Just a dark-skinned man who smelled like sweat and earth.

Guess it was now or never.

"Was your relationship with my father complicated?"

Her mother turned and submerged her hands in the suds. "Yes. It was complicated because *he* was complicated." Her mother paused and stared out the window, which overlooked the backyard. "No. That isn't true. He was a simple man in a complicated world. He loved me, but when I started to grow, he either couldn't or wouldn't grow with me."

Rashida waited, almost holding her breath so her mother wouldn't stop talking.

"He felt threatened because I wanted more out of life than being a wife and mother. We separated when I was pregnant with you. I took Karla and came to the States and started college. He followed, and for a while, the four of us were okay. And then we weren't."

Her mother resumed scrubbing pots and pans. Rashida guessed the conversation about her father was over. But she needed to ask one more question. "Is he still here? In the States?"

Her mother shrugged. "I don't know. After the divorce, I lost touch with him."

Staring down into the sudsy water, her mother asked, "What will happen to your relationship with Elliott if his application is approved?"

"I told you there is no relationship."

"So why have I seen him twice in the last week when I

haven't seen you with anyone in the year since Alex moved to San Francisco?"

Rashida couldn't answer that question.

"So, I repeat. What will happen if the zoning committee votes in his favor?"

"My goal is to try to get him to change his mind and withdraw the application or to accept one of the compromises."

Her mother frowned. "You mean you need his father to change his mind, don't you? It's his father's project, right?"

Rashida nodded. She kept forgetting Elliott stood in for his father while he recovered. At dinner a few nights ago, he'd spoken of working for his dad straight out of post-graduate school rather than starting a business in historical restoration. He hadn't wanted to disappoint his father. That gesture said his dad had a lot of influence over Elliott. But did Elliott have any influence over his father?

Had he discussed the community's alternatives with his father? Or just decided his father wouldn't be interested?

Her stomach pitched. Somehow, she had to get him to present those alternatives. Time was running out.

The next afternoon, Rashida arrived early at Grammy's place to drive her to the market. She didn't want her grandmother to get the idea she could jump behind the wheel.

With her court date coming up, her grandmother didn't need additional charges on her record like "driving with a suspended license."

Rashida walked through the house, calling her grandmother's name. No Grammy. Heart thudding behind her ribs,

Rashida checked for the old Cadillac. She let out a sigh of relief when she spotted the car parked in its usual place.

Maybe her mother had driven Grammy to an appointment.

"I spoke with her about an hour ago," Rashida's mother said. "As far as I know, she had no plans to leave the house. She's probably sitting on someone's porch, chewing the fat."

"Thanks, Mom. I guess I panicked."

Rashida walked down the street to Mrs. McClain's house. The old lady didn't answer when Rashida knocked. *Please don't let the two be together with Mrs. McClain driving.* The last time they'd been together, Elliott had ended up in the hospital.

But Mrs. McClain's car was in her garage.

The faint squeal of voices drew Rashida's attention to Mrs. Parker's house, two doors from Mrs. McClain's. Just as Rashida reached Mrs. Parker's steps, her screen door flew open and the three women came charging out.

"What's wrong?" Rashida asked as she walked up onto the porch. When she got a good look at the elderly trio, she drew back in surprise. They were drenched.

Mrs. Parker shook herself like a wet dog, and Grammy tried to wipe her face with even wetter hands.

"What happened?"

"The pipes burst," Mrs. McClain said, peering up into Rashida's face.

"Water is shooting everywhere," Mrs. Parker said. "Ruining my new floor."

Her "new" floor had been installed fifteen years ago. Rashida remembered Grammy carrying on about the expense... and then wondered if she could get her floors replaced, too. Rashida didn't know anything about plumbing, but she did know they could turn the water off from the outside meter. "Do you have a wrench?"

Mrs. Parker shook her head.

Rashida didn't bother to ask her grandmother. There'd be no tools in her grandmother's house. Her grandfather, when he'd been alive, could make anything grow, but that was the limit of his handyman skills.

Rashida called Marty Hollins. The call went straight to voicemail.

"I'm going to have to call a plumber, Mrs. Parker," Rashida informed the elderly woman.

Her grandmother's neighbor's eyes grew wide as saucers. "I don't have the money for a plumber."

Rashida patted her hand. "Don't worry about it." *How much could it be?*

She called several plumbers in the area, and the best she could do was one who could make an emergency call in about four hours to the tune of two hundred fifty dollars.

"How about that nice friend of yours?" Mrs. McClain said, blindly peering into Rashida's face.

"Who?" Rashida asked. She could only mean Elliott, since Rashida had brought no one other than him around.

She hated to disappoint Mrs. McClain, but Elliott in his expensive clothes and shoes didn't appear to be someone who knew about replacing pipes. Drawing them into a blueprint— yes. But taking out the old and putting in the new? Rashida didn't think so.

Then again, he did surprise her with a camping trip...

"The one who came over for brownies the other day," Mrs. McClain supplied. "The one I hit with my car."

"Elliott?"

Mrs. McClain touched Rashida's arm. "Yes. Yes. That's the one."

A nice young man who is going to destroy your neighborhood. But, of course, she didn't say that. She also didn't tell Mrs. McClain she doubted Elliott would drop what he was doing to rush down to the Millhouse area and fix a plumbing problem.

She glanced at the house. Water trickled out from beneath the screen door. Did they have the luxury of waiting on a plumber to show up? No. She needed to get over her objections to Elliott Quinn. Even if he could only turn off the water entering the house from the city's main valve, Mrs. Parker would be ahead.

She dialed his number.

He was there in record time. And he even had tools.

"Where'd you get the tools?" she asked when he arrived.

He lifted an eyebrow. "You don't think I had them in my car?"

She clamped her lips together to prevent a grin. "You don't strike me as the type of guy who carries tools around."

"I don't," he admitted. "I stopped at one of Dad's projects and the foreman lent me these."

She followed him to the water meter. He used a crowbar to pry off the water meter's lid. Using a wrench, he twisted one of the valves, then with long strides, he made for the house. He reappeared a moment later and gave them a thumbs-up.

The ladies hugged each other.

Rashida watched with a half smile. She didn't want to rain on their parade, but they seemed to have forgotten Mrs. Parker had a pipe that needed the services of a plumber to the tune of two hundred fifty dollars.

Most of the water had drained out the front door, but as Rashida made her way toward the kitchen, there was still enough standing water to ruin furniture and the floors.

She found Elliott in the kitchen, going through the pantry.

"What are you doing?" she asked.

"Looking for a flashlight."

"Why?"

He stopped rooting around and stared at her. "Because it's pretty dark under the sink. And I can't see the problem without some light."

"You don't have to worry. A plumber is coming in a couple of hours."

"I can have it fixed before then."

She scoffed. No way.

He pulled his head out of the pantry. "What was that for?"

"What?"

"That sound you made. Like you doubt I can repair the pipe."

Although he had a body that told her he did more than sit behind his desk, she doubted his ability to do manual labor. "Can you?"

"I'm going to try. As soon as you find me a flashlight."

Mrs. Parker had a flashlight in the nightstand by her bed.

Elliott maneuvered into the cabinet, leaving Rashida to stare at his hard thighs. Heat flashed through her body as she remembered gripping those very thighs on the beach when she—

"You okay, dear?" Mrs. Parker had materialized at Rashida's shoulder.

"Yes, ma'am. Just a little warm in here."

"I know what you mean."

Was it Rashida's imagination or was the old lady also checking out Elliott's body?

He scooted out from underneath the sink. "I can't repair it."

Just as she thought. Now they'd have to wait on the plumber.

"I'll have to go to a home improvement store and get a new pipe."

Rashida's face must have shown her surprise and her doubt.

He placed a dirty forefinger under her chin, tipping her face up to his.

"Yes, Rashida. I know how to replace a pipe." He had the audacity to kiss her lightly on the lips.

Her stomach dipped and twisted and righted itself.

Mrs. Parker tittered. "You kids are so cute."

"Let me give you some money for the pipe," Mrs. Parker demanded.

Rashida wondered how much money the old lady had to give. She'd not asked how much the pipe would cost.

"No problem. I have a builder's account with the store."

"Oh, that's good," Mrs. Parker said.

Rashida stared at the clutter pulled from underneath the sink.

Mrs. Parker touched her arm. "He's so nice. It's wonderful that he has an account, and they are going to give him the pipe."

Rashida clamped her lips together to keep the sigh from spilling out. The poor dear didn't understand Elliott would still have to pay for the pipe. She'd come to understand Elliott a little better, though. Generous and dependable. Just the type of guy to get under her skin.

• • •

While Elliott replaced Mrs. Parker's busted pipe, Rashida, Grammy, and her two friends with brooms and old towels tried to rid the house of as much standing water as they could.

Afterward, the three ladies retired to Grammy's house while the large industrial fans Elliott rented while at the builder's store did their job.

"Are you hungry?" Rashida asked him as they walked to her car. He had unidentifiable stains on his slacks, and his expensive shoes were ruined.

"I'm always hungry. What did you have in mind?"

She was so going to regret this. "Do you want to follow me to my apartment? You can clean up there while I whip up something to eat." She couldn't believe she'd made the offer. Her apartment was her sanctuary.

"You cook?" The wicked gleam in his eyes told her he was baiting her, taking the weight away from what they both knew was a significant shift in their relationship.

"Okay. Turnabout is fair play."

"I'll follow you," he said quietly.

It took fifteen minutes from Grammy's neighborhood to Rashida's apartment in Decatur.

"Nice," he said when he crossed the threshold.

"It's small," she said in defense of her place but was pleased he liked it.

"Cozy."

She tried to see her apartment through his eyes. Bright and bold colors both on the walls and the fabric of the sofa, chairs, and pillows. Color lifted her spirits.

He walked around the living room, studying the artwork. Black-and-white charcoal prints of African women with their children.

"Did you sketch these?" he asked.

She laughed. "My art talent is limited to stick figures. But you…" She remembered the guidance he'd given Marty's granddaughter.

Elliott turned, waiting for her to finish her sentence.

"You're an artist, aren't you?"

He lifted his shoulders in a casual manner. "It relaxes me."

When he didn't elaborate, she said, "Let me show you the bathroom." She glanced down at his shoes. "Sorry about your shoes."

He shrugged. "They can be replaced."

Her apartment, a studio-sized affair, housed the living room, dining area, and kitchen in one open space. The one bedroom and bath were located down a short hall. She handed him fresh towels and pointed him in the direction of the bathroom.

While he cleaned up, she put water on to boil for pasta then pulled out veggies for a penne pasta salad. Simple but filling.

Later they worked side by side, chopping vegetables. He smelled of her lavender-scented soap.

"Thank you for helping Mrs. Parker. It means a lot to her… to me."

"She wanted to do something to pay me back." He stopped chopping, and a stricken look passed over his face. "She's not going to bake brownies, is she?"

Rashida laughed. "She's a great baker. Consider yourself fortunate if she does." She pointed toward the refrigerator. "Grab a beer."

While he rooted around in the refrigerator, she added the chopped vegetables, fresh basil, parmesan cheese, cherry tomatoes, and Italian dressing to the cooled pasta then tossed.

They ate in her living room.

"You can cook," he said after his second serving.

"Thank you, but that wasn't cooking." She knew her limitations.

"Accept the compliment."

She flushed. "Thank you."

To take the attention off her shortcomings, she asked, "Do you want to play Monopoly?"

"As in the board game?"

"Yes. Is there any other Monopoly?"

He rose and picked up his plate and beer bottle then moved toward the kitchen. "I haven't played since I was a kid."

"Good. That should make beating you a breeze." She followed him into the kitchen. "Want another beer?"

"Nay." He held up his almost empty bottle. "Better just have one."

She rinsed the dishes before placing them into the dishwasher. Standing next to her, he fingered the pots of herbs that crowded the windowsill.

An orange, hazy light filtered in through her south-facing window, giving the kitchen an otherworldly appearance. The sound of running water, dust motes dancing through fading sunlight, and Elliott standing next to her at the sink gave the scene a sweet, domestic feel.

"Thank you for inviting me over." He curled a loose strand of her hair around her ear then trailed his finger down her neck, leaving a path of heat.

"The least I could do." Her voice cracked.

The only sounds were the quiet hum of the refrigerator, the *tick-tock* of the wall clock, and her heart jitterbugging against her ribs.

She held her breath in anticipation of his next move.

His finger traced her collarbone, leaving goose bumps as a parting gift. She found it difficult to draw a breath. Each attempt caused a hitch in her chest.

As he explored each dip and hollow of her throat, she studied his lips. If she leaned forward ever so slightly, she could capture his full lower lip between her teeth.

His breath fanned her cheek. The not-unpleasant scent of yeast filled her nostrils. She stood on tiptoes, bringing her mouth within a breath of his.

Her brain sent her signals. *Abort. Abort. Abort.* But her body sent her stronger more urgent messages. *Closer. Taste. Lick.*

Her mouth touched his. Lightly. Then withdrew. Those same lips that often looked so uncompromising were surprisingly soft. She hesitated for one heartbeat then dove in for a more intensive exploration.

Then his tongue came out to play. The yeasty taste of beer invaded her mouth. His tongue danced with hers, guiding, leading. He maneuvered his body until the sink was at her back and his strong thighs pressed into her front.

She skimmed her fingers over his jaw. The bristle of hair tickled her skin. He needed a shave. She needed him.

Why fight the connection between them? Why deny what they both wanted? She lifted her gaze to stare into his eyes gone suddenly dark. There was a question there. She didn't analyze it. Her body knew the answer.

Taking his large hand, she led him down the hall to her bedroom.

To her bed.

CHAPTER SIXTEEN

Yellow pillows were piled deep on a cream-colored duvet. Splashes of different shades of yellow dotted her bedroom. Must be her favorite color. The thought drifted into Elliott's head and was forgotten as she started to shed her clothes. First her hip-hugging jeans fell, then the scrap of bright blue material that was her thong. Her thighs were smooth and defined. Her stomach had a slight pouch, which beckoned his lips to kiss.

She cocked her head then raised an eyebrow. "You planning to join in?"

He couldn't stop the smile that spread across his face. As serious as their encounters had been, she always made him smile. "Just enjoying the show."

"I'd like to enjoy it, too."

"I'll do my damnedest to make sure you do."

He did a slow striptease for her. Taking his time with the buttons on his shirt, he slowly exposed his chest.

She sat cross-legged on the bed. "Is that all you got?"

He whipped the shirt off and twirled it around his head to the beat of some tuneless melody running through his head.

After tossing the shirt, he cocked his hip then unbuttoned his slacks. He paused then started rocking his hips.

She clapped her hands, which only encouraged him. He was a horrible dancer and rarely got on the dance floor, but now he performed for her. For her smile and for her laughter.

He slid his trousers slowly down his legs, getting a jolt of pleasure when the laughter left her face and hunger entered her eyes.

When she wet her lips, he almost stumbled over his pants, trying to remove them faster. His cock pulsed. He was tired of the striptease.

Dressed only in his boxers and holding her gaze, he moved slowly toward her.

She rose onto her knees. When he reached her, she melded her body to his—skin to skin. He closed his eyes and reveled in her softness. Her warmth. The touch of her lips.

She slid her arms around his neck. "Elliott?"

The question in her voice brought to the surface their differences in the last couple of weeks. He didn't want to think about what kept them apart. He wanted to be in this moment. To feel her arms around him. To be inside her.

Pulling her down with him, he stretched out on the bed. They were face to face. Hip to hip. He traced her features. Her large brown eyes, her nose, and her strong jawline. "Let's enjoy this. We'll worry about tomorrow…tomorrow. Okay?"

She nodded. "Condoms are in the top drawer."

With his lips, he traced the squarish jaw, the full soft lips, the dip at the base of her neck. He inhaled the flowery scent of her, traveling down her body. Lapping at her nipples, her belly button, and lastly at the bud at the apex of her thighs.

She tightened her fingers in his hair, whispering his name urgently. He took his time tasting her, inhaling the womanly fragrance of her, reveling in the clench of her muscles around his tongue.

"Elliott."

"Hmmm."

"Please."

He lifted his head. "What?"

"Please…inside…I want…" Her words were breathy and disjointed.

He wouldn't be rushed. He wanted to take his time tasting her, letting the honey blossom on his tongue. When he felt her explode and spasm around his fingers and tongue, he raised his head. Her eyes were squeezed shut, and her chest rose and fell like bellows. Her skin had flushed dark with her orgasm.

"You with me?" he asked.

"Hmmm." A slow smile spread across her face.

He tore open the condom, rolled it on, then sank into her warmth. Arms braced on either side of her head, he took one breath then two before beginning to move.

Her hands roamed his back, massaging the muscles then kneading them. He felt her urgency even though he wanted, needed, to take the explosiveness of their lovemaking down a notch. If he didn't, this show would end quicker than either of them wanted.

But her needs were more important than his. He rose onto his knees and positioned her legs over his arms. The penetration was deeper. He tried to go slowly, but the walls of her core tightened around him. Pulsed around him. He gritted his teeth, trying to suppress the urge to pick up his speed. But she took the decision out of his hands. Gripping his forearms, she worked her body on his cock. The bed creaked with their motion. The room filled with their incoherent words.

"Need you," he whispered. "Need…"

Sweat beaded and ran down his face and dripped onto her breasts. His breath exploded from his lungs in harsh bursts.

Damn. His heart jackhammered in his chest.

"More. Give me more, Elliott."

"I—"

Her walls clenched around his cock and held him tight like a glove. His body and mind couldn't take any more. His balls tightened. He was ready to blow.

Leaning forward, he captured her mouth with his and pumped through her orgasm and his.

Later, he lay on his back staring at the ceiling. Beside him, Rashida was still. He lifted a damp curl off her neck, and a hot rush of protectiveness shot through him.

Something shifted in his chest, like two tectonic plates moving apart then coming together. She was important to him, and the feeling had nothing to do with sex. He buried his face in her damp, salty neck.

"I've been thinking," she said.

"Don't think." He was afraid that whatever she said would destroy this fragile moment. But she wasn't listening.

"Do you think your father understands the significance of what he's doing?"

Elliott groaned. And just like that, they were on opposite sides again. The fragile tie that had held them together was broken.

"He understands. Trust me."

Crushed rocks pinged the undercarriage of Rashida's car as she drove around the circular drive of Marcus Quinn's home. Shielded by six-foot shrubs, the massive two-story pink stucco house sat back from the road.

She said a silent prayer then exited the car. It was important that the elder Quinn see that the Millhouse neighborhood and Quinn Enterprises could work together.

A young woman in scrubs answered the door, and Rashida felt a moment of guilt. She hadn't wanted to impose on Elliott's father. Not while he still recovered. But there were only five days left before the zoning committee met to make their final decision.

"My name is Rashida Howard. Mr. Quinn is expecting me."

A frown screwed up her attractive face. "Ah…" She glanced over her shoulder into the interior of the house. "Does his son know you're visiting?"

"Who is it, Rebecca?" a male voice called from within the house.

"It's a Ms. Howard, sir."

"Let her in."

The nurse stepped back so Rashida could enter.

She got a general impression of high ceilings, a massive staircase, and flowers everywhere.

"Up here, young lady."

Rashida moved toward the bottom of the curved staircase then craned her neck until she spotted Marcus Quinn standing on the second landing above the foyer. He appeared much thinner than his website pictures.

"I'm sorry to bother you at home." She bit back the fact she knew he'd been ill. She didn't want him to think his frailness compromised his ability to make decisions.

"No matter," his voice echoed down to her. "What can I do for you? You mentioned something about one of my projects?"

"Yes, sir. I wanted to speak to you about the Millhouse area."

"Millhouse?" He appeared confused. "What questions could you possibly have? The job hasn't started yet."

"I know." She glanced around. "Is there somewhere we could talk?"

"Come up." He waved to her. His body swayed slightly. He gripped the banister for support.

The nurse made a move toward the stairs.

He waved her away. "Bring us something to drink."

As Rashida climbed the long staircase, she regretted her decision to circumvent Elliott. The old man didn't seem well enough to answer her questions.

"Come to my bedroom."

Rashida looked for the nurse. She'd disappeared.

"I'm not going to bite." Brilliant green eyes stared back at her from under bushy eyebrows. "Now tell me, what's brought you to my house?"

He hobbled down a carpeted corridor. She followed, stepping in and out of sunlight that filtered in through a window onto an Oriental runner.

"My grandmother lives in the Millhouse area."

Marcus walked through an open double door, and Rashida stopped at the entry. A hospital bed sat front and center. There was only one chair in the room.

"I don't usually come to a man's bedroom on the first date." Technically, that wasn't a lie. It had been a hotel bed, not Elliott's.

Mr. Quinn turned slowly, and she witnessed a spark of humor in those familiar eyes. "Forgive me. There's a sitting area farther down the hall."

After they were seated in a small alcove with two high-backed chairs upholstered in blue fabric, he folded his hands in his lap. The veins stood out like ropes on his pale skin. He wore a plain white shirt that looked like he'd borrowed it from a much bigger man.

"Now start from the beginning," he said.

"My grandmother lives in the Millhouse neighborhood. I—we believe if you build a commercial building in that residential area, the property values will change."

"For the better," he interjected.

"Yes, that's true. But the residents who currently live there are elderly. They won't be able to afford their homes after a few years."

He adjusted the flower arrangement that sat on a glass table between them. "What do you propose?" He held up a finger before she started speaking. "Because I'm listening doesn't mean I will change my plans for the area. But go on."

Her stomach did a queer pitch at his words. "I spoke with Elliott—"

"You know my son?" His eagle eyes probed her face.

She nodded. "We're acquainted." Which wasn't a lie.

"Go on."

"I proposed to him that you could build a nursing home or a community center instead of the shopping area. Either of those could benefit the neighborhood and make a profit for you."

"And my idea of a marketplace wouldn't benefit the area?"

He studied her from behind eagle eyes. He had a commanding presence, which didn't appear dulled by illness.

"Elliott mentioned the shops were upscale. The residents couldn't afford the services, and after a few years, the tax base will increase, so they won't be able to afford their homes, either."

"And you mentioned all this to my son?"

"I did."

"In the time you spent with my son, did he tell you I vetoed those ideas?"

Rashida's stomach twisted. "He didn't think you would be interested in the two options."

"And you thought you would come and personally ask me to change my mind?"

She straightened her shoulders. "I'd hoped you would see how the compromises might help both you and the community."

She was saved from pleading by the arrival of the nurse with a tray of iced tea with lemon.

"Thank you," Marcus said after she placed the tray on the table.

The nurse hovered, glancing from Marcus to Rashida.

"Thank you," the elderly Quinn repeated with a sharper tone and a dismissive glance.

Rashida didn't pick up her iced tea because she knew her hands would tremble. He had to know by her coming to his house that communication had broken down between her and Elliott.

"Now, young lady. Those two businesses wouldn't begin to offer the compensation I need out of this project."

What more could she do? She wouldn't fall on her knees and plead. Instead, she rose. "Thank you, Mr. Quinn, for your time."

With as much dignity as she could, she walked down the stairs and out of his house.

CHAPTER SEVENTEEN

Rashida's doorbell rang. She glanced at the kitchen clock. Eight p.m. Who would be visiting at this time of night, and especially without calling?

She peered out the peephole.

Elliott.

Her traitorous pulse quickened.

Contrary to what her heart said, she really didn't want to see him right now. His father had blasted a hole through her last-ditch attempts to save her grandmother's neighborhood.

Without opening the door, she asked, "What do you want, Elliott?"

Silence.

She could almost feel his surprise.

"I hope my dad wasn't rude to you."

Obviously, her not opening the door to let him into her apartment wasn't what Elliott had expected.

"He wasn't." Her pride wouldn't let him know how off-balance and humiliated she'd been by her talk with his dad this afternoon.

"The fact we're talking through a closed door tells me otherwise."

Rashida unlocked then opened the door but didn't step

back to admit him. "Okay, now we're talking face-to-face."

She drank him in. He was dressed in a light blue chambray shirt and wore jeans that molded to muscular thighs. His dark hair curled slightly at the ends and appeared wet. She shut her eyes briefly, but the image of a naked Elliott stepping out of the shower still burned against the back of her lids.

"May I come in?" He lifted his arms to show flowers and wine.

How long would she play this childish game? She wanted to see him. Making him wait on the steps like a naughty child would not change the conversation she'd had with his dad.

She stepped back to allow him entry.

"What happened?" he asked when she'd shut the door behind him.

She shrugged. The gesture was more to make him think the visit with his dad was no big deal when it had been anything but. "He just informed me our alternatives wouldn't work."

Elliott placed the presents on the waist-high bar separating the kitchen from the living space. He tucked his hands in his jeans pockets and rocked back and forth on his heels. "Do you remember when I mentioned that Dad needed to make money on this project?"

She nodded. She remembered him alluding to hard times for his dad's business. But the Quinns had money and contacts, they could weather whatever financial rough spot they were currently going through.

"He's facing bankruptcy. With the right renters in the space, the bank might back off some. He needs businesses willing to pay well for renting the space."

"So, a community center wouldn't have done it." A fact that Marcus had already very bluntly told her. Why was she so dense? This project was never going to go well for her grandmother's neighborhood.

Elliott shook his head.

Walking to the kitchen, Rashida said, "I need wine."

As she hunted for the corkscrew, she sensed rather than saw Elliott enter the kitchen.

"Don't think badly of him. He's a good guy. He's had some lousy business breaks in the last ten years."

Rashida stopped hunting and gave Elliott a sour look. "Excuse me while I cry."

Elliott straightened from the column he'd been leaning against. "What's that supposed to mean?"

"I saw your father's house. Enough said."

Elliott ran a hand over his face. "My mother had the money. You already know that Dad's family came from old Cabbagetown."

Elliott eyed the wine bottle. Rashida pulled a glass from the cupboard and left it on the counter. She wasn't in the mood to play hostess.

He poured them both a glass. "Dad probably thought what happened in Cabbagetown could be duplicated in Millhouse. With its proximity to Atlanta and the rail system, he probably felt a commercial property in that area would be a sound bet. The area also has history, which adds to its attractiveness."

"He didn't think about what his building would do to the residents?" Rashida asked.

Elliott studied the depths of his glass. "I'm sorry to say he probably didn't think past buying the land."

The wine turned sour in her mouth. "You keep saying 'probably.' Weren't you privy to what was going on in your father's head?"

"No one other than Marcus Quinn is privy to what goes into the decisions he makes. Least of all me. Remember, I have my own company."

The more Rashida learned about Marcus Quinn, the less she liked him. She studied Elliott through her lashes. Where did *he* stand? Did he give a damn about the Millhouse neighborhood and its residents or was it all about saving his father's company? She knew the answer. This guy had loyalty written all over his face. He would walk across hot coals for his dad.

"Why are you here?" she asked. "You could have called and asked the same questions and gotten the same answers."

Over the last few weeks, she'd come to realize strong emotion made his eyes almost black like they were now.

"I like being with you." He placed his glass carefully on the counter then turned to face her. "In fact, my whole day is spent watching the clock until I can either hear your voice or see your face. Preferably the latter."

Her stomach quivered at his words.

He moved toward her. "And you feel the same," he said, stopping when their shoes touched.

"I—I... You're full of yourself."

He cupped her face in his large, warm hands and stared into her eyes. A shiver ran over her body. "Tell me I'm lying."

She opened her mouth to tell him just that, but instead she found herself kissing him. Open-mouthed and with lots of tongue.

Hours later, they lay in her bed, legs entwined, with moonlight filtering in through her plantation blinds.

"One of us is going to lose," she said.

He didn't respond. She turned her head on the pillow to

see if he was awake. He studied the coffered ceiling as though he were doing a thesis on its construction.

"What's going to happen?"

He turned so he faced her. "To us or to the neighborhood?"

"To us," she whispered.

He reached for her, pulling her into his body. "Depends on what we want. I can tell you what *I* want."

"What?" she said into his shoulder.

"I want you. No matter how this turns out."

How did she feel about him? At times she thought she might love him. But could that love survive her grandmother's community being torn apart? She didn't know the answer to that question.

Even though Elliott's father had rejected the community's compromises, she had to keep fighting. She couldn't let her grandmother's neighborhood be destroyed. She had to find a way.

L ater that morning, Elliott stuck his head into his partner's office before heading to Quinn Enterprises. "Got a moment?"

"Sure," Chris said. "Let me grab a fresh cup of coffee." He stepped over balled-up sheets of drafting paper that had fallen short of the wastebasket.

In his office, Elliott took off his jacket and sank into his desk chair. He missed his space. It had none of the pomp and circumstance of his dad's place. Just a desk, chair, pictures of his home designs complete with the elevation, and a minifridge stocked with water and assorted drinks. He didn't have a Ms.

Silverman to field his calls, run his errands or interference for him. Here he could decompress. Something he couldn't do in his father's Buckhead suite of offices.

"What's up?" Chris asked, dropping into a black leather swivel chair. "It's not Wednesday."

Wednesday was the day they went over the business of Luxury Designs, Inc.

"I need a level head," Elliott said.

"That I've got. Refereeing between a four- and five-year-old, a man's got to have his wits about him."

"Do you remember me telling you Rashida had come up with compromises for other options for the Millhouse site?"

"Yeah. What were they? A laundromat or a nursing home?"

Elliott shook his head. "Nursing home or community center." He massaged his temple— something he'd done a lot recently. "She went by my father's house to see him."

Chris's lips quirked. "The girl's got some cojones. But let me guess. It didn't go well."

Elliott leaned back in his office chair. The chair tilted backward, allowing him to stretch. "You got it."

Chris took a sip of coffee, studying his partner over the rim. "You're worried about her?"

Elliott eased his chair back to the floor. "Is it that obvious?"

"Sure, it is. I worry about Crystal constantly."

"But she's your wife."

Chris smiled. "You know you have all the signs of being in love, don't you?"

Elliott digested those words. Yes, it was true. He'd been halfway in love with her from the moment she'd stepped out of that Uber weeks ago. His respect and regard for her had been growing over this short period of time. "This is so messed up.

I need to figure out how to make this all work."

Balancing his mug on his crossed leg, Chris said, "You're not going to make everyone happy."

"I know." Elliott sank his head in his hands.

"But Rashida's idea of a compromise isn't half bad. You just have to make sure it's the type of compromise your father would agree on."

Elliott dropped his hands and let his body slump back in his chair. "Compromise isn't a word in Dad's vocabulary."

"Maybe Redding could help."

"How?"

Chris stood and popped the vertebrae in his back. "Redding wants the community to come on board with changes in the neighborhood, right?"

Elliott nodded, not sure where this was leading.

"Redding tells your dad he needs the community to be happy. When they're happy, he's happy. And a happy investor spends or, in the case of your dad, loans money."

Elliott eyed his partner. "What's the guarantee the community and Dad will come to a meeting of the minds?"

"A mediator. A neutral party. Someone with no vested interest."

Elliott mulled the suggestion over. It was a brilliant idea and possibly the only way everyone would get some of what they wanted.

"Who do I call?"

Chris moved toward his office. "I'll find a name for you."

Could helping Rashida and his dad be this easy? God, he hoped so.

• • •

When Elliott arrived at the Quinn Enterprises building around nine a.m., it was to find his father working behind his desk.

"What are you doing here?"

"Good morning, Son."

"Dad, *what* are you doing here?" Elliott's shock at seeing his father made him repeat the question like a parrot who only knew one line.

His father rose and walked around his work area to stand in front of Elliott. "I'm back at work."

His father's suit was new, tailored to fit his now-slimmer figure. So he'd been planning this day for a while, because Marcus Quinn did not buy off the rack.

Recovering, Elliott studied his father, looking for signs of distress. "Did the doctor give you clearance to return to work?"

His dad cocked a bushy white eyebrow. "I'm my own man, Son. I decide when I return to work. It was time."

Elliott translated that to mean his father's doctor didn't know his patient had returned to work prematurely. "Dad—"

His father held up his hand. "This isn't up for discussion. I've called a meeting. Robert should be here in a moment."

A flush worked its way up from Elliott's chest until his tie felt like it had a stranglehold on his neck. Of all the crazy stunts to pull. This was why his father had had his heart attack. Not following medical orders. Not listening to his body then driving that body beyond its limit. Some people never learned. And as sad as it was, you could only leave them to their own devices.

Elliott turned and made for the door.

"Where are you going? Erickson's coming."

Elliott didn't bother facing his father. He was too angry. "You don't need me any longer. I'm going back to my business.

I've neglected it too long."

"But, Son, you know what's happening with this Millhouse project."

"Erickson will bring you up to speed."

Elliott's strides ate up the distance to the elevator. He jabbed the call button as if his actions would make the car come quicker.

He loved his father, but the man was an immovable rock, great in business but not so much when it came to personal care. His father was an adult. If he cared that little for his health, then Elliot could do nothing.

Chris glanced up in surprise when Elliott stepped into his office. "Forget something?"

"Dad returned to work."

Chris reared back. "Why?"

Elliott ran a hand down his face. "Who knows? Maybe he thought I wasn't doing the job. Funny how he returned after his conversation with Rashida. I told him I thought it was too soon. But you know what it's like trying to move an immovable rock."

"Yeah. I've seen you beat your head against that rock for the last ten years."

Elliott pointed to his office. "Give me a minute to cool down then send me over the details for the Mapleton subdivision."

An hour later, he was at work on new floor plans when the chime on the outside door rang. Elliott walked to his office door and peered out. His father and Robert Erickson stood in the vacant reception area.

"I'm sorry about returning without giving you a heads up," his father said. "But I need your help for just a while longer."

His father still didn't get it. But Elliott wasn't in the mood to debate, plus his father looked pale. Better to let him have his say and hopefully the old man would take himself home. "Sure. What do you want, Dad?"

Elliott shook hands with Erickson and then directed the two men into his office.

His father dropped into the black leather seat Chris normally propped his long-legged body into when they were meeting in Elliott's office.

"We need a plan just in case the zoning committee doesn't approve the application," Erickson said.

Elliott frowned, confused. "Why do you need a plan? Just sell the land."

His father shifted in his chair. "I need to recoup my losses quickly. The property was on the market for over a year before I purchased it."

Which explained why his father had bought it so cheap.

"Sell it to Redding," Elliott said.

"He said—"

"Forget what he said." Elliott looked from his father to Erickson. "Redding will move on that neighborhood whether you get approval or not. He'll build residential and won't need zoning approval. If you build, it will make the deal sweeter for him, but I'll bet my business that's Redding's plan."

"Doesn't matter. Doesn't matter," his father said. "The vote will go our way."

What was up with his dad? One minute he wanted a contingency plan and the next he was certain the vote would go his way. *Was his old man losing it?*

Elliott glanced over at the lawyer to get a bead on what was happening with his dad and to see if he could read what

Erickson was thinking. The man's face was as blank as a whiteboard.

His dad speared him with a probing intensity. "You impressed on Hartwell the necessity of voting yes, didn't you?"

"No. I didn't."

His father blinked slowly like a lizard sunning himself. Elliott knew it wasn't calmness but astonishment that his son hadn't jumped into action as he'd been instructed.

"What do you mean you didn't? Didn't what?"

"I didn't speak to him about the application." Elliott rose from his seat. "Dad, I felt that it was dishonest."

"Dishonest!" A vein started to throb in his father's forehead. "It's the way business is done. He does us a favor, and sometime down the road we return that favor."

Rashida's face flashed in Elliott's mind. She wouldn't have thought very much of him if that was the way he did business. And what she thought of him meant a hell of a lot. More than his father's anger.

"I think we should let the process work," Elliott said. "That's what it's there for. The committee will decide what's best for the area."

His father popped out of his chair and started to pace. "I thought I taught you better than this. If you want something, you have to seize it. You've got to make it happen."

"Marcus, calm yourself," Erickson said.

Elliott's dad threw the lawyer a look that should have melted the man's bones.

"I'm fighting for my business, in case either of you are interested. I'm not going to sit on my ass and take whatever's dished out. Even though it appears that my son operates that way."

His dad was at the door, hand on the knob, when he turned. "Is it that woman? What's her name? Regina? Has she let you into her panties and you've lost your edge? Well, I hope not. I didn't raise you to be pussy whipped."

His father flung open the door. "I'm building on that land. And no one's standing in my way." He marched out.

Erickson rose to follow. "I'll calm him down."

After the men had left, Elliott stared out the window onto their office's tiny backyard. He'd never been like his father, who had a no-holds-barred approach to business. Take no prisoners. That had never been Elliott, and it was the reason he'd ventured out on his own. He admired his father but not his business ethics.

And his father's opinion about Rashida? Yes, she'd let him, but he had a mind of his own. He would do what was right for both his father and the woman he loved even if it killed him.

CHAPTER EIGHTEEN

Rashida parked her car in the church lot. Even at seven p.m., humidity still clung to the day. She'd dressed in a long-sleeve top because the interior of the church was always frigid. She wasn't the first to arrive, based on the number of cars already here.

Because Elliott had such faith in the mediation process, she was willing to suspend her disbelief and seal her doubts away in a dark corner of her mind. Frankly, something radical might be the only answer to get through to Elliott's father.

She made her way down to the basement.

Deep in conversation, Elliott and a fortyish male in a pinstripe suit stood off to the side. At a long rectangular table, Reverend Clemmons and Marty Hollins were the only others present. She took a seat on the opposite side of the table.

The reverend had announced during Sunday service that there would be mediation talks this week at the church. Rashida had no idea how many people would be present.

Ricky Thompson strode in. He'd grown from a gangly kid to a muscular, fit guy. He nodded at everyone but made straight for Rashida.

"Hey." He leaned over her and placed a warm hand on her shoulder.

"Hey, yourself." Rashida didn't need to look at Elliott to know he watched her and Ricky.

She patted the chair next to hers. "Have a seat." She hoped the act of sitting would force Ricky to remove his hand from her shoulder without her having to ask him. It did.

"Any idea how this is going to go?" Ricky's eyes were trained on Elliott and the mystery man.

Rashida followed his gaze. "None."

Elliott glanced at his watch. Tension radiated from his body. Rashida figured his unease had something to do with his father not being here.

He pulled out his phone, but the sound of footsteps made him lift his head. Marcus Quinn and the lawyer she recognized from the protest—what was his name? yes, Erickson—walked through the door. Elliott put away his phone, and his shoulders dropped. So he had been worried his father wouldn't show.

"Let's get started," Elliott said, moving to the head of the table.

"I'd like to introduce Patrick Carey. He will tell you about himself and what he hopes we can accomplish." Elliott stepped back but didn't take a seat.

Patrick Carey took Elliott's place. "I'd like to thank you all for coming out tonight and for inviting me." His gaze landed on each of them, a cordial smile on his lips. "I hope I can help you find solutions for the situation you face. The fact that you are all here tells me you think there is some merit to these discussions.

"I'm an attorney with Lewis, Strong, and Anderson. We have offices in Midtown, Chicago, and Denver. We specialize in corporate law, and my particular specialty is mediation."

Patrick pointed to the table to the right of the one they

now occupied. "I'd like everyone to move to the round table." He waited until everyone had complied.

"This is a cooperative process. One in which everyone is equal. There are no heads or leaders. Think of me as an impartial facilitator."

He waited a beat. "This may be a short or long process depending on how strongly you as a group want to come to a consensus."

"Let's talk about ground rules. I'll ask questions for my clarification. One person speaks at a time. Everyone should be respectful of the other's opinions. If at any time these rules break down, we'll take a five- or ten-minute recess. If we still can't respect each other, then we'll adjourn for the evening. Let's start by everyone introducing themselves and their interest in this gathering."

The reverend stood. Even though Rashida knew the minister's story and what he wanted for the community, she listened to every word carefully.

She hated to be so cynical, but based on the tightness of Marcus Quinn's lips and the stone-like set of his face, he would probably be less than cooperative.

Before she knew it, Patrick nodded at her.

"I'm Rashida Howard. I'm representing my grandmother, Eula Robinson. I lived with her here in the Millhouse area as a child. I know how much the community means to her and how tight the bond is between the residents. Building on Millhouse Road would destroy the fabric of this community and displace the elderly and poor who would not be able to hold on to their modest homes."

Across the table from her, Elliott's father shifted in his chair. Rashida didn't look at his face but stared at Elliott's instead. He tapped a finger against his lower lip, and a frown had furrowed his forehead. He seemed to be internalizing the tension floating around the room. Rashida thought that strange, since he had less at stake than anyone present other than the mediator.

Ricky rose. His chair caught in the threads of the thin gray carpet.

"I'm Ricky Thompson, a homeowner in the community. My grandparents raised me here in Millhouse. When they died, I inherited their house. The area holds a lot of memories for me. I wouldn't want to see it destroyed."

"Thank you, Mr. Thompson," Patrick said.

He turned to Elliott's father. Marcus rose—his shoulders rigid, his head and color high.

"I'm Marcus Quinn, CEO of Quinn Enterprises." He stopped. His mouth worked, but no words came out. Rashida could see the struggle in his face.

She was struck by the difference between father and son. Humor ran through Elliott's personality, which put people at ease. But there was no lightness in Marcus Quinn's manner. To Rashida, he was overbearing and entitled, with the personality of an old ram. The only person he would work well with was another ram. He appeared to be struggling with his anger. She hoped he wouldn't implode.

He threw a glance at his son. Elliott returned it with a nod.

Marcus drew himself up. Rashida knew by that one gesture that the old man, for all his gruff manner, loved and valued Elliott. It made her impression of the man soften—a little bit.

"I purchased the property on Millhouse Road to build a commercial structure to lease to small businesses."

Rashida glanced at Elliott. He stared at the carpet, but

his jaw was a series of ropes and ripples. His tension radiated over to her. *Breathe, baby. Breathe.*

She felt an overwhelming need to go to him, to hold him and stroke his back. He had such goodness in his soul. The fact he'd organized this meeting when it brought him nothing made her love him more than she already did.

Goose bumps sprang up on her arms. She *loved* him.

"I thought I was doing something good for the community." Each word seemed to be pulled from Mr. Quinn. "Building it back up. But it appears I was wrong." He lowered himself slowly into his chair—the gesture of a tired and unwell old man.

Patrick, who'd been standing against the wall through the introductions, came back to the table. "Thank you, Mr. Quinn."

He glanced around the room. "I'd like each of you to tell me what you hope this mediation process will accomplish. Then, after everyone has spoken, we'll set another date to meet. I'm aware we have a deadline looming, so I hope we can reach an agreement within that time frame."

Everyone said pretty much the same thing. They wanted to maintain the community the way it was.

When it was Elliott's father's turn, he didn't rise. "I've said all I'm going to say."

His lawyer, who'd introduced himself earlier but had said nothing during the evening, leaned forward and whispered something in Marcus's ear. The man's color flamed, and his gaze appeared to be locked on a spot across the room.

Would the process fall apart at this point just because one stubborn old man refused to engage?

Rashida's childhood flashed before her eyes. Sitting in her grandmother's kitchen, peeling onions until she cried, frying green plantains, reading in the shade of the oak trees in the cemetery. Was there nothing she could do to make this man invest in this process—this process that meant so much to the rest of them?

"Mr. Quinn?" Patrick Carey prompted.

Marcus sat stiffly in his chair, his large-knuckled hands gripped tightly together.

She sent a pleading gaze to Elliott's. *Do something. Say something.*

When it appeared Elliott wasn't going to speak, she cleared her throat. "Mr. Quinn?"

The old man turned toward the sound of her voice. "Would you like to come to dinner at my grandmother's house tomorrow?"

She didn't know where that idea came from. She'd just opened her mouth and the invitation sprang out. If he accepted, and she doubted he would, she would have to plead with her grammy not to poison him, no matter how much that would solve all their problems.

Every eye rested on Elliott's dad. The silence seemed to drag out forever.

"I don't—" He glanced over at his son. Silent communication seemed to pass between the two men. Then he dropped his gaze to his hands as if the answers to all his questions were written across his knuckles.

He raised his head and stared at her for one heartbeat. "I could do that."

A collective sigh went up from everyone. The mediation process was not dead.

• • •

The silence that greeted Rashida's announcement the next morning was so profound she could hear the bees buzzing around the wildflowers in Grammy's yard.

Then the three old ladies woke from their individual shock almost at the same time.

"You did *what*?" The words came from Grammy's mouth, but from the expressions on Mrs. Parker's and Mrs. McClain's faces, they felt the same.

"I invited Elliott's father here for dinner. Tonight," Rashida repeated.

She had called her grandmother early that morning and asked her to invite the other two ladies over. To help the news go down sweeter, Rashida had brought pastry from Mama Mambo's. The baked goods sat on the small table in the middle of the porch, untouched.

"What were you thinking?" This came from Mrs. McClain as she squinted up at Rashida from her position on the swing.

Rashida's grandmother was doing a slow shuffle around the porch—her imitation of a pace.

"I wanted to give him a face and a story with each name in the community. We're a faceless mass to him right now. He doesn't know Mrs. Parker makes the best brownies."

Mrs. McClain humphed.

Rats. She cleaned her misstep up quickly. "Or that Mrs. McClain lives in the oldest house in the neighborhood."

From Mrs. McClain's smile, Rashida knew she'd redeemed herself.

She caught her grandmother's gaze. "I'm sorry if you think it's a bad idea. I thought I was doing the right thing. I'll call him and say dinner is off."

She dug in her purse for her cell. Mr. Quinn would love

nothing better than to get out of this invitation. When she'd invited him, he'd looked so pained, you'd have thought someone had pulled every tooth out of his mouth with a pair of pliers.

"What time tonight?" Grammy asked.

"Huh?" Rashida glanced up from scrolling through her contacts.

"I'm gonna need some help," Grammy said. "Mamie, what do you want to make?"

Dressed and sitting on Grammy's couch at six thirty p.m., the ladies watched the clock. Rashida tapped her phone against her thigh, waiting for a call from Elliott with some excuse that his father had contracted Ebola and wouldn't be able to make it.

Thirty minutes later, Elliott's Range Rover pulled into her grandmother's drive.

"They're here," Rashida said. Behind her, the women twittered like blue jays.

She stepped onto the porch to greet their guest.

"Sorry, we're late," Elliott said as he closed the driver's door. "Traffic was a bear."

The passenger door opened, and Elliott's father climbed out. His eyes were hidden behind aviator glasses, and his movements were slow.

"So glad you could make it," Rashida said. Should she shake Mr. Quinn's hand? There was an awkward moment as they stared at each other.

"Thank you for inviting me." His tone said he'd rather walk over hot coals than be here.

Rashida glanced at Elliott. He turned his palms up in a what-can-you-do gesture.

"Let me introduce you to everyone," Rashida said. She turned to lead the two men into the house only to find everyone standing on the porch. She made the introductions.

Once inside, Elliott's dad took his sunglasses off and looked around the front room. "Lovely home." He glanced at Elliott. "Craftsman?"

Elliott shrugged. "Technically, yes, but someone made some modifications along the way."

Mrs. Parker and Mrs. McClain looked at each other, having no clue what the men talked about.

"It's a style of house," Rashida said to the two. "Like a ranch-style house."

"Ah," they said almost in unison.

Grammy appeared with large glasses of refreshment. "Iced tea?"

While Grammy passed out drinks, Rashida steered Elliott into the kitchen, hoping the three friends would engage Mr. Quinn in conversation and break the ice.

"What happened?" Rashida asked Elliott once she got him in the kitchen.

He leaned against the refrigerator, one leg crossed over the other at the ankle. "He'd decided he wasn't coming. Said he was feeling weak. When I said I'd drive him to the emergency room, he recovered."

"How are you doing?" She studied his face for signs of stress. He'd appeared pretty tense the night before when he'd stopped by her apartment after the mediation. She'd helped him relax.

"Better." He pushed off the refrigerator and gathered her

in his arms. "Actually, much better now."

He planted open-mouthed kisses in the juncture between her shoulder and neck. She sighed, leaning into his body, feeling the hardness of his thighs and the growing bulge of his cock against her stomach. Her hands drifted from his shoulders to his ass, pulling him closer.

The creak of a floorboard made her eyes fly open. She jerked out of Elliott's arms.

The kitchen doorway was empty. She could have sworn someone had been there watching them.

"What's wrong?" Elliott stared into her face, his eyes the color of a murky sea.

"Someone was there." She pointed to the door. "I think it might have been your father."

Elliott's face twisted in a frown. "Why do you think it was him?"

She swallowed against the sudden lump in her throat. "The ladies would have said something. Giggled or scurried off." She placed her hand on Elliott's chest. "What if it was him and he saw us?"

Elliott grasped her face between his large hands. "It's okay."

"No, it's not. I wanted to keep this"—she made a hand motion between their two bodies—"separate from the issue with your father's construction project. Now, he'll think I'm trying to get to him through you."

Elliott's lips twitched, and an eyebrow lifted. "You're worried he'll think you're screwing me over to the dark side?"

She narrowed her eyes. "Funny."

He pulled her back into his arms. Her head rested against his chest. The rhythmic sound of his strong heartbeat comforted her.

"Don't worry about my father. Why did you invite him to dinner?"

She pulled back so she could look him into his face. "I don't know. I was grasping at anything to get his cooperation. Dinner just popped into my head."

She stepped out of his arms. Her stomach ached as if she'd eaten bad scallops. "Not such a good idea, huh?"

"I don't know. At least we'll have a fine meal out of it." He looked around. "Maybe I can persuade my father to try the mango chutney?"

She laughed. "Too funny."

Rashida strained to hear what was going on in the living room as she and Elliott brought food to the dining room table. She caught bits and pieces of conversation between the women but no rumble of a male voice.

During the meal, an awkward silence hung like smog over the table, the only sound the ping of silverware on plates.

Rashida took a deep breath. "Mr. Quinn, Elliott tells me that your family lived close by."

Elliott's father lifted his head and looked first at Rashida then Elliott. "It seems you and my son have gotten quite close."

She bit her lip, but the action couldn't stop the flush of heat flooding her face. So it had been him she'd heard outside the kitchen. She couldn't very well say they were only friends. Not after he'd caught them in a clinch.

Elliott came back with the save. "We're getting to know each other."

Marcus grunted. "Is that what you call it?"

Elliott patted his mouth with a napkin but not before she caught the twitch of his lips. How could he laugh at a time like this?

"You grew up in the area?" Mrs. Parker asked. "Where?"

Rashida threw her a grateful smile. Mrs. Parker had always been the peacemaker between the kids when Rashida had lived here. Always the one supplying them popsicles.

Elliott's father smoothed his napkin in his lap. He seemed almost reluctant to talk about his upbringing. "Cabbagetown. My grandparents lived in the area and worked at the Mill."

"It would be nice if we could preserve Millhouse like they did Cabbagetown," Mrs. McClain said. She blinked at Marcus through her thick, dirty lenses.

"Just think how proud your grandparents would be that you had a hand in preserving an area so close to Cabbagetown." A gleam came into her grandmother's eyes.

Rashida's stomach fluttered. She prayed Grammy wouldn't ruin dinner.

"They probably had friends and family that lived right here in Millhouse," Mrs. Parker said.

The ladies lobbed that idea back and forth like a tennis ball over the net.

Marcus placed his napkin carefully and with precision on the dining room table. "Ladies, Cabbagetown and Millhouse do not resemble each other. Without giving you a history lesson, a hundred years ago, Cabbagetown was a bunch of one-story shanty-like houses built for the mill workers at the Fulton Bag and Cotton Mill plant.

"The Milhouse area was a more upscale area. I guess you would say it was the area for Atlanta's middle class. So when you talk about preserving the two areas, they have nothing in common other than they are close to downtown Atlanta."

Rashida wasn't sure if the old man was being condescending or truly wanted to inform them about Cabbagetown's history.

She glanced at Elliott for a clue, but he kept his eyes glued to his plate.

"You sound like you admire our community," Grammy said.

"It is beautiful," Marcus said. "I do admire it, and because I admire it, I want to build something here that will make it even better."

Rashida saw the spark building in her grandmother's eyes and knew there was about to be an explosion.

"More chutney, Mr. Quinn?" Rashida asked.

He waved the dish away.

"If you admire it so much," Grammy said, "why are you trying to destroy it with that building you're constructing?"

Marcus puffed out his chest.

Oh. Oh.

"Mrs...?"

"Robinson," Grammy snapped.

"Mrs. Robinson, you haven't seen the blueprints. It's a beautiful building that will fit within the existing look of the area. It can only improve what's here."

Grammy leaned so far over the table, Rashida thought she'd fall face first into the peas and rice. "Improving the area would be creating a park. Not running old folks out of their homes. But you're not interested in beautifying the area. Admit it," Grammy said, "you need to make money, and a park won't do it."

"Grammy." Rashida reached out a hand to stop her grandmother's tirade.

Face a beet red, Marcus Quinn pushed back from the table. "Thank you for dinner." He nodded at the ladies then threw a pained smile at Rashida. He turned to Elliott. "I'll call an Uber."

"Go with him. We'll take care of everything," Rashida said.

"Thanks," Elliott said. "I'm sorry it didn't turn out better." He held her gaze. "I'll call you later."

"Well, that was a bust," Grammy said when the Quinn's vehicle pulled away.

"I've never seen such an uptight man," Mrs. Parker added.

"I have," Mrs. McClain said. "My Herbert. God rest his soul. I used to tell him his boxers were wedged in his you-know-what."

Mrs. Parker and Grammy laughed.

Rashida didn't. Her spur-of-the-moment plan had been as helpful as tits on a boar—something her grandfather always said. She could have used his wisdom about now.

This mediation had better work because she'd run out of ideas on how to save Grammy's neighborhood.

Headlights from oncoming traffic pulsed in and out of the SUV as Elliott and his dad traveled up I-75 North. His father stared out the passenger window, and for the first few minutes of the ride, Elliott didn't attempt to engage him in conversation. He had his own issues to work through.

As much as he wanted to put his company on the map, he was beginning to believe his prospective partnership with Redding would violate his personal code of ethics.

Maybe his and Chris's company would never make big money. Maybe they were destined to be a small business rather than one that raked in millions every year. But the little community of Millhouse had a uniqueness to it and a core of individuals who considered themselves family. And you didn't break up family.

"Your girlfriend didn't accomplish what she wanted."

Elliott glanced over at his father then back at the road. His father was probing. He wanted to know how serious Elliott's relationship with Rashida was. He decided to ignore that probe and address the rest of his father's statement. "What did she want to accomplish?"

"She wanted to change my mind about building in Millhouse." His father turned to face him. "As if you didn't know."

"That's not news, Dad."

His father snorted. "I didn't raise you to be led around by your dick."

Elliott counted to ten and only spoke when he was sure he had complete control of his anger. "Why did you accept the dinner invitation?"

"She put me on the spot."

"You've been on the spot before, and it never bothered you."

"I needed to at least pretend to compromise."

Elliott moved around a slow-moving vehicle. "Why? For whose benefit?"

"For Redding's, of course. He holds the purse strings."

"I think he wants you to make a real effort," Elliott said.

"Please. I know men like Redding. Whatever gets them the results they need."

"If you're serious about keeping your business afloat, compromise. Come to an agreement with the Millhouse residents then get your finances back on solid ground so you don't have to compromise the next time."

For the first time Elliott could remember, his father didn't have a comeback.

CHAPTER
NINETEEN

Elliott showed up at Quinn Enterprises the next morning at ten a.m.

Phone caught between her head and her shoulder, Mrs. Silverman jerked her head in the direction of his father's office.

Robert Erickson sat in a chair in front of Elliott's dad's desk. His father stood at the window, looking down on the parking lot.

"Good morning," Elliott said to the room at large. "You wanted to see me?" He directed the question at his father's back. Elliot was still frustrated and fuming from the outcome of their dinner the previous evening.

Before Marcus could return Elliott's greeting, the intercom buzzed. Marcus jabbed the button.

"Mr. Redding is on line two." Mrs. Silverman's voice floated ghost-like through the office.

More confused than ever, Elliot mouthed, "What's going on?" to Erickson.

The lawyer shrugged. Concern creased his haggard face.

Obviously, sometime between the period he'd dropped his dad off at home last night and this morning, his father had made a decision and wanted to talk to Redding. What had he decided?

He mimed for his father to put the call on speaker. The old man shot Elliott a glare hot enough to melt the hairs on his arms.

For a moment, he thought that his dad would refuse.

"Mr. Redding, my son and lawyer are in the office. If it's okay with you, I'm going to put this call on speaker."

Redding must have agreed, because Elliott's father punched the conference button.

"Good morning, gentlemen." Redding's high tenor floated across the room. "What do I owe the pleasure of this call at seven o'clock in the morning?"

Elliott winced.

Had his father known that Redding was on the West Coast? With a shock, Elliott realized the two men had never spoken. All the communication had gone through him because his father had been on medical leave.

"Redding, it's a pleasure to finally talk to you. This is Marcus Quinn, CEO of Quinn Enterprises. I wanted to introduce myself and to thank you for your generous offer to finance the Millhouse project."

Elliott held his breath. Something in the way his father spoke made him wonder if the old man was planning to turn down Redding's money. If he did, it would be the death of Quinn Enterprises. But it would set Elliott free from an obligation that he was beginning to feel was not right for his company.

Elliott glanced over at Erickson. The lawyer leaned forward in his chair, his gaze glued to his client's face. The man's posture and his stiffness told Elliott more than words could. Erickson also had his doubts as to how this conversation would go. Obviously, he and Elliott's dad hadn't discussed this call beforehand.

"No problem," Redding said. "Glad to know you're feeling better. How are things going with the community out there?"

How was the old man going to handle this question? Would he lie?

"Met with members of the community just last night. I'd say things are going well." His father drummed his fingers on the desk. His knee bobbed to some invisible stimulus.

"Glad to hear that," Redding said. "How's the community taking the plan for your building? The last time I was in Atlanta, things weren't going well."

Elliott rubbed the spot on his hip where old Mrs. McClain's car had clipped him.

"Your son informed me that he has everything under control. I assume that everything is still under control and moving forward?"

"It is." Elliott's father's fingers drummed faster on the desk. "I wanted to talk to you about a formal agreement. We've not put anything on paper, and I would feel more comfortable about moving forward with something in writing."

Redding chuckled. "Yes, I imagine you would. But I would feel more comfortable if I had something concrete that said the community is on board with your project and that there would be no more…ah, let's say conflicts of interest."

His father's face tightened with anger. He wasn't used to being dictated to by anyone. That he needed Redding's money must infuriate him. And that the venture capitalist had him by the balls must enrage him even more.

"How are the designs coming along, Elliott?" Redding asked.

He and his father locked gazes. Did his father know

that his funding from Redding was dependent on both the community's cooperation and Luxury Designs working with Redding?

Redding was playing hardball. Elliott didn't want to put his father in this position. He had been thinking that this venture might not be the right one for his company. But where would this leave his father? On the one hand, if Elliott withdrew, it would allow his father to continue his project on his own terms. Even if it meant bankruptcy.

But could he do that to his father? No, he couldn't.

"Things are going fine. My partner and I have come up with a few floor plans that we'd like your opinion on."

Elliott sensed rather than saw his father relax.

"Send them to me anytime," Redding said.

"We'll draw up a formal agreement with the community today," his dad interjected. "I'll send the agreement over as soon as it's signed."

"Wonderful. I'll look forward to receiving it. Once I do, I'll have my accounting department cut you a check so you can get started. Now, I must start my day."

An audible *click* indicated that Redding had ended the call.

"Dad, why didn't you offer to sell the property to Redding? It would have solved all your problems."

His father rose slowly from his desk then straightened the cuffs of his suit jacket. "Because that's not the man I am. I'll see you this afternoon at the church."

Elliott had been dismissed.

• • •

Rashida drove to the church with her stomach twisted like a pretzel. After the fiasco at dinner last night, she had her doubts about whether Marcus Quinn would show up today.

When she entered the meeting room in the church basement, Patrick Carey was the only one present. They exchanged polite conversation while they watched the clock.

Within ten minutes, everyone had arrived except Elliott and his father. Just when she thought they wouldn't come, Elliott appeared at the door, and a minute later, his father.

"Mr. Quinn, it's so good to see you." By the vigor with which Carey pumped the old man's hand, the mediator had also had his doubts about Marcus returning. "How was dinner last night?" Patrick glanced from Marcus to Rashida. "Productive, I hope."

"Dinner was fine," Marcus mumbled. He didn't look in her direction, just dropped into a seat next to Elliott.

"Good. Good." Patrick clapped his hands together. "Okay, let's get started." He glanced around the table.

"Yesterday we spoke about what everyone hoped to get from this negotiation. Mr. Quinn"—Patrick glanced at Elliott's father—"I think we left off with you."

Rashida held her breath as Marcus Quinn lumbered to his feet. Dark circles ringed his eyes and his skin had the unhealthy pallor of someone who'd spent little time in the sun. His hands had a fine tremor. The man needed more rest.

Rashida glanced at Elliott. Did he know how fragile his father was? From the intense scrutiny he aimed at his dad, he knew.

Marcus Quinn cleared his throat. "My son informed me that I made a procedural error after I purchased the Millhouse property. I should have called for a meeting of the community residents and informed them of my plans for the land. Bypassing that step has created a great deal of stress and ill feeling. I apologize."

He lowered his body slowly into his chair and clasped his hands together on top of the table.

What had made Marcus admit to this oversight? He was an architect. He knew all about zoning and the process. She found it hard to believe this was an oversight on his part. And why admit it and try to make amends now?

She had to believe Elliott had something to do with his father's change of heart.

From his seat at the opposite end of the table, Patrick Carey said, "Thank you, Mr. Quinn. I'm sure those present appreciate your candor."

Rashida was not going to say that technically the whole community should be present for this discussion. Since she and Rev. Clemmons had polled the community, she figured that would suffice.

Rev. Clemmons rose from his chair. He cleared his throat. "I know I speak for the whole community when I say that we are glad Mr. Quinn is willing to open the discussion up to us no matter the lateness of that decision."

She kept her face as blank as possible. She didn't dare smile, but she heard the reprimand in the minister's words.

Rev. Clemmons turned to Elliott. "The community was polled a few weeks ago, and I believe our suggestions were given to Mr. Quinn's son."

Rashida squirmed in her chair, remembering her visit to Elliott's office and the performance she'd given. She didn't dare look at him.

"Those choices haven't changed," the minister continued.

"We would support a nursing home or a community center being built on the land." He paused. "Those two choices would benefit the community the most."

Patrick turned to Marcus. "What do you think, Mr. Quinn? Would one of those choices suit your purposes?"

Marcus was silent for a moment then cleared his throat. "Yes. The community center would work." The old man didn't look at the minister or the mediator. He fixed his attention on the painting on the wall where Jesus hung on the crucifix.

Rashida knew the old man's hand had been forced. But by whom?

Rashida stared into Elliott's eyes and moaned in ecstasy. The timbre of her voice washed over him, leaving goose bumps.

"My God…" Her lashes fluttered.

Elliott swallowed. His throat suddenly dry.

She pulled the plastic spoon from between her lips in a slow tease, leaving a trail of chocolate on her mouth, a trail Elliott wanted to lick off.

"I should be suspicious of anyone who doesn't like ice cream, but at this moment, you the man," Rashida said.

The coldness of the ice cream gave her words a slight lisp. She sank her plastic spoon again into her cup of double chocolate and rocky road.

They sat outside the ice cream shop in her grandmother's neighborhood. Shadows crept in slowly from the surrounding trees, heralding the end of the day. Inside, the owner wiped down tables in preparation for closing.

"Glad I could make your day."

"You and your father have made my year. What did you say to your dad to get him to compromise?"

No way could he tell her about the agreement with Redding. Because he'd have to inform her about the role the venture capitalist wanted Luxury Design, Inc. to play in the redesign of Millhouse.

"I think after the ladies brought up Cabbagetown, it started him thinking. Then one thing led to another."

Actually, they'd argued half the night. And then there'd been that call with Redding.

"What's next?" she asked.

"Carey will draw up the agreement and get Dad and your representative to sign. Everyone will get a copy."

She stirred the ice cream in the cup until it was one soupy mess. Then she scooped up another spoonful and deposited it on her tongue.

Elliott took a big gulp of his now-tepid water.

"It's such a relief. I can't wait to tell Grammy."

He gave her a weak smile. She didn't notice. She was happy. The load she'd been carrying had been lifted from her shoulders. It now rested on his.

He traced the outline of her chilly fingers wrapped around the cup of ice cream.

How long could he wait before he told her about his deal with Redding? He dreaded that moment. Because once he told her, it would be the end of their relationship.

• • •

"Seems strange having you here every day."

Elliott turned away from the window that overlooked

the office's small backyard. Chris had dropped into a chair, the ever-present coffee mug in his hand.

"Seems strange to *be* here every day. But I'm glad I'm back."

"Your dad and Redding ironed out their terms?"

"Yeah." He sighed. "Once Redding had the agreement Dad signed with the Millhouse community, the money flowed."

"Great. You didn't tell me about the beach. How was it?"

Elliott looked at his partner in surprise. "Man, that's been over two weeks ago."

Chris shrugged. "You've been busy putting out fires. Personal takes a backseat."

Elliott rubbed his neck. "You're right. A lot has happened since then. The trip seems a lifetime ago." He wished he could go back to those carefree two days.

"Other than the sand fleas, it was great." He thought back on the beginning of the trip. "Rashida's not a camper. I really blew that, but I think she ended up enjoying it."

"From the looks of you, she's not the only one who had a good time."

Elliott tried to hide his happiness but couldn't. "I think she's the one."

Chris paused with his mug to his lips. "You're shitting me."

"We have a long way to go, but for me..." He ran his hand through his hair. "Yeah. She's the one." He moved away from the window. "I just need to convince her." *I just need her to understand.*

Chris raised a brow. "Convince her? That doesn't sound good. I thought two people usually arrived at that stage in their relationship together."

"Normal people," Elliott said. "Like you and Crystal. Rashida and I started out on opposite sides of a battleground.

Except she was more at battle than I was."

"When do I meet this goddess?"

"Soon." Elliott sat on the corner of his desk. "But something's been bothering me."

Chris, cool and collected as always, took a sip of coffee then said, "Spill."

"I don't think this thing with Redding is right for me." He pushed off the desk and started to move around the room.

"Will you find a chair and park your ass in it?" Chris demanded. "You're making me dizzy. Just tell me what's on your mind."

Elliott stopped pacing and went back to the window. He was about to jump out of his skin. "I feel like a hypocrite. I encouraged this mediation process, knowing full well Redding wants to buy their homes and put up luxury ones."

"The residents don't have to sell," Chris pointed out.

Elliott dragged a hand through his hair. "You know the price point of our homes will drive up the tax base."

"Well, there's that. But will selling be such a bad thing? They can hold out for top dollar. Unless you think he'll try and undercut home prices," Chris said.

"Frankly, I just don't know." A sour taste filled his mouth. "Great businessman I am, right? I relied on my father's lawyer to vet this guy."

"You want us to withdraw from the project?"

This was the part that bothered Elliott the most. Chris had a wife and two kids. He needed the money from this type of project. It would allow him to save for his children's education. Take his family on nice vacations.

"I don't want to deprive you of this kind of money."

Crossing his legs at the ankle, Chris stretched. "Are you

trying to say I'm not ethical?"

Chris was the most honest and ethical man Elliott knew. It was why he wanted to be in a partnership with him. "You know I'm not."

They sat in silence for a moment.

"If Redding wants this to happen, there are other architects out there who won't hesitate to make the Millhouse area into the dream community he wants us to build," Chris said.

"That's what's driving me insane."

"We have to find a way to safeguard the community."

Something occurred to Elliott. "Maybe dangle another carrot in front of Redding."

"Like what?"

"I don't know, but I better come up with something quick. The zoning committee is meeting tomorrow night. They're making their decisions. If my father's application is denied, Redding could move right in."

"Hell, he could do that anyway," Chris said.

"Yeah, but I'm betting he wants to see how commerce does in the area. If it draws the attention of the up-and-coming homebuyer, he'll know he can't lose. He'll start buying up the properties before anyone else can."

"Then we need to get our brains in gear," Chris said.

Rashida wasn't surprised to open the door and find Elliott on the other side. She would have been more surprised if he hadn't shown up. The sight of him filled her with a warm, gooey feeling. And she was not a warm, gooey kind of woman. At least she hadn't been before she met him. Not even with

Alex.

"How was your day?" he asked when he stepped into her apartment.

"Not very productive." She walked to her open computer on the bar and closed the article she'd been working on for the magazine—Georgia barrier island cuisine.

Elliott pointed at her computer. "I can leave if you need to work."

She lifted an eyebrow. "Right. You drove all the way over here to turn around and go."

One side of his mouth ticked up. "I don't want to, but I will if you need to work."

She studied him for a long moment. His eyes told her he didn't lie. He cared enough about her to respect her decisions. She'd never had a man who'd subjected his desires to hers. Definitely not Alex. He could have turned down his promotion when she told him she didn't want to leave Atlanta. He hadn't.

And if I loved him, I would have gone with him.

"I'm fine," she said. "At a good stopping point. Have you eaten?"

He shook his head. When she turned to go to the kitchen to see what she could whip up, he caught her arm.

"Let's order in."

"It's no problem."

He pulled her into his arms. "I didn't come over to have you cook for me."

He buried his face in her neck. Something he seemed to enjoy. "Just want to be with you," he mumbled into her skin.

Her arms curved around his back and pulled him closer. Some of the worry and tension about the meeting tomorrow seemed to seep out of her body. "I'm glad you're here."

His hands traveled down her body then gripped her ass, bringing her closer. A groan rumbled up from his chest. "Too many clothes."

She stepped out of his arms. After pulling her shirt over her head, she dropped it on the floor. She turned and started down the hall to her bedroom, dropping her bra, her shorts, and lastly her thong. By the time he made it into her bedroom, she was on the bed, her legs spread in invitation.

"I'm hungry," he said.

She grinned at him. "Then eat."

Gripping her hips, he pulled her to the end of the bed.

She was turned on by the raggedness of his breathing and the hunger in his eyes.

He slipped his arms under her legs, lifting then pushing them toward her chest, opening her to his hungry gaze. His kisses started at her knee and trailed to the juncture of her thigh and hip. He treated the other leg to the same tender care, stopping both times just before he reached her mound. He allowed his warm breath to tease her clit before he retreated.

Rashida squirmed, pushing herself toward him, wanting to feel his mouth on her, needing to feel his tongue delve into her wetness. "Please…"

He repeated the torture to each thigh, this time getting closer to the spot where every nerve screamed. Finally, he sat back on his heels. "What do you want, baby?"

Her stomach was a mass of knots, her sex throbbed to each beat of her heart.

"Lick me."

He did as she commanded. His tongue started at her opening and swiped up to her clit, where it lingered, hovered, then closed around that sensitive bundle of nerves and sucked.

Bracing herself on one elbow, she gripped the back of his head, holding him in place, so he couldn't stop the exquisite torture of his lips and tongue. Her legs trembled, and her breath came in ragged bursts. Her heart beat an erratic dance in her chest. She needed... What did she need?

She tried to hold back a moan, but she couldn't. It tore its way out of her throat. "Elliott..."

"Hmmm." His head lifted from between her thighs, lips coated with her juices, hair damp with sweat.

"Please." The word like a plea she couldn't hold back.

He seemed to know what she needed, because he stood, pulled a condom from his pants pocket, and dropped it on the bed. Next, he stripped off his shirt, pants, and shoes. His cock raged, bobbing.

She moved forward to capture the salty precum, which dripped off the tip. Intoxicating. She opened her mouth wider, capturing the bulbous head between her lips and sucking it deeper into her mouth.

"Damn." The word seemed pulled from his chest. "Rashida. Baby. Stop." He gripped her hair. "Don't make me come."

She released him then ran her tongue around her lips, still tasting him.

He reached for the condom, but she plucked it off the bed before he touched it. Her fingers shook so hard it took two attempts to rip the foil package and slip the latex over the steely pipe between his legs. Then she scooted back on the bed.

He stared into her eyes. "I know this probably isn't the right time to tell you this, but I love you."

The words ripped the air right out of her lungs.

He didn't wait for her response. The mattress dipped under his weight as he advanced toward her. Slipping his arms under her legs, he took a ragged breath before plunging.

Rashida closed her eyes against the exquisite fullness. Tears slipped from between her closed lids. She wrapped her arms around his neck as he began to move.

Gliding one hand between their bodies, he circled her clit with his thumb as he pumped into her wetness. The sound that escaped her throat was a whine that escalated until it could break glass.

Wave after wave of contractions traveled up from her center and spread out to the rest of her body. She held him tight, her mouth buried in his neck as her orgasm ravaged through her body.

Later, she lay awake, listening to him sleep. She stroked his chest, loving the comfort she felt having him in the bed next to her. "I love you, too." She whispered the words in the darkness, promising herself she'd say them in the light of day when she found the courage.

"I know," he said, gathering her close.

From his vantage point at the back of the county auditorium, Elliott watched people entering through two sets of doors on opposite sides. His father and Erickson had seats toward the front.

The place filled up quickly. People were wedged in tighter than starter homes on a fourth of an acre lot. The seven men and women who would make the final decision were already on the stage, conversing among themselves.

If Rashida didn't get here soon, she wouldn't find a seat.

Finally, he spotted her grandmother's gray hair bobbing through the crowd with Rashida directly behind her.

His pulse sped up. That he had the privilege of knowing what made her moan and beg made his chest tight. And the knowledge she loved him made an idiotic grin spread across his face as he advanced through the crowd toward her.

When he reached her side, he touched her elbow. She jumped, but her frown quickly dissolved into a smile.

"Hi," he said.

"Hi," she answered back.

Oblivious to the people moving around him, he stared into her eyes, hoping he communicated the way she made his world revolve.

"There's Mamie," Grammy shouted to Rashida.

Elliott followed the direction of Grammy's finger. Mrs. Parker sat two rows back from his father. There was a vacant seat beside the elderly woman.

"You go ahead, Grammy." Rashida raised her voice to be heard over the noise in the room. "I'll meet you after this is all over."

Her grandmother gave him a disdainful look before shuffling toward the front of the auditorium. Guess he had his work cut out for him with Rashida's grandmother. She was determined not to like him, but for Rashida, he would do whatever he had to.

He touched her arm and pointed toward the back wall.

"I was afraid you wouldn't make it," he said once they were situated.

"It took a while to convince Grammy she shouldn't drive."

He chuckled. She looked frazzled. Her eyes were wide and her face dewy. She was beautiful. He wanted to drag her from this overcrowded venue and take her someplace private where he could love her thoroughly.

"When does she appear in court?" Elliott asked.

"Later this week."

Unfortunately, he was going to add one more unpleasant thing to her plate. He would tell her what Redding wanted from him. He hoped she'd forgive him. For a while, he'd lost sight of what was important.

He touched her face. "Everything is going to be okay." Was he reassuring her or himself?

A gavel banged.

"We'd like to begin."

Elliott turned his attention to the front of the room. The

speaker was James Hartwell.

He waited a few moments for conversation to die down. "I am Commissioner James Hartwell, and I call this meeting to order."

Rashida shifted restlessly beside him. What was bothering her? He touched her arm. She glanced at him, and he gave her what he hoped passed for a reassuring smile.

By the time the commissioners had worked their way around to the Millhouse application, which was fourth in line, Elliott's stomach was tied in knots. How was his father doing? Was the suspense getting to him? This project could make or break him.

"We have reviewed the Millhouse application and the recommendation of the Planning Committee members. Would the applicant like to say a word?"

His father stood and made his way to the microphone at the side of the room. He moved slowly. Even though he'd returned to work without his doctor's permission, he looked thin but healthy.

"You have five minutes, Mr. Quinn," Commissioner Hartwell said.

"Commissioners and audience, I am Marcus Quinn, CEO of Quinn Enterprises. My firm plans to build a commercial structure that will make the Millhouse community and city of Atlanta proud." His voice was firm and filled with conviction.

Elliott's heart filled with pride. This man was still fighting at sixty-six, long after most men his age had retired.

"Our hope is the building will attract high-quality businesses whose stores will in turn bring traffic and monies into this community. Monies that can be used to support the infrastructures, roads, schools, and libraries in the area and enrich the lives of everyone in the community. We hope the commissioners will see the benefit of such a building and vote yes for the change of zoning from residential to mixed use."

"Does the Millhouse community wish to speak?" Hartwell asked.

"No, Commissioner Hartwell." The speaker was Marty Hollins, the guy who'd been arrested with Rashida. "We have come to an agreement with Mr. Quinn on a commercial structure that would benefit both Mr. Quinn and the community."

It appeared the Quinn Enterprises application was the last of the evening. The commissioners turned their microphones off and conferred among themselves.

"What's bothering you?" Elliott asked her as they waited for the vote.

She shook her head. "I don't know. I just can't make the butterflies in my stomach settle. I know theoretically I shouldn't worry. We signed an agreement with your father, yet..."

She gnawed on the inside of her cheek.

Elliott pulled her close and rubbed her shoulder.

The sound of a door shutting drew Elliott's attention away from Rashida. His breath caught in his throat, and a vise squeezed his chest. Monroe Redding stood near the entrance, his gaze roaming over the people in the auditorium. Was he looking for Elliott's father?

Elliott's attention was drawn back to the front of the room by the gavel pounding.

"We're ready to read our decisions," Hartwell said. "There is an appeal process for all decisions."

He began to read. "The Holmes application is approved." Applause.

"The Compton application is approved with conditions."

Conversation rose in the auditorium. Hartwell looked up from his sheet then waited for the voices to die down. The audience took the hint.

"The Ingram application is denied." Voices rose again, and again, Hartwell waited.

Elliott's stomach churned. His gaze went to his father, who sat as immovable as concrete.

"The Quinn application is denied."

Stunned, Elliott couldn't move. He'd known this was a possibility but couldn't believe his father had lost. He looked at his dad. His father hadn't moved from his seat. He appeared to be oblivious to the decision.

"I'm sorry." Rashida's touch was warm on his arm. "I know your father needed this to be approved."

"Thanks." He glanced once more toward the front of the auditorium. "I need to go."

She gave his arm a squeeze. "I understand. I need to get Grammy."

"Elliott."

Both he and Rashida turned at the sound of his name. Elliott had forgotten about Redding.

"I'm sorry about the decision and the repercussion on your father's business." The venture capitalist looked suitably remorseful. Not that it would impact him to any degree. "I want you to know the zoning commission's decision doesn't affect my plans for the Millhouse development."

"Maybe we can grab a drink after I see my father home," Elliott said. No way did he want to have this discussion in front of Rashida. His plan had been to talk to Redding after the vote tonight. To tell him he was no longer interested in his offer.

"I wish I could," Redding said, "but I need to be in

Baltimore tomorrow morning. Why don't we do a conference call tomorrow afternoon? I'm looking forward to seeing the floor plans you and your business partner have designed for the Millhouse area."

He clapped Elliott on the shoulder then moved off into the crowd.

Elliott closed his eyes briefly, wanting to turn back the clock and have this conversation with Rashida earlier.

"What Millhouse development? And what floor plans?" Her face crinkled in confusion.

Elliott turned to her. "I'd planned on talking to you later—"

"Talk to me now."

Her eyes were cloudy, and they roamed over Elliott's face.

Someone shouted congratulations to Rashida. She didn't acknowledge them.

He ran his hand through his hair, wishing he could yank it out by its roots. The pain wouldn't be any worse than seeing the look of distrust in the eyes of the woman he loved. "Redding is the guy you..." He was going to say, "the guy you just met," but Elliott hadn't introduced the pair.

"Redding is an investor. He offered to finance the Millhouse construction for Dad."

"In exchange for what?" Deep grooves lined her forehead. "Why would he make the offer?"

"Because Redding is interested in the Millhouse neighborhood."

"To do what?"

"Buy homes, then remodel them or tear them down and build new ones."

"This is my grandmother's neighborhood we're talking about?" Her voice was box-cutter sharp.

"Yes." Why hadn't he talked to Redding sooner?

"And what, exactly, is your company's role in all this?"

"Redding wanted us to design the floor plans for these new homes."

An array of emotions from confusion, to fear, to anger moved across her face. "New homes that would take the place of those already there? Homes that belong to my grandmother and her friends?"

He felt like he was drowning in quicksand.

"So, this thing"—she moved her hand between their bodies—"has been about building your company?"

"No. No—" He reached for her, but she moved back to avoid his outstretched hand, stepping on a woman's foot in the process.

The woman threw her an annoyed glance.

"I thought—" Rashida's eyes were bright, and her mouth trembled.

He could barely get words through the tight muscles in his throat. "Rashida, I love you. I'd never—"

But she'd already turned and walked away.

Rashida lifted her head off the sofa and blinked against the morning sun blasting through the kitchen window. Her head throbbed, and her eyeballs felt encased in sandpaper.

She needed to get up, brush her teeth, and shower, but she didn't have the energy. She'd spent last night plotting murder and berating herself for getting involved with Elliott when she wasn't crying.

Her cell lay on the coffee table. Around three a.m., she'd

shut it off. Elliott kept blowing up her phone. She didn't want to talk to him. She never wanted to talk to or see him again.

Every time she thought about how he'd used her, a deep, crushing weight fell on her heart. She didn't have time for this remorseful whining and crying. She had to get on with the rest of her life.

She'd almost found a place of peace when a knock sounded at the door. She held her breath. Maybe whoever it was would go away.

The knock came again. This time more insistent. She knew without opening the door who stood on the other side.

She flung open the door without checking the peephole. The morning sun almost blinded her as it highlighted the auburn streaks in his dark hair. "What the fuck do you want?"

The fact she'd resorted to profanity, which she rarely did and never at him, should have been a warning to him, but he appeared unaware.

"May I come in?"

She would have slammed the door in his face, but his foot was in the way.

"Just five minutes then I'll leave."

When she didn't respond, he said, "*Please.*"

She wanted to scream more profanities in his face, but she couldn't think of them fast enough, plus she wanted answers to questions that had kept her up all night. His betrayal was like a sore tooth she couldn't stop probing.

Without answering, she left the door open and walked back to the sofa and plopped down, crossing her arms and legs.

He stepped across the threshold. His presence filled up her small space. The scent of sandalwood wrapped around her, making her think of the times they'd made love and she'd fallen asleep with her nose buried in his chest.

Now, dark circles ringed his eyes and his hair stood on end as if he'd run his hands through it several times. Good. She wanted him to suffer.

"I'm turning down Redding's offer." He dropped into the low-back chair opposite her, his legs spread, his elbows resting on his knees. "I meant to do it sooner, but—"

"But you were hedging your bets," she finished for him.

He rubbed his forehead, making a red mark appear between his eyebrows. "I honestly don't know what I planned to do. The offer was flattering, and our company needed both the recognition and the money."

He ran a hand over his unshaven face, the sound like sandpaper.

She let the words sink into her chest, let them carve their way into her heart. "Have you been working with him from the beginning?" She could barely get the words out.

"Rashida, I—"

"Just answer my question."

"No. Just since Mrs. McClain hit me with her car."

She wanted to say something hateful like *Mrs. McClain should have finished the job.* But the idea of Elliott not being in the world was too incomprehensible for her to contemplate.

"Why?" She could barely clear the word past the lump in her throat. She blinked against the pinpricks of pain behind her eyelids. "Why didn't you tell me about your plans? Why let me believe you cared about this community and its residents?" She'd almost said "cared about me." "You must have laughed at me when I came to you with those compromises." The words were thick in her throat.

He reached for her. She jumped up, taking a position

against a far wall, and he settled back on the sofa.

Why had she let her guard down? She'd let this man get under her skin. Get next to her heart. Hadn't she learned from her relationship with Alex? Hadn't she learned not to trust a man? Obviously not.

"I'd never laugh at you. I admired your dedication to your grandmother's community. I admire *you*." His last words hung in the air like lead balloons.

Like a child, she wanted to put her hands over her ears to block out his words.

"I've just been a novelty for you. The Millhouse neighborhood and its residents have been a novelty."

His face twisted. "You know that's not true. I care for them, especially those three old ladies."

"Why did you come?" The words were hard to get out because her face felt as hard as an overdried mask. A mask that would crack with one more wrong word from him.

"I'm turning down Redding's offer."

"You said that already. And why should I care?"

He stood and walked toward her. "Because I think we can work together to save the community. Save it from investors like Redding."

She laughed. "I noticed you didn't say save it from your father. I know he can appeal the decision. He could still get approval for what he wants to do in Grammy's neighborhood."

"My father's project could have actually helped the community."

She stared at him in disbelief, and then uncontrollable laughter burst from her lips. "Do you hear yourself? You're still sprouting daddyisms. You haven't changed. I hope your father realizes what a good puppet he has in you."

A vein pulsed in his forehead. "I'm no one's puppet."

"Come back when you've worked that all out." She walked to the door and flung it open. "Actually, don't come back. Ever." She was done with pleasantries and courtesy.

He walked slowly toward her, his gaze never leaving her face. But when he reached her, he leaned so far into her space she thought he was going to kiss her.

"It's not over," he said.

"Yes, it is. You just haven't admitted it yet." She wanted to push him out the door, but she was afraid to touch him. Her traitorous body would have pulled him into her embrace instead of rejecting him. She kept her arms rigidly at her sides.

When he walked through the door, she slammed it behind him.

She waited until she heard his footsteps echo down the stairs before she let fresh tears fall.

Elliot rode the elevator up to his father's office after leaving Rashida's apartment. He intentionally kept his mind off the disaster that was his love life. Because if he didn't, he'd be of no help to anyone, not to his father and not to Luxury Design, Incorporated.

He and Chris had postponed talking with Redding until later in the afternoon to give Elliott time to check on his dad. On the drive home last night, his father had refused to talk about the decision or what it would mean for his company.

When Elliott stepped into the Buckhead office, his father and Robert Erickson were huddled over papers spread out over the desk.

His father's eyes were bloodshot and his face pale. Elliott's first inclination was to call his dad's physician, but he knew it would do no good. His father would continue doing business, but this time from his hospital bed.

"Your dad and I were talking over his options," Erickson said. "I suggested he sell the Millhouse property. Maybe Redding would be interested in buying it. A quick sale would provide some needed capital. Your dad could use the money to complete his other projects."

Erickson focused his attention on his long-time client. "I also suggested he think about retirement after these projects are completed."

His dad straightened. "No way in hell I'm retiring. I'll make that decision when I'm good and ready. And I definitely won't be leaving the game with my tail tucked between my legs."

"I wish you would consider retiring, Dad."

His father shot him a look that would have melted steel rafters. "Like I said. When Hell freezes over."

Too late, Elliott knew he'd used the wrong tactic. He decided to backtrack. "What is your short-term plan?"

His dad paced the room. "Appeal the zoning commission's decision. But more immediately, find a new backer." He turned to Erickson. "You found Redding. There must be someone else out there willing to lend me the capital."

The old lawyer massaged the muscles in his neck, his face now as gray as the suit he wore. He looked every bit of his sixty-plus years. Years of working with the likes of Marcus Quinn would do that to a person.

"Investors would want a guarantee the money they lent would return a profit. At this point, the best you could hope for is to break even after paying your creditors and making payroll for the two remaining high rises. But it's all dependent on selling the Millhouse property quickly and profitably then investing the money back in your remaining businesses."

His father sank into his desk chair then rested his head on the back of the seat.

Silence reigned.

His father raised his head and speared Elliott with a look. "Where does this leave you with Redding?"

"It doesn't," Elliott said. "Chris and I are turning down his offer."

His father's face flooded with thick, thunderous anger clouds.

"Why?" His father's voice sounded like it came out of a strainer.

"Redding wants to move on the Millhouse area. He isn't interested in the community as it is. He wants to create mini mansions. Chris and I don't want to destroy neighborhoods, so we're walking away from the opportunity."

"That's bullshit," his dad shouted. His face flushed with color. "You're letting that woman and her family dictate how to run your business. Sex and business don't mix, Son. Haven't I taught you anything?"

A drumming pulse pounded behind Elliott's eyes, turning the world red, drowning out sound, almost rendering him speechless. "Is that what happened with Mom? You just wrote her off because your business meant more to you than she did?"

His father's face drained of color. His mouth worked like a stroke victim who couldn't form words. Elliott had caught him by surprise. Obviously, a discussion of his marriage was the last thing he'd expected.

"Ah...I'll just step outside and make a call." Erickson walked stiffly out of the office.

His dad reached for a water bottle that sat on his desk. He took a swig then leveled a hard-as-nails glare at Elliott. "You don't know what you're talking about. You were just a child."

"I was with her every night when you didn't come home for dinner. I watched her drink until she fell asleep on the sofa. I'd wake her and she'd cry as she stumbled up the stairs to bed with me behind her in case she fell. Not that a ten-year-old could catch her."

"And it's not the life I want for myself." His pulse pounded in his ears until he thought *he'd* be the stroke victim. "I want to leave the job at six and be home for my wife and any children I might be fortunate to have."

"With this Millhouse girl?"

Elliott propped his fists on his dad's desk and leaned toward the man who'd given him life. "Her name is Rashida. And yes, with Rashida. Do you have a problem with it?"

Elliott waited for the heat of his father's anger. But it never came.

His dad scrubbed a hand over his pale face. "If that's what you want, Son."

With his breath coming fast and hard, Elliott pushed back from his dad's desk.

"I loved your mother." His father seemed to have shrunk in his chair. "Don't ever doubt it. I was just trying to make enough money so we didn't have to live off hers. I wanted to be my own man. That plan backfired." His father stared at the far wall, seeing something only he could visualize. "By the time I was thirty-five, I was a widower raising a young son. Something I would have gladly changed, if I could."

This was the first time his father had discussed Elliott's mother with such frankness.

Elliott willed his breath to slow. "I'm glad you loved her. I've wondered my whole life."

His father rose from his desk and came to stand in front of Elliott. He'd always thought of his father as bigger than life. The last couple of months had worn him down. He was a shadow of the man Elliott remembered.

"I did love her. And I know I don't say this enough, but I love you and admire the man you've turned into." His father placed a hand on Elliott's shoulder. "I know that man has developed despite having me as a father."

His dad turned and walked to the window. He was silent before looking over his shoulder at Elliott. "If Rashida is the woman you want, then you have my blessing."

His father chuckled. The sound this time held amusement. "I would expect nothing less of my son than to go after the woman he wants and say to hell with anyone who stands in his way, including his dad."

For the first time in the last twenty-four hours, Elliott's spirit lifted. "Thanks, Dad. I'm hoping she'll have me." He didn't mention he doubted Rashida would let him back in her life. But he hadn't given up hope.

CHAPTER
TWENTY-ONE

A knock rattled Rashida's apartment door the next morning. Heat raced up her body and flooded her face. Didn't he ever give up? She stalked to the door and flung it open.

Her sister stood on the other side. Karla's face was a frozen mask, devoid of expression and bleached of color—all except her red-rimmed eyes.

"What's wrong? What happened?" Rashida asked as she pulled her sister inside.

"Do you have coffee?" Karla asked.

"Sure." As she led the way into the kitchen, Rashida snuck glances at her sister. Her powder-blue suit looked like she'd slept in it. Had she even been home? In fact, Karla looked like Rashida felt—emotionally bruised and battered. "What—?"

"I need a moment. Please."

Rashida lifted the mugs from the cabinet then pulled out a Mountain Roast pod, her sister's favorite, and dropped it into the Keurig. Her stomach churned with the anxiety and tension flowing from Karla.

Rashida waited until the last drop of coffee had dripped from the coffeemaker before she placed the mug in front of her sister, who'd plopped her slender body on one of the barstools.

Karla's fingers shook as she added sugar and poured in

Amaretto creamer. She took a cautious sip then placed the cup back on the counter.

"Kenneth is cheating on me." The words fell into the room like the first hack of an ax in a silent forest.

Rashida paused in the act of putting a pod of Mountain Roast into the coffeemaker for herself. "How do you know?"

"I caught him."

Karla had spoken so calmly Rashida had to make sure she'd heard correctly. "How?"

"He left his cell phone on the counter in the kitchen and went up to take a shower." Her sister took a big gulp of her coffee. "He got a text…" She shrugged. "I read it."

Rashida stopped stirring her hazelnut creamer, afraid she'd miss something.

"He was smart enough not to have programmed anyone's name into his phone, so I didn't know who sent the text. The message included only three numbers."

A hotel room number. Rashida thought the words but didn't say them out loud. She sipped her coffee and grimaced. She'd forgotten sugar.

"I followed him to a downtown hotel. Gave him fifteen minutes then went to the front desk and identified myself to the registration clerk. I said I'd locked myself out of the room. I lucked out…" Tears glittered in Karla's eyes. "Kenneth had used his real name. Stupid bastard. I showed my driver's license and the clerk gave me another key. It was providence I should catch him."

She took another sip, leaving Rashida hanging onto her words.

"I used the key and caught him in the act." Now tears leaked from her eyes. "She…she was so young." She swiped at the trail of tears. "It was almost comical. He jumped out of bed naked as the day he was born, his *thing* deflating even as he told me this wasn't what it looked like."

Rashida wanted to laugh at the picture her sister painted, but she suppressed the urge. Instead, she enveloped her in a hug. They clung to each other like they used to when they were children, when it was just them and their mother against the world. Now here they were, the cycle repeating itself—a new generation crying over a man.

Rashida stepped back from her sister. "What are you going to do?"

"I don't know." She picked up her mug, stared down into it, then pushed it away, giving up all pretense of drinking.

"You can stay here."

Karla shook her head, causing strands of hair to loosen from her bun.

"At least until you figure out what you're going to do."

Her sister didn't respond but stared at the counter as if she could see her future written in the swirls and veins in the granite.

"You could always go home and toss his clothes out in the yard and set fire to them."

A smile played around Karla's mouth. "Don't give me ideas."

"I'll even help you, and I'd enjoy it."

The silence stretched out between them. "I mean it, Karla. You can stay here. Tomorrow is soon enough to figure out what you want to do."

"I'd like that."

"Good."

While they sipped their coffee, Rashida allowed her

thoughts to drift to Elliott. She hadn't seen him in twenty-four hours, and she missed him. Missed the promise of the relationship they could have had. Missed his strong arms around her.

At least she had avoided getting her heart broken like her sister's.

No, who was she kidding? Her heart was just as shattered as Karla's. The only difference—Elliott had sacrificed what they could have had for a business deal. Somehow that felt colder and more heartbreaking.

Elliott woke with a dream of Rashida fresh in his mind. And from the erection he sported, his body had thought the dream was real. He remembered her shapely legs wrapped around his hips, her heels digging into his ass while he'd pounded into her heat.

He threw back the sheet and swung his legs out of bed. Burying his face in his hands, he groaned. How could he have made such a mess of this?

Eight weeks ago, he'd been deep in his routine of work, work, and more work. Now he couldn't draw a straight line with a ruler.

Rashida wasn't answering his calls or texts, and he'd be damned if he'd sit outside her apartment like a lovesick puppy.

He needed a long workout, hot coffee, and a cold shower. He headed toward the exercise room on the other side of the apartment and jumped onto the treadmill.

His jog lasted all of twenty minutes before he gave up. He showered, grabbed a cup of coffee, and did what he'd said he wouldn't do—drove to her apartment.

Acid churned in his stomach. The coffee wasn't helping. He took a deep breath and stepped out of the car. When Rashida's apartment door opened, he was momentarily confused. The face framed in the doorway wasn't the one he'd expected.

For a moment, he was at a loss for words. "Hey, Karla. Ah…is Rashida here?"

She studied him for a long moment. What had Rashida said about him?

Karla stepped out of the apartment but left the door ajar. "She isn't here. This is her day at the food bank."

"Oh." He ran his free palm over his forehead then turned and stared out at the parking lot. He'd rehearsed what he was going to say to her the whole drive over. Now what was he going to do?

"I'd ask you in for coffee, but it looks like you've got that taken care of." Karla nodded toward the paper cup he still clutched in his hand.

"Okay, well…I guess I'd better go." But his feet didn't move. It was as if his body knew once he left this place, he'd lose his connection to the woman he loved.

He turned back to Karla. "Can I take you to lunch?"

The request caught her off guard. He could tell by the widening of her eyes. "Why?"

"I need to talk to someone." He took a deep breath and exhaled. "I need advice. I can follow you in your car."

She glanced back inside the apartment. "Sure. Give me five minutes."

Ten minutes later, she stepped out dressed in jeans and a T-shirt that looked familiar. He must have stared too long at the shirt, because a sad smile flickered across her face.

She plucked at the garment. "I'm staying here for a while. No clothes." A pained expression crossed her face. "Long story."

She locked the apartment door. "Where do you want to go for lunch?"

"I'll leave it up to you."

He followed her into downtown Decatur, a quaint area with shops and eateries surrounded by well-maintained homes with a small-town feel.

She took him to a pub where they ordered food and took seats at a table in the restaurant's small outside space.

The sun was warm on his back, and here and there water puddled on the sidewalk, evidence of the late morning rain.

"What's the deal with you and my sister?" Karla said.

"I...I fucked up."

Karla placed her soda back on the table without taking a drink. "With Lissa Cloyd?"

"Lissa? What—?" He racked his brain trying to figure out what she alluded to.

"I saw how she looked at you at the benefit. I thought maybe you were trying to have your cake and eat it, too."

"Lissa and I are friends. In fact, she and Rashida are closer than Lissa and I are."

"You've cleared that up. Okay, spill. Why do you think you're the cause of the breakup?"

Elliott told her everything, including that his father still had a chance to get the zoning committee to reverse their decision.

"And this Redding wants to gentrify my grandmother's neighborhood?"

Elliott rubbed the back of his neck, trying to loosen the

knot that had formed at the base of his skull. "Yes. And he doesn't need the zoning board's approval, since his changes will be residential, not commercial. I need to figure out a way of safeguarding the neighborhood from other developers, because if not Redding, then some other real estate interloper will come in with plans to change the community," Elliott said.

The waitress arrived with their food. Elliott's burger no longer seemed appealing. He took a sip of his water but wished it were beer.

Karla cleared her throat. "Maybe I can help. I can create a postcard to advise homeowners about what makes a good sale. They can be armed with the facts, so they're not taken advantage of and can get a good price for their home." She unwrapped her silverware. "Scratch that. My cards might be interpreted as self-serving and hasten property sales."

She took a bite of her salad then pointed her fork at him as she chewed. "The trick is to get Redding interested in something else."

"Like what?"

"Undeveloped land. Something close to Millhouse so the same amenities would be there."

Elliott smiled for the first time in a while. "Do you think you can find such a property?"

"I can try." She took a sip of her soda. Placing the glass back on the table, she said, "You need to figure out a way to safeguard the neighborhood now *and* in the future."

Elliott thought about Patrick Carey. Maybe the lawyer could help him or at least point him in the direction of someone who could.

"I might have that covered."

• • •

At zero dark thirty, Rashida remembered why she was not an exerciser. Each footfall jarred her skull and rattled her brain. Her legs felt as if fifty-pound weights were tied around her ankles, and her skin itched from sweat trickling between her breasts and down her face. Her mouth was as dry as a desert and twice as gritty.

Determined to get her life back on track and move on from Elliott, she'd taken up Monique's challenge and joined her friend for a predawn run.

So here she was pounding the pavement as the morning sun peeked over the horizon and traffic started to increase along Ponce de Leon Avenue.

She hauled her exhausted body a few more feet before she stumbled to a stop, bent over, and placed her hands on her thighs.

Monique jogged back to her. "Breathe, don't pant."

"Easy…for you to say." Rashida's lungs cried out for air, so she tried to drag in the life-sustaining substance slowly, but her pounding heart and her wheezing lungs wanted more. Demanded more. "There…are better…ways to exercise. Like… inside an air-conditioned…gym."

Monique scoffed. "Who wants to breathe in someone else's sweat and watch reruns of *Law and Order*?"

"Right now? Me." Rashida waved her friend off. "Go on without me. Just remember where you left the body."

Monique jogged in place. Sweat glistened on her dark skin. "We only have half a mile more. Speed walk if you can't run."

Rashida twisted her head so she could look up at her friend. "You don't understand. My legs are on strike."

Her friend's face softened. "You'll get through this, Rashida. In a year's time, you won't remember this pain."

"What?" Rashida sputtered. "Are you insinuating that I'm out here killing myself for a man? A treacherous man who lied to me even as he was screwing me?"

Monique shifted her gaze away from Rashida's and stared out at the increasing traffic. "Just saying. It'll get better."

"And what about Karla?" Rashida asked. "Will it get better for her?" She was horrified to hear the crack in her voice.

"I'm sorry about Karla," Monique said. "Did you show her the video?"

"Couldn't." Rashida straightened and drew a deep, slow breath in her lungs. "It would have hurt her too much."

"And finding him in bed with that young thing hurt less?"

"Point taken."

She could only imagine her sister's pain.

"Let's walk," Monique said.

While they walked, Rashida took her mind off Elliott and studied the neighborhood in the early morning light. "I wish I had the money to buy one of these estates."

The Druid Hills area had always been one of the grandest neighborhoods to Rashida, with its sprawling homes built on lots of acreage.

Monique studied the houses with a disinterested eye. "Too rich for my blood."

"Do you know it was the second planned suburb after Inman Park?"

Monique mopped her face with the towel she carried. "Is this from the architect boyfriend?"

Rashida ignored her friend's reference to Elliott. "I've always had an interest in beautiful homes and neighborhoods, but like you, I can't afford them."

They passed a bronze marker. These signs were found

all over Atlanta, denoting some major historical happening. This one referenced the march of Union General William T. Sherman's troops through this area on the way to the sea during the last days of the Civil War.

Rashida stopped. Elliott had said something weeks ago about the historical significance of the Millhouse area.

She hadn't lied to Monique about this outing being for her. "Okay, let's finish." She held up a finger when her friend started to grin. "I'm speed walking. Meet you back at the car."

An hour later, with tight muscles protesting, Rashida limped into Grammy's kitchen with a bag of bagels and cream cheese.

Mrs. McClain was there, sipping coffee from a saucer. She said it cooled the hot drink quicker. Rashida took her at her word. If she'd tried it, she'd be wearing the coffee.

"Good morning, ladies." She bent to kiss her grandmother on the cheek.

Grammy glanced at the clock and back at Rashida. "You just getting in from the club?"

"No, I went running."

"Was someone chasing you?" she asked.

"Ha ha. I'm trying to get in shape."

"You're already in shape." Her grandmother shook her head. "You young people. Always wanting to be thin as a pencil."

Rashida plated the bagels and placed a knife on the table for the cream cheese. She then lathered cream cheese on her cinnamon raisin bagel.

Mrs. McClain contributed to the conversation by clucking her tongue. "There was a time when women with meat on their bones was a sign of good health. You couldn't get a job if you looked too thin. Made your employer think you had the consumption."

Rashida looked at the elderly woman out of the corner of her eye. "What century was that?"

A ghost of a smile played around the old woman's mouth. "My granny would tell me stories about when she was young and working in the houses of rich folks."

Mrs. McClain had to be in her eighties. If her grandmother told her these stories about her youth, this must have been around the turn of the twentieth century.

Rashida thought about the palatial homes in Druid Hills. "Where did she work?"

"Right here," Mrs. McClain said. "In the Millhouse area."

Grammy put creamer for the coffee onto the table.

"This area had people wealthy enough to have servants?" Rashida asked.

The elderly woman held up a finger. "One family. The Maier brothers. They owned the mill. My granny worked there until she was fired."

Curiosity piqued, Rashida asked, "Why was she fired?"

With thin, misshapen fingers, Mrs. McClain reached for an everything bagel. "Mrs. Maier said my granny tried to entice her brother-in-law into sin."

"Was your grandmother able to find another job?"

"Not until after my mother was born five months later."

Rashida's mouth dropped. "The brother-in-law?"

Mrs. McClain nodded. "But he did right by her."

Rashida stopped chewing. *He married her?* No. Impossible in the South where anti-miscegenation laws were on the books until 1967. "How did he do right by her?"

"He built her the house I live in. Been passed down from

my grandmother to my mother, and finally to me."

"How many years ago?"

Mrs. McClain chewed carefully. "Mother was born around 1906. What does that make it?" She glanced at Rashida.

"One hundred fifteen years ago." Rashida stared at her grandmother's friend. She knew Mrs. McClain lived in the oldest home in the neighborhood, but she'd had no idea the house was over a hundred years old.

A germ of an idea made her forget all about the bagel she'd been starved for. "Do you have pictures of the neighborhood from back then?"

"No neighborhood then. Just our place, the gristmill, the Maiers' home, and the cemetery."

Oh my God! She'd forgotten all about the cemetery.

"Where was the old mill?" Rashida asked.

"On the property we've been protesting about." Mrs. McClain grinned, cream cheese caught between the spaces of her teeth.

Nothing had ever looked so beautiful to Rashida.

The elderly woman meant the land Quinn Enterprises had purchased.

The idea that started on the jog this morning began to take shape.

Rashida sat at Karla's kitchen table, staring into her second glass of Cabernet Sauvignon as her sister prepared a salad. Kenneth had moved out earlier in the day, so Rashida had come over to lend her sister moral support.

"Are you going to be okay?" Karla asked. She peeled a

cucumber over the garbage disposal.

Rashida frowned. "I should be asking *you* that, shouldn't I?"

"I'm fine. Never better."

Right. The last twenty times her sister blew her nose wasn't because of seasonal allergies. How did you handle separating from your husband of eight years? Was it eight times harder than separating from someone you'd known less than a year? If so, then her sister's heart must be pulverized by the pain.

"You didn't answer my question," Karla said. "Are you okay?"

Rashida took a gulp of her wine. Forget sipping. It didn't numb the pain fast enough. "Sure, why?"

Her sister rolled her eyes. "I know about Elliott."

Rashida's blood sped through her veins like a Japanese bullet train. "Know what? There isn't anything to know."

Karla sliced cucumber into the salad bowl. "I know you two broke up."

Rashida laughed. Her grip on the fragile wine goblet was tight enough to break it. "We weren't together. Wait..." Her wine fogged brain tried to work through what her sister had just said. "How did you know we were together? I didn't mention it."

Karla threw cherry tomatoes onto the lettuce. "We haven't been very close, not like sisters should be. I wasn't there for you when you and Alex broke up. I should have been. I'm sorry."

Rashida waved away her concern. "Our breakup was nothing compared to this one with Elliott."

Karla studied her. "I didn't want you to make the same mistakes in love I did."

"Too late."

Her sister's face melted, and tears flooded her brown eyes.

"Don't do that," Rashida whispered. She got up and went to her sister, pulling her into a hug. "If you start crying, you'll make me cry. And the way I feel now, I might never stop."

"Were you in love with him?"

Rashida released her sister and went back to her wine. She swirled the contents of the glass around. The crimson liquid coated the sides of the goblet then slid down to settle with the remaining wine in the bottom. "I thought so, but the man I was in love with didn't exist. He was a mirage." She laughed. "Aren't those the words of a song? The love I saw in you was just a mirage."

"One of those oldie groups," Karla said. "The Temptations, or was it The Miracles? I'll have to ask Mom. But you're evading the question. Were you in love with him?"

"Yes. No. I don't know. And if I was, it doesn't matter now. He clearly wasn't in love with me. He was just using me."

"Are you sure?"

Rashida frown at her sister. "Of course I'm sure. And why are you questioning me about it?"

Her sister divided the salad into two bowls. "Because I believe he's in love with you and he's pretty miserable."

"Good. Wait…" Rashida put one hand on her hip. "Just how do you know that?"

"Because he told me."

Rashida leaned forward so she could see into her sister's face better. "When did you see him?"

"A couple of days ago, when I stayed at your apartment. He came by to see you. You weren't there, so he took me to lunch."

"And the two of you talked about me?"

Karla pulled a couple of bottles of salad dressing out of the refrigerator. "You were all he talked about. He wants to get you back. And he wants to save the neighborhood."

"Save the neighborhood? I'm confused. His father's application was denied. Grammy's neighbors don't have to worry about his business changing the area."

"Marcus Quinn isn't the only person Millhouse has to worry about. You've heard of a man named Redding?"

Rashida nodded. "He was at the zoning meeting."

"He wants to buy property in the area and either tear the houses down or remodel them, if possible," Karla said.

"Did Elliott tell you Redding wants him to be the architect on this reimagined neighborhood?"

"He did. He also said he turned the job down." Karla slid a salad bowl toward Rashida. "Redding is just one investor. There'll be others. Elliott wants to set up a governing board that will put in place restrictions on buying into the neighborhood."

Rashida snorted. "I don't trust him. He's proven himself to be as ruthless and devious as his father."

Karla studied her. "He really hurt you, didn't he?"

Rashida could still feel Redding's words slamming into her chest, ripping the veil of illusion caused by love off her eyes. The pain had been searing.

She moved the salad around in her bowl. She wasn't hungry, and from the way her sister eyed her salad, neither was she.

"We don't need him. I've been working on something," Rashida said. "Do you know anything about the process involved in getting an area declared a historical landmark?"

"Enough to know it takes forever. Why?"

"I want to look into it. See if that designation could save

Grammy's neighborhood to keep it from falling into the hands of investors."

"I have a suggestion," Karla said. "But you're not going to like it."

"What?"

"Elliott is into historic restoration, isn't he? I bet he knows a lot about historical landmarks."

Rashida narrowed her eyes. "You two talked a lot."

"We did. And he's willing to help. If you really want to help Grammy and her neighbors, you won't let your pride stand in the way."

Rashida didn't want to deal with Elliott, but she didn't want Grammy and her friends to lose their homes, either.

She was an adult. She could meet with Elliott without letting her feelings get in the way. Without letting her heart get in the way.

E lliott's office was a small house in Inman Park, complete with a wide front porch and comfortable deck furniture with cushions.

Rashida stood outside his front door, gathering her courage and mental fortitude around herself like a cape. She could do this. She wiped her sweaty palm on her dress then turned the knob.

A chime sounded when she opened the door. She stepped into an airy space with two doors several feet apart on the right. A desk sat at the base and to the left of a wide staircase.

Two comfortable chairs were arranged around a low glass coffee table to the left of the front door.

"Be right with you," a voice called out.

The house, although small, gave the illusion of openness. The floors were darkly stained hardwoods and were protected from foot traffic by a wide red patterned rug. Rashida didn't know much about rugs, but it appeared expensive.

"Can I help you?" A tall, dark-skinned Black man stood in the open door of the last office.

"Is Elliott in?"

"Not at the moment." He moved toward her. "My name is Chris Hollins. I'm Elliott's partner." He held out a hand.

She shook it. "Rashida Howard."

"Rashida." His face erupted in a wide, white-toothed smile. "Glad to finally meet you. Elliott talks about you frequently. Can I get you something to drink? Coffee? Soda?"

"I'm fine. I'll just wait over here." She pointed to one of the comfortable-looking chairs in the reception area.

It had been almost two weeks since the zoning committee's vote and two days since her conversation with Karla. Rashida had finally overcome her pride and made an appointment with Elliott to ask for his help with the Historical Registry.

Instead of going back into his office, Chris, still smiling, perched on the corner of the desk.

This is one happy guy. Rashida shifted in her chair.

"I can see why he's so enamored with you," Chris said.

Heat crept up her face. She glanced at her phone. "We have an appointment. I guess I'm a little early." She didn't want Chris to think she was so desperate to see Elliott she'd stopped by without being invited.

The door chimed.

Elliott stepped inside, closing the door behind him. He took in Chris on the desk. "What are you—"

Rashida rose from her seat, and Elliott's head swiveled in her direction. He didn't speak for what seemed like forever, then a lopsided grin transformed his face. Her heart stuttered.

Dressed casually in khakis and a white dress shirt with long sleeves rolled up to his elbows, he looked tan and healthy. She wanted him to be pale and pining for her.

"Hi," he said. He looked from his partner to her. "I assume you two have met."

"We have," Chris smirked.

Elliott narrowed his eyes at his partner. "Come into my

office, Rashida." He extended an arm to the first door on the right.

After pointing her to an empty chair, he went directly to his desk and powered on his computer. He didn't utter a word as he waited for his computer to start up.

She glanced around. Probably once a bedroom, his sunny office had a small fireplace and windows on three sides. His desk overlooked the front porch and the street.

"I want to get your opinion on something I designed."

He turned the monitor to face her then walked around his desk until they stood side by side. The woodsy scent of his cologne danced around her head until she was dizzy. She wanted to lean into his solid body and stay there.

"It's a mock-up of a gristmill."

She pulled her thoughts away from having carnal knowledge of his body and stared blindly at the computer screen. What did he want her to say? "It's nice."

He chuckled. "I walked the property Dad purchased on Millhouse Road. Did you know there was a creek behind the building?"

She shook her head. "I knew there was a well."

"A well? There are remnants of the old millhouse but no well."

She turned to him. "Of course, there—"

Grammy had always mentioned the well when they were children, but now Rashida realized it had all been a way to keep them off the property.

"The gristmill is long gone, but the house's stone foundation is still there."

She could hear the excitement in his voice.

"I thought it would be a great idea to reproduce the gristmill and at least shore up the foundation. It might expedite your application. We could also build a stone fence around the cemetery, with an entrance."

Why was he doing all this? For her? No. She wouldn't let her thoughts run down that track. That way led to heartbreak. "It's lovely."

He swung the monitor back to its original position. "I was serious when I said I wanted to help save the neighborhood. I think establishing a governing board would be a good way to go. It would further safeguard against any investor who wants to change the neighborhood to something other than its current historic look. What do you think?"

She didn't know what to think. When Karla had suggested Elliott might be able to help, never in a thousand years did she think he would come up with this elaborate plan.

"The credit goes to Chris," he said. "I told him I wanted to help you in some way to protect the neighborhood. Once we walked the area and then the property my father had purchased, Chris thought reproducing the historical feel of the area would be a great idea."

"Where would the money to do all this come from?"

Elliott shrugged. "There are ways of raising money. The chamber of commerce might be of help. The neighbors could provide the labor for the cemetery gate."

"What about Mr. Redding?"

"Karla has located undeveloped land we think might work for him. Chris and I have done a mock-up of a new community complete with a few floor plans. We're presenting this to him in a couple of days. He should like it. It's not too far from the Millhouse area and has many of the same amenities, close to downtown, and near the MARTA station. We're pretty confident he'll go for it."

Elliott seemed to have forgotten one important detail.

"What about your dad?" she asked. "This gristmill is on his land."

Elliott laughed. "Trust me, Dad's getting compensated. He's donating the land to the community and writing it off his taxes. Plus, this grand gesture is getting him some publicity, and his bank wants to be a part of that publicity, so they're donating funds. There will be a placard on the site with everyone's name who's donated to the project. And his bank is working with him to reevaluate his finances and come up with a plan to help him become solvent."

"Why are you doing all this?" She had to know, even if it hurt.

He held her gaze. "You know why."

Her heart seized then restarted as though an electric current had been passed through it. "I think this is all wonderful," she rushed on before he could say any more. Before he could make her believe he still cared. "When do we start?"

The choir's voices built to a crescendo, the sound almost rocking the church's foundation. The voices dropped to a whisper, and the organ's fading notes left goose bumps on Rashida's skin but a lighter feeling in her soul.

"Let us pray." Reverend Clemmons bowed his head and led the church in the ending prayer.

After the service, as some of the congregation filed out of the sanctuary, Rashida stopped and said hello to a few friends.

She made her way toward the exit. Up ahead, she heard the minister's booming laughter. She made for the other exit to bypass him. She wasn't ready for any soul searching. Knowing as much about her business as he did, the minister would have her reaching deep to examine the events in her life. And he'd do all this without uttering a word. Just by looking at her with those intense eyes.

"Sister Howard."

Crap. She turned slowly, a jovial smile that she didn't feel plastered on her face. People maneuvered around him like eddies of water around an immovable rock.

When they reached each other, she was the first to speak. "Reverend Clemmons, a wonderful sermon."

He grabbed her hand in his massive one. "I didn't see your mother today."

Rashida scrambled quickly for a lie that wouldn't bruise his ego. "She came to the early morning service." Junior ministers conducted the early and evening services. Traditionally, the head minister, Reverend Clemmons, conducted the eleven o'clock service.

"Ah…" He nodded while holding her gaze with his earnest one. Rashida knew from the knowing look he gave her that he had conducted the early morning service. She decided not to say anything more, because she was doomed to dig herself a deeper hole.

"Would you join me in my office?"

She glanced longingly at the exit. The double doors stood open. Sunlight slanted in and gleamed on the highly polished floors. Escape beckoned.

"Of course," she said.

He led the way to the back of the church, stopping to say

hello to a church member here and there.

Once inside his office, he removed his vestment. He'd left the door open, and Rashida could hear congregation members calling to one another.

"Why is your mother avoiding me?"

Rashida hadn't expected him to be so blunt.

"You know I have deep feelings for her."

Rashida could only nod. She didn't know what to say. Her mother was a very private woman. She hadn't discussed her feelings about the minister with her daughters. Rashida sensed her mother didn't dislike the man. It was more a case of her being unwilling to play the June Cleaver to his Ward. Reverend Clemmons gave Rashida every indication of being a traditional male who expected his wife to play a traditional role in their relationship.

Essie Howard was not a traditional woman. She'd been on her own without a man in her life for twenty-five years. Even if she loved the reverend madly, Rashida couldn't see her mother taking a backseat to him.

"If I were a man with a poor self-image, I'd think she didn't like me."

Rashida wanted to laugh. The minister had a good heart, but he could be overbearing at times.

"She respects you, Reverend. But I think she feels another woman would be a better complement to your personality."

The minister sat at his desk with his massive hands resting on his equally impressive chest and stomach. His usually jovial smile had disappeared. "I love your mother, Rashida."

She couldn't stop her jaw from dropping. *Holy shit. Forgive me, Lord.* Did her mother know?

"I'm asking for your approval to court her."

Holy moly. "What if she doesn't feel the same way about you?"

A faint smile twisted his full lips. "She does."

Ahhh. How did she say this delicately? *My mother tries to avoid you at all costs.* Case in point: her not coming to the eleven a.m. service. "How can you be so certain of that?" She liked the minister for all his chauvinistic ways. She didn't want to see his heart broken.

His eyes twinkled. "I know."

"It's great to be that certain," Rashida said. "Not all of us can be that lucky." She cringed. Had that just come out of her mouth? It sounded bitter.

"Do you want to talk about it?" Reverend Clemmons asked.

Rashida laughed, but the sound lacked humor. "Not enough hours in the day."

The minister's seat creaked as he shifted position. "Is this about the young Mr. Quinn?"

"Elliot, Alex..." Her mouth twisted. "Take your pick."

"Alex?" The reverend raised an eyebrow. "That was the young man that moved away?"

She guessed the minister had been keeping close tabs on the family. "Yes...ah...we broke up about a year ago."

"You loved him very much?"

Had she loved Alex? She thought back over the years. Maybe in the beginning there'd been some excitement in their relationship. But the last year or two, that excitement had been missing. And it hadn't even bothered her. Had she checked out of the relationship before he had? Had that been why he sought love somewhere else and left for San Francisco? It didn't excuse his infidelity, but she understood it.

"No. I just realized I didn't. In fact, I'm not sure that I ever did." She stared at the folders neatly lined up on the reverend's desk. Why had she been holding on to this resentment of Alex? Why had she placed the blame for the disintegration of their relationship on him when it had been her?

She shifted her attention to Reverend Clemmons. "I didn't love him. At least not in a long time."

"And Elliott?" the minister asked.

She didn't want to hear his name. It was like a knife twisting in her heart. "It doesn't matter if I love him. He doesn't love me."

"Are you certain?"

She remembered Elliott's words...well, his implied meaning. That he was doing the historic restoration on the gristmill property for her.

The minister must have sensed her uncertainty. He rose from behind his desk and took her hand in his. Her hand almost disappeared inside his larger one. "Imagine yourself at fifty. Living alone without him. How does that feel? Or running into him at a restaurant and being introduced to the woman who became his wife."

Instead of me. She tried to smother the image of Elliott waking up beside some faceless woman every morning. The vision made her insides twist and her heart heavy.

"Does he go out of his way to make you happy?"

Rashida thought about the amount of work he'd done to ensure the Millhouse neighborhood was approved for the National Registry. Of persuading his father to attend the mediation talks. Of pleading his case to her sister—a woman he barely knew.

"I think your heart knows the answer." The minister released her hand then slipped into his suit coat. "Let's lock up." He indicated she should precede him out of his office.

The building had grown silent, and her thoughts were loud. As they walked toward the front of the church, his words sank in.

He locked the exterior door and pocketed the keys. "Life is short. Don't take too long to let him know how you feel."

CHAPTER TWENTY-THREE

Rashida sensed the moment he stepped into the bar. The air seemed to shift in the room. Raindrops glittered in his dark hair and spotted his white shirt.

She sat in the same bar they'd occupied several months ago when she'd stormed from the Quinn Enterprise offices and sought refuge from the heat in this frigid place.

While he scanned the bar for her, she scanned him. His slacks couldn't hide his muscular thighs, and his white shirt, rolled up to his elbows, couldn't hide his strong forearms. Her pulse beat an erratic dance in her veins, and her mouth needed every drop of the water in her glass.

He nodded his head in acknowledgment when he spotted her.

"Hi," he said as he slid into the seat across from her. She sat in the same booth they occupied that evening they met.

"Hi, yourself. What are you drinking?"

"Scotch," he said, looking around at the small crowd.

"Not McCallan 18?"

He shrugged. "I can live with a house scotch."

She smirked. "I invited you for a drink. Drink what you want." She held up a hand for the waitress.

When the young woman arrived, Rashida said, "McCallan

18 on the rocks and a margarita top shelf with salt around the rim."

The waitress hurried off.

Rashida's pulse beat thickly through her veins as his gaze traveled slowly over her features. "How have you been?" she asked, hoping conversation would stop his scrutiny.

"Doing good." His mouth lifted at the corner in that easy grin of his. "How about you?"

"Good." *Missing the hell out of you.* She'd last seen him at the gristmill's dedication ceremony two months ago. Pride had kept her from going up to him and telling him how much she missed him. But time had expired on her pride keeping them apart.

The waitress arrived with their drinks. After placing Elliott's on a cocktail napkin in front of him, the waitress gave him a smile that lasted too long for Rashida's liking.

"Thanks," he said, his attention already returning to Rashida. "How're your grandmother and the other ladies?"

"Mrs. Parker and Mrs. McClain are doing fine. Grammy..." Rashida shrugged. "Maybe not so fine."

Elliott paused, his drink halfway to his mouth. A frown creased his forehead. "What's wrong? Is she ill?"

"She lost her license."

"Ouch," Elliott said. "What happened?"

Rashida licked the salt off her glass before sipping her margarita. She needed this drink. "She failed the sight exam and has been running me, Karla, and my mom ragged."

"Well, I guess that explains why Mrs. Parker drove the three of them up to the construction site every day."

Rashida chuckled. "That was because she was the only one of the three that could drive." She tucked an errant strand of hair behind her ear. "What were they doing up at the site?"

Elliott's gaze seemed to be locked on her ear. "Ah... bringing us food. I had to tell Chris what was safe to eat."

She laughed, remembering Mrs. McClain's brownies. "How's your dad?"

"Slowing down. He's sold off a big chunk of his business, and with the reconsolidation by the bank, his finances are in better shape. Maybe in a few years I can get him to retire." Elliott laughed. "Who am I kidding? At least he's agreed to move into a condo, so I'm selling the house."

He lifted his drink to his lips, watching her over the rim.

The silence stretched out awkwardly.

"Why did you call?" he asked.

Her gaiety died. "Ah..." She arranged the extra cocktail napkins on the table in a neat pile. "I'm thinking of buying a house."

He put his glass on the table. It hit with a clunk, the liquor splashing up the sides. "That's great. Where?"

"One street over from Grammy." She shrugged, trying to be nonchalant about what she was going to ask. "I wanted you to take a look at the place and give me your opinion. You know...about remodeling it. It needs a lot of work."

The waitress chose that moment to return with a menu. "Would you guys like to order food?" She looked from Elliott to Rashida. Rashida shook her head.

She swallowed. *Now comes the hard part.* "I'll need a roommate, because with the renovation costs and the mortgage, my resources would be stretched to the limit. Do you know anyone looking for a place to stay?"

His face scrunched up, and he tilted his head in confusion. "No—"

"I know I'm not an easy person to live with, but I have a lot of good qualities. I'm loyal, I'm a good listener, and I've been told I'm a good lover."

His head snapped back. "What?"

She smiled. "Just testing to see if you were listening."

"I—" He shook his head. "How much of what you just said was real?"

"All of it."

"You want me to find you a roommate?"

"Sure. Male or female. It doesn't matter."

He stared at her, obviously confused.

"But only if you're not interested." She rearranged the cocktail napkins again, fanning them out this time.

He drained his drink then placed the glass on the table. "You want us to move in together?"

Her lungs couldn't pull in enough air. He didn't appear overjoyed at the prospect. Maybe she could pretend it was a joke. *No.* She'd come this far. She needed to put her feelings on the table. No more hiding behind a wall. "Yes. I do."

She could barely hold his gaze. The intensity was too much.

"I thought you'd stopped loving me," Elliott said.

Her heart flopped over and over, coming to land against her ribs. She tried to read what was behind those darkened green eyes. "I stopped trusting you, but I never stopped loving you."

He reached out and covered her hand with his. The touch of his hand made her feel like she'd found a safe place.

"Why did you wait so long to contact me?" he asked. "I've been going crazy, trying to give you space."

Her lungs relaxed, and she drew in a deeper breath. "I had to learn to trust my feelings for you. To not be afraid to love you."

"Are you still in love with me?"

She nodded.

He rose then slid into the booth beside her. He traced her earlobe then ran his thumb across her lips. The muscles tightened in her abdomen.

"I've wanted to do that since I walked in the door," he said.

"I've never really thanked you for all the work you did getting the neighborhood ready for its National Registry application."

"I did it all for you."

Heat rushed into her face. *God, she was acting like she was sixteen.*

"How about dinner?"

She was so flustered she couldn't follow the change in conversation. "What?"

"Dinner. Food. Sustenance."

She looked at him a long moment. "Where?"

"The Ritz."

She glanced out the window then shifted her attention back to him. "Okay. Dinner. But visiting the rooms above the restaurant is out of the question."

But of course, they did.

EPILOGUE

Three years later…

"You look beautiful." Rashida's mother adjusted the dress on her daughter for the millionth time.

Rashida turned left then right, eying herself critically in the mirror that one of her mother's friends had the foresight to bring to the church.

Around them the rest of the bridal party giggled, gossiped, and galivanted around the church's small dressing room, half clothed. The air was filled with the scent of perfume, foundation powder, and nervousness.

"Ten minutes," Rashida's mom called out like a staff sergeant, which caused more laughter and scurrying about.

"Here are your flowers." She stuck a bouquet of white lilies and orchids into Rashida's trembling hands. Her mother met her eyes and smiled. "Just breathe. You'll be fine."

"Speak for yourself," Rashida mumbled. She could barely breathe in the dress. Mindful of the hour Karla had spent on her makeup, Rashida settled for giving her mother's hand a squeeze.

"Where is Karla?" her mother asked.

"She went to make sure Jamal was seated on the bride's side of the church." Jamal was her sister's fiancé.

The door to the dressing room opened, and Grammy stuck her head through the opening. The sound of music filtered in. "The bridegroom showed up, so I guess there's going to be a wedding."

Laughter filled the room. Rashida never doubted he'd show up. He'd wanted this wedding sometimes more than the bride.

"Okay, ladies, line up. It's showtime," Rashida's mom said.

Rashida didn't know how her mother could be so calm. The bridesmaids filed out to take their place in the vestibule outside the sanctuary. Rashida pulled up the rear.

The church was filled with well-wishers. The hum of conversation could be heard with the doors to the hall closed. This was the wedding of the summer. Of the year.

The doors opened, and the bridesmaids, one by one, glided down the aisle toward the pulpit.

Faces blurred. Whispers blended. The music swelled as Rashida moved down the aisle. She gave Elliott's dad a watery smile. He returned it with a thumbs-up.

At the front of the church, she locked on Elliott's reassuring smile and let it steady her as she floated toward him.

When she took her place, she could finally relax and return his smile.

Then the traditional wedding march began to play. The doors at the back of the sanctuary opened again.

Essie Howard filled the opening, looking radiant in a royal blue gown and matching veil.

Rashida snuck a peek at the groom. He'd conducted hundreds of weddings, but she guessed when it was your own, it was different. For one moment, she thought they might need smelling salts. A profusion of perspiration trickled down the side of the big man's face. In contrast, her mother walked serenely down the aisle.

It had taken three years, but Reverend Clemmons had worn her mother down. Rashida knew that wasn't true. Essie Howard, soon to be Essie Howard-Clemmons, was a strong-willed woman. That she was here, about to marry, meant she loved the minister and felt he was the right man for her.

As the reverend lifted the bride's veil, Rashida's gaze drifted to Elliott, who stood across the aisle with the other groomsmen. He locked eyes with her the way he'd done eighteen months ago, when he'd lifted her veil and they'd pledged themselves to each other.

Now, love filled his eyes as he mouthed, *I love you.*

She caressed her small baby bump as she mouthed in return, *I love you, too.*

ACKNOWLEDGMENTS

I'd like to thank my long-time critique partners: Mary Barfield, Pamela Varnado, Sharina Harris, and LaShon Hill for their exemplary efforts in bringing my plot ideas down from the rafters and making my words shine.

A big thank-you to Elizabeth Pelletier, CEO of Entangled Publishing, who gave me the opportunity to bring Elliott and Rashida's story to print. I'm in awe of your visionary business acumen.

Lydia Sharp, thank you for your expertise, your patience, and your courtesy.

Thank you to my agents: Amanda Leuck and Sandy Harding of Spencerhill Literary Agency, two wonderful ladies, who held my hand through the traditional publishing process.

A special thanks to the Cultural, Interracial, Multicultural Special interest Chapter of Romance Writers of America (CIMRWA) who sponsored a contest that allowed my work to come to Liz Pelletier's attention.

And to all the Entangled Publishing staff who worked hard to bring *The Hookup Dilemma* to the bookshelf: Riki Cleveland, Jessica Turner, Stacy Abrams, Curtis Svehlak, Heather Riccio, Bree Archer, and Elizabeth Stokes, thank you.

A special thanks to illustrator, Keisha Archer, for the creation of *The Hookup Dilemma*'s beautiful cover.

Any facts about gentrification and real estate that are in error are strictly my own. The Millhouse area is a fictitious Atlanta location.

*Turn the page to start reading the
heartfelt and humorous new book
from debut author Elle Cruz.*

CHAPTER ONE

Some people chased a high by doing drugs. Claire had never understood that. The best high she'd ever experienced was seeing peoples' reactions to her homemade sugar cookies.

Claire was a cookie artist. She could make literal masterpieces with a few bags of piped royal icing on a slab of dough. It was ironic, really, because she couldn't draw to save her life, yet she could recreate Van Gogh's *Starry Night* on a giant cookie. She discovered this talent quite by accident. Five years ago, she was on YouTube looking for recipe ideas for her cousin's school bake sale, and she somehow stumbled upon sugar cookie decorating.

She'd fallen down the rabbit hole and never returned from Wonderland.

Claire Ventura's life-long dream of becoming an entrepreneur was so close, yet so far. She aspired to become a full-time cookie decorator, with plans to sell her creations online, and offer tutorials and classes. But two little obstacles stood in the way. One: mustering up the courage to actually leave her day job and follow her dream. And two: breaking the news to her traditional Filipino family that she would *never* pursue a job in medicine or science.

It was Friday morning. Everyone at her grandmother's assisted living facility knew what Fridays meant. The staff's faces lit up as Claire came striding in, rolling her fold-up cart full of goodies. She was going to knock their socks off today.

"Good morning, Miss Claire," the receptionist said.

"Good morning, Rose," Claire replied as she signed in. "You sound cheerful this morning. I wonder why?" Claire removed a cellophane-wrapped cookie from her cart—and she got the reaction she was hoping for right as Rose's eyes landed on it.

"Oh my goodness, Miss Claire, I can't believe it," she cried. "It's a rose! I couldn't eat this. It's so pretty. I am never going to eat this."

"You have to eat it," Claire said. "That's part of the magic. Not only do you get to enjoy how pretty it is, but you get to taste how delicious it is too."

"Thank you so much," Rose gushed again. She clutched the cookie to her heart like it was a long-lost family heirloom. "You are the sweetest thing."

"It's the least I can do for you and the rest of the staff. You are always so nice every time I call, and everyone takes such good care of my lola."

Her first stop was a success. On to the next.

She rolled her cart down the carpeted hallway toward the nurses' station. After dropping off a box full of flower-shaped cookies and receiving the "oohs" and "aahs" she lived for, she headed off toward her grandmother's room.

Claire rolled her cart to the elevator and punched in the secret code to access the second floor. Lola had only been living there for about three months, but it was a tough transition. She was diagnosed with Alzheimer's a few years ago, and it steadily got worse. No one in her family was prepared for how drastically it would change her. It all came to a head a few months ago when the caregiver at Lola's house called Claire, frantically screaming that Lola had disappeared. It turned out Lola had decided to go for a walk. She was found five miles away at a strip mall.

Five miles.

How she got there was beside the point. Afterward, Lola wasn't the same. She stopped having conversations. She stopped acting like herself and became a complete stranger. Lola couldn't live alone in her house any longer, so they moved her into the locked Alzheimer's unit at the assisted living facility. This sudden change scared everyone in her family, but not Claire. Lola was still Lola, despite whatever illness she had. Claire had never given up hope, and she came to visit her every single day.

The elevator door slid open. Claire stepped off and walked across the vestibule to the locked doors. She punched in another code, and the doors slowly opened. The Alzheimer's unit was decorated with accents of love and nostalgia. Old black-and-white photos of the residents who had served in World War II and Korea adorned the walls. Vintage wedding pictures and photos of smiling family members also hung there, paying homage to the residents who left their lasting impression on the world.

Ornate red paisley paper covered the walls. The carpet was a plush, dark green shade with deep gold accents. The wood grain paneling along the walls might have seemed outdated, but Claire liked the personal touch. It seemed so much more like a home than a facility.

She rolled her cart down the hallway and around the corner to the right. Lola's door was wide open.

"Lola, I'm here."

Claire walked into the room and stopped short when she

saw her favorite nurse there, studying the picture frames on Lola's dresser.

"Oh. Hi Allison," Claire said. "How are you?"

"Fine, thanks. I just finished giving your grandma her meds."

Lola was clean and dressed, sitting primly in her armchair like a faerie queen upon her throne. Her eyes were trained on the talk show TV host, but she showed no signs of engagement or comprehension. A green-and-white crocheted blanket was draped over her lap. The pointed tips of her brown snakeskin flats peeked out from the hem of her pink-and-blue floral dress.

"So how has she been?" Claire asked as she took a seat at the edge of the bed beside Lola's armchair.

"Pretty stable so far. She woke up once last night and started to wander, but she was easily redirected. She went right back to sleep. Do you mind if I ask you a question?"

Claire paused, then said, "Not at all. What is it?"

"I never took the time to look at your grandma's pictures before," she said. "They're so interesting. She has a huge family."

"She sure does. She gave birth to eleven children at home. Sometimes the midwife couldn't get to her in time and she had to birth them on her own."

"Wow. How many grandkids does she have?"

"Thirty-five."

The nurse's face lit up. "Amazing."

"It's Friday, Allison. You know what that means." Claire plucked another cookie out of her rolling cart and handed it over.

"Oh my god, is this an orchid?" she exclaimed. "You made this all by yourself? How in the world do you do this? It's gorgeous."

"Yes, it's a dendrobium orchid," Claire replied. "My lola's favorite flower."

"I can't accept this. It's too nice. This must have taken hours to make. How much is this? I can pay."

"No, it's a gift," said Claire. "It was no trouble at all. It's the least I can do for all the great care you give to my grandmother."

"This is professional grade work," Allison said, admiring the cookie. "Is this what you do for a living?"

"No. It's just a side-hustle."

"Side-hustle?" Allison asked in disbelief. "No way. You've got talent. This could seriously be a full-time business. I'm sure people would pay good money for this kind of work."

Claire shrugged dismissively, even though Allison had given voice to her greatest unspoken dream.

"Did you want me to stay to help your grandma finish her breakfast?" Allison asked.

"No, I can do it." Claire waved her off. "But thank you."

"Out of curiosity, what's inside your cart?" Allison asked.

"Magazines. She loves the tabloids." Claire hefted out a stack of magazines with bold, bright headlines across the covers.

"Really?" Allison said with an amused laugh. She picked up one of the magazines and started flipping through it. "How funny is that?"

"I know. I've tried reading a lot of different things to her, but the tabloids with the short, snappy articles and all the pictures of celebrities seem to engage her on some level."

"Uh, yeah, I know exactly what engages your grandma," Allison said with a hearty laugh. "Look at the headline on this one. *Summer Special: Hollywood's Hottest Hunks at the Beach.*"

"Oh my gosh, how ridiculous." She couldn't help but laugh at the outrageousness of the title and the pictures of half-dressed male celebrities across the cover. "You know what they say. There might be snow on the roof, but there's still a fire in the furnace."

Claire and Allison burst into laughter. Lola flicked her eyes over to them for a brief second, then stared back at the TV.

"Oops, I think we startled her," Allison said. "I don't blame her one bit for liking these stories. They're trashy, but so much fun."

"Go ahead and take it," Claire said. "There's plenty more where that came from."

"Are you sure? You don't like to read these?"

"No." Claire shook her head emphatically. "I can't stand the tabloids. I get them strictly for Lola."

"Really? What's not to like? Look at that six-pack. Working in a place like this makes me appreciate this kind of male beauty."

"You are so funny," Claire said. "But I'm not really fond of celebrities."

"Why not?"

"I'm not into all of the glamour and pressure, and being in the spotlight constantly. I'm an introvert. I just don't understand that lifestyle. And all the wealth makes me uncomfortable. Those celebrities have enough money to end all kinds of suffering, but they'd rather put it toward something ludicrous, like a collection of private jets, or handbags the price of a house."

"I never looked at it that way," Allison said. "I still think they're fascinating, though. Thanks for the cookie and the magazine."

Allison left, and Claire eyed the breakfast tray set up beside Lola.

"Are you hungry?" Claire asked.

No response.

"Okay. Here's what's on today's agenda. I'll help you eat breakfast, then we'll read some magazines. Then, we'll watch some TV, and I'll go home. Does that sound good?"

No response.

A little twinge of hurt speared through Claire's heart. She tried her best to keep up a cheerful appearance in front of Lola, but sometimes the reality of her disease hit hard. Claire's memories of Lola pre-Alzheimer's were so vivid. She was a warrior spirit in the body of a tiny woman who once chased down a chicken thief with a huge bolo knife back in the Philippines. She was also a gentle soul who read stories of Filipino folklore to her grandchildren to share her heritage and keep it alive in their hearts. She was so full of life, Claire wondered how there was enough energy left over for the sun to light the skies.

It was beyond difficult seeing her reduced to this sick, frail shell, but Claire wouldn't give up. She imagined Lola trapped inside her body, watching everything happen all around her, helpless to interact with the world the way she used to. Claire always believed the real Lola was in there somewhere, and that she understood and appreciated everything Claire did for her.

Claire picked up a spoonful of oatmeal and held it up to Lola's lips. She took a tentative bite.

"Good job." She hated patronizing her, but she had to admit it worked sometimes. "Here—keep eating. It tastes so good. Oatmeal is your favorite." Joy ignited in Claire's heart when Lola took the spoon and slowly began to feed herself.

"Progress is progress," Claire whispered, happy to accept any victories having to do with Lola, no matter how small. She picked up one of the magazines. "I have some good ones for you today. Allison took the one with the half-naked hunks, but it's okay. Here's one with all the attendees of the MET gala. You'll love it."

An hour or so later, Claire was almost ready to go. She placed the magazine pile in a corner of the room beside the dresser. There was no use in rolling her now empty cart out of the facility. She folded it up and tucked it flat underneath her arm.

"I'm going now. I'll see you tomorrow, okay?"

"*Nakuha mo ba?*"

Claire dropped the cart. It struck the carpeted ground with a muffled crash. The shock of hearing her grandmother speak for the first time in weeks stole her own words for a brief spell.

"Oh my god. In English, Lola. English. I can't understand Tagalog."

Lola paused and leaned forward. After a painstaking minute, her lips finally found the straw, and she took a very slow sip of orange juice.

"Did you find it?" Lola asked finally.

"Find what?"

Instead of answering, Lola sat back in her armchair, settling into the comfortable cushions. She pointed towards the nightstand with her lips. Claire whipped towards the nightstand, scrutinizing it for anything unusual.

"What are you looking for?" Claire asked as she walked to the nightstand. She was so excited she thought she'd explode in a cloud of sparks.

"The key," Lola replied. "You open the box inside my closet."

"But...there's no box inside your closet." Claire opened the door and peered inside at her clothes all neatly lined up on hangers.

"Ay nako," Lola said with a sigh. "Look there."

Bewildered, Claire turned toward the nightstand again. Sure enough, there was a small rusted key on top that she hadn't noticed before. It was partially obscured by a white crocheted doily. A trill of excitement ran through her as she picked up the key and scurried back to Lola.

"What is this for?" she asked.

"To open the box."

"What kind of box?"

"Treasure," Lola whispered. "It's a treasure chest."

Claire hesitated. At first, she was excited about her talking again, but if all her words were delusional, there'd be no use in hoping she'd get better.

"Why so sad?" Lola asked. "Stop frowning. You go find it now."

As Claire drove down the jacaranda-lined street to Lola's house, she slowed her car to scan the driveway. Good. None of her family had arrived yet. She wasn't sure why she didn't want her family to know about what Lola said today. Maybe she was scared of what they'd think. Or maybe she wanted it to be a secret between her and Lola, in the unlikely event there was some truth to her bizarre words. Claire still had some time to get to the bottom of this little mystery.

The family had plans to sell Lola's house to help pay for

her rent at the assisted living facility. It was the end of an era, and her family was going to meet up there today to finish clearing out the rest of the house.

Claire parked and then zipped up the porch steps, unlocking the door and shutting it quietly behind her. The aroma of vanilla and lavender clung to the air—remnants of Lola's favorite candles her family still lit out of respect for her.

She headed into the hallway, her bare feet padding softly against the hardwood floor. Most of the home had been emptied out already. Only a few pieces of furniture made it over to Lola's new apartment. The rest had either been sold or divvied up amongst the family members. Only the garage and storage shed needed to be cleared out.

Stepping up to Lola's old closet in her empty room, Claire confirmed her suspicions—it was empty, too. She didn't know why she'd even bothered. She and her sisters had emptied out this room themselves, sorting everything out into two piles: stays with Lola, and stays at home. Lola was probably hallucinating.

Unless...

Claire rushed toward the back of the house and quickly slipped her feet into the old pair of flip flops sitting on a little rectangle of carpet. The garage was in a separate structure behind the house, faithful to the design of the old Craftsman style homes in this area of Long Beach. Lola and Lolo (may he rest in peace) bought the house about forty years ago. Since then, the only home modification was adding a second story to the garage structure, thus turning it into a little studio apartment. It was the only other place Lola could have been referring to...and it was the only place that hadn't been emptied yet.

She rushed up the stairs on the side of the garage structure and opened the door to the apartment. Claire sighed at the huge piles of Lola's belongings still gathered there. This would certainly be a beast to sort out. She skirted around the stacks of sheet-draped furniture and opened the closet.

"Holy cow," she breathed. The closet was full. It was going to be nearly impossible to sort through all these boxes and clothes and—

"Holy cow!"

Her eyes landed on a small chest fashioned from a dark-stained wood. It was almost obscured by a pile of crocheted shawls. For some reason her eyes went straight to it—as naturally as it would have been drawn to a beam of light in the darkness.

Claire leaped toward it, shoving a stack of plastic containers out of her way. It toppled to the ground like a crumbling tower. Could there be something in there that Lola wanted only her to see? Did she break free from the shackles of her illness for just a moment to give Claire a special message?

She placed the key into the lock and twisted it. The lock must have been broken because the key fit loosely inside.

The day Lola took a sharp decline from Alzheimer's was the day a part of Claire's heart died. The woman who'd loved and guided her was not the same. She would never be the same. The possibility of disappointment was almost too much to bear. Could the contents of this chest give Claire some sense of reassurance?

Steadying her hands, she slowly opened the lid and saw... Nothing.

CHAPTER TWO

"Ate, are you up there?"

The sound of her younger sister's voice jarred Claire. She wasn't sure why the emptiness of the treasure chest devastated her so much. Lola had dementia, for goodness' sake. Was it realistic for her to expect something to come of her words? Lola could not even remember the date. Sometimes she didn't even recognize her own children. Smoothing her palms over the chest's smooth surface, Claire traced her fingertips over the grooves, trying to get a grasp on her sadness so she could chuck it far, far away.

"Ate!"

Claire shut the lid and covered it back up with the shawls.

"I'm up here. I'm coming down."

Claire put on a cheerful face and bounded out of the apartment like there was nothing wrong. As the second of three sisters, Claire found herself forced into the role of the peacemaker. The diplomat. The voice of reason and the calm in the storm while the two opposing forces, youngest sister Rochelle and eldest Samantha, rocked the boat whenever they saw fit to do so. Despite their differences, they loved one another fiercely. It was one of the things Lola had insisted upon. Family first.

The Lord only gave you each other, Lola would say. *That's why you should not quarrel.*

Rochelle was standing inside the back door to the main house with a plastic grocery bag dangling from her arm. Oversized square-framed sunglasses perched on her nose, flattering the oval shape of her face. She looked absolutely chic in her loose, short white Bohemian dress with puffy long sleeves.

"Nice dress, Ro," Claire said.

"Thanks, ate," Ro said with a big smile. She stepped aside so Claire could enter the house. "It was on the clearance rack at Urban Outfitters. Seriously, it pays to be an XX-Small. Did you see Lola already?"

"Yes. Why?"

Rochelle pouted in disappointment.

"Aw," she drawled. "I went to the store and bought her a whole bunch of magazines. I even got her the *In-Touch* exclusive. The one with the hot guys at the beach? I paid extra for that special edition."

"You know how I feel about celebrities," Claire said.

"Yeah, and you are the only straight female in the whole world not affected by this hotness. Did you see how sickeningly *hot* Nate Noruta looked on the cover? There should be a law prohibiting him from going anywhere wearing clothes. Not only is he hot, but he's rich as hell. There's an article in here about the latest vacation home he bought. It's this sprawling estate at Lake Como in Italy. It cost him twenty-two million dollars."

"Good for him."

Claire was used to Ro's larger-than-life personality. Ro was by far the most outgoing and charismatic Ventura sister. When they were kids, she always stole the spotlight and wanted to be the center of attention. Yes, she did hog the karaoke machine at every family party. And yes, she did strive to snag every lead role in their school's dance and theatre productions. Clearly the birth order theory won out with this one.

"Oh, it looks like everyone else is here too." Claire headed toward the front door where there was a commotion on the porch.

"Ate, wait."

The abrupt change in Ro's tone stopped Claire in her tracks.

"What?"

Ro pushed her sunglasses up over her forehead. Her brow furrowed a bit as she studied Claire.

"Are you okay? You seem…kind of sad."

Claire scoffed, conjuring a smile that she hoped didn't seem fake. Damn. Her little sister was good. Either she had magical powers of empathy, or she knew her ate far too well.

"No," she said, feigning cheerfulness. "Trust me. Everything's fine."

Claire turned brusquely away from Ro's dubious eyes. Fortunately, the arrival of the family put the impending interrogation to an end. They came streaming into the home in the familiar hustle and bustle that filled her heart with comfort. Claire's mother, Irene, and three of her sisters came in carrying plastic bags full of food. They headed toward the kitchen in a flurry of Tagalog chatter. The two youngest cousins ran into the living room, excited to play in an open space unimpeded by furniture.

Claire and Ro greeted each of the aunties with a polite kiss on the cheek. They tried to kiss their youngest cousins, but they darted out of the way, far more concerned with their game of tag than the business of properly greeting adults.

"Your Tita Chriss is here too," Mom said, her lips stretched into a tenuous smile.

Claire's heart dipped in dread. Tita Chriss. Claire loved the woman about as much as a niece was obligated to love her aunt. She had always considered herself the unspoken matriarch of the family, even when Lola's mind was intact. The reasons? Because one, she was the eldest. And two, most importantly, she was rich. Tita Chriss was self-made, investing in real estate and making risky financial moves that proved to be very lucrative. Along with the wealth came a sense of entitlement—her unspoken designation as head of the family, and that everyone was subject to her rules, judgments, and expectations.

"Really?" Claire asked. "I thought she was in Italy."

"I know. It surprised me too," Mom replied. "She ended up coming back early."

Tita Chriss made an entrance and whipped her sunglasses off. The whole atmosphere seemed to shift as she surveyed the room, and her younger sisters immediately approached to greet her. Even though Tita Chriss was rich, she dressed modestly, and even drove a sensible car. Chrissandra Ilagan Santos showed the world her wealth through her extravagant handbags and homes.

That was one of the many places where Claire and her aunt differed. Claire was never into fancy accessories. The most expensive purse she owned was a black leather Coach bag she received as a high school graduation gift twelve years ago. She bit her lip as Ro strode up to Tita Chriss and fawned over her new designer shoulder bag.

Claire squashed her nervousness and approached Tita Chriss just as her older sister Samantha walked in. The hard look in Sam's eyes made Claire's heart flutter. Something was off, but now was not the time to address it. Claire kissed her aunt and knew she was obligated to make pleasantries, even though she would rather be doing anything else.

"How was Italy?" she asked with a smile.

"Oh, same old, same old," Chriss replied with a dismissive wave of her hand. "I was getting a little tired of my house in Positano. I think I'm going to sell it for something bigger and higher up on the cliff. But it was nice and relaxing. A good change of pace after working like a dog for all these months without a break. And what about you? Have you found another job yet?"

Claire's jaw tightened. Her fight or flight senses tingled, but the obedient niece in her stayed glued to the spot.

"No, I'm not looking for another job," she replied lightly. "I already have a job."

Tita Chriss scrunched up her nose.

"You still work at that little bookstore?" she asked incredulously. "But you graduated with a degree. Shouldn't you be doing something better, like teaching? Or maybe you should try to get into nursing school. I'd be happy to help. I've already put so many of your cousins through nursing school. I can do it for you too."

And there she was, coming in red-hot. Tita Chriss always targeted Claire and made her the focus of her haughty disappointment. For some reason she never really bothered Ro, even though Ro didn't have one of the "pre-approved" professions in Tita Chriss's mind. Maybe it was because Ro refused to take any of her shit and wasn't intimidated by her. But Claire couldn't help being intimidated by the woman. And perhaps that was why she was always the target.

"Thank you, but I'm fine for now." She shifted uncomfortably as two of her aunts perked up their ears. "I'm a senior seller at the Book Nook. It's one of the most famous indie bookstores in Northern America."

"No offense, but that's a high school job," Chriss said. "I can't believe you poured so much money into a college degree and you ended up doing absolutely nothing with it. You should take life a lot more seriously. Like me. I'm a strong, intelligent, independent woman. I utilized my talents and resources to the max, and now I'm a millionaire. If you worked hard, you could be like me. Lola and Lolo didn't come all the way to America to see their future generations waste their time. Lola would be very disappointed in you."

Claire was blindsided. Tita Chriss had always been hard on her, but today she went too far. If Claire had the courage, she would have told her aunt she didn't give a shit about her money, and that she'd rather be poor than get her kicks out of harassing others. But she wasn't brave enough. The fire in her sputtered and the words lodged deep in her throat.

"Tita Chriss, that's not fair," Ro said. "You're not giving Claire enough credit. You don't know it yet, but she's thinking of starting her own cookie decorating business. She's really talented, and she's drawn a lot of interest online already. Right, ate?"

Heat flared up Claire's neck and into her cheeks. Ro was trying to be helpful, but Claire knew this information would do nothing but trigger Tita Chriss.

"Cookies?" Tita Chriss giggled, and the sound of it tied Claire's stomach in a knot. "You can't be serious."

"I'm…kind of considering it," Claire mumbled.

"Ate, Chriss, the food is ready," Irene called.

Claire almost collapsed with relief. Her mother would never outright disagree with Tita Chriss, but she still had the sense to swoop in and save her daughter when she needed help.

"We'll talk more about it after lunch." Tita Chriss pasted on a grin and swept into the kitchen to dig into the Chinese takeout laid out across the pale-blue-tiled counter.

The rest of the family converged on the food as well, but Claire hung back. Tita Chriss's words stung so badly, Claire would be surprised if she woke up the next morning without scars somewhere. And the last thing she said hurt the most: *Lola would be very disappointed in you.* How could Tita Chriss say something so cruel and careless?

Something came over Claire, and she found herself backing away from the kitchen. She didn't know if it was shame or fear, or some combination of both. But after all that happened today, the last thing she wanted to do was wait for more berating from her disapproving aunt.

Without a word, she turned and left through the front door.

Look for
*How to Survive a
Modern-Day Fairy Tale*
wherever books are sold.

APRIL may FALL

April Davis totally has her life in order. Ha! Not really. Yes, she's the Calm Mom—a social influencer with a reputation for showing moms how to stay calm and collected through yoga—but behind the scenes, she's barely holding it all together. Raising tiny humans alone is exhausting, but that's just the chewed-up cherry on the melted sundae of her life. Her kids aren't behaving, her husband left her for his skydiving instructor, and her top knot proves she hasn't showered in days.

Then a live video of the "always calm" April goes viral...and she's most definitely not. Enter Jack Gibson, April's contact at the media conglomerate that has purchased April's brand. The too-sexy-for-his-own good Jack will help clean up April's viral mess, and even work with her to expand her influence, but toddler tea parties and a dog with a penchant for peeing on his shoes were definitely not part of the deal.

Now April's calm has jumped ship quicker than her kids running from their vegetables. Not to mention, the sparks flying between her and Jack have her completely out of her depth. Forget finding her calm—April's going to need a boatload of margaritas just to find her way back to herself again.

Two powerhouse authors bring you a hilarious tale of one woman's journey to find herself again.

back *in the* burbs

by Tracy Wolff
New York Times Bestselling Author
and
by Avery Flynn
USA Today Bestselling Author

Ever have one of those days where life just plain sucks? Welcome to my last three months—ever since I caught my can't-be-soon-enough ex-husband cheating with his paralegal. I'm thirty-five years old, and I've lost my NYC apartment, my job, my money, and frankly, my dignity.

But the final heartache in the suck sandwich of my life? My great-aunt Maggie died. The only family member who's ever gotten me.

Even after death, though, she's helping me get back up. She's willed me the keys to a house in the burbs, of all places, and dared me to grab life by the family jewels. Well, I've got the vise grips already in hand (my ex should take note) and I'm ready to fight for my life again.

Too bad that bravado only lasts as long as it takes to drive into Huckleberry Hills. And see the house.

There are forty-seven separate HOA violations, and I feel them all in my bones. Honestly, I'm surprised no one's "accidentally" torched the house yet. I want to, and I've only been standing in front of it for five minutes. But then my hot, grumpy neighbor tells me to mow the lawn first and I'm just...done. Done with men too sexy for their own good and done with anyone telling me what to do.

First rule of surviving the burbs? There is nothing that YouTube and a glass of wine can't conquer.

it's

raining

men

Don't drink and text.

Even on the cusp of forty, I had to learn that the hard way. After discovering my best friend, who I was supposed to grow old and single with, got engaged, I drowned my loneliness in one too many Old Fashioneds and woke up with thirty-nine responses from every available man in my phone. Yup, I even texted my plumber...and he turned me down.

Apparently, my liquor-infused text said that while I don't need a man, maybe I'd be down for a constant sidekick for movies, plus-one invites, and dinner on the table after my grueling shifts as a concierge doctor—till death do us part...and was anyone in?

Through the absolute mortification of thirty-seven rejections, shockingly, I realize two men have said yes. Behind Bachelor Door #1 is Rob, my old high school crush: the comfortable, dependable boy-next-door. Behind Bachelor Door #2 is Darius, the exciting, flashy news reporter about to hit it big. Does this mean I'll have to get out of my yoga pants and actually go on dates now?

Dax, the local bartender who got me into this disaster in the first place—remember the Old Fashioneds?—can't believe I've given up on finding true love. What does a tattooed, broody twentysomething know about carving out a future for yourself, anyway?

Too bad the further into this hot mess I get, the less I know abut who I am. And I'm going to have to figure out exactly what I need if I ever want to find a true happily ever after.

AMARA
an imprint of Entangled Publishing LLC